ABOUT THE AUTHOR

Lucy Booth was born in Suffolk, then moved with her family to Solihull, Cyprus and Lymm in Cheshire, where she attended Manchester High School for Girls before studying Behavioural Sciences at Nottingham University. On graduating, Lucy moved to London to pursue her career as a freelance producer for adverts and music videos.

In 2011 Lucy was diagnosed with breast cancer resulting in surgery, chemotherapy and radiotherapy. Undaunted, Lucy not only continued working and writing her blog (lucifersboob.blogspot.co.uk) in a typically forthright and humorous fashion but felt the urge to write a novel. *The Life of Death* is the result.

In 2014, the aggressive cancer returned. However, Lucy was determined to live her life to the full and to finish her novel.

Lucy was funny and brave and an inspiration to all who knew and loved her; she never allowed her cancer to define her and remained upbeat and positive until her last days.

Lucy died in August 2016, aged thirty-seven.

The Life of Death

Lucy Booth

unbound

This edition first published in 2019
Unbound
6th Floor Mutual House,
70 Conduit Street,
London W1S 2GF
www.unbound.com

Text Design by Ellipsis, Glasgow

A CIP record for this book is available from the British Library

ISBN 978-1-78352-710-6 (trade pbk)
ISBN 978-1-78352-712-0 (ebook)
ISBN 978-1-78352-711-3 (limited edition)

Printed in Great Britain by CPI (UK)

The Good Man at the Hour of Death

When from this life Heaven calls the Just away,
Serene he does the pleasing call obey.
Of all offense he finds the conscience clear,
And all is Hope and nothing to fear.

Thomas A. E. Chambers (1724–1789)

I

I HAVE LIVED THE LIVES OF MORE SOULS THAN I can count. My husbands have loved me, scarred me, cherished me, scared me. I have outlived them all. My children have feared me, welcomed me, run to me and run away. I have caught them all.

I am there when you are born. When you cross the road. When the live wire frays in a Bakelite plug. I am there in the hospital canteen, by the frozen pond, in the carbon monoxide fug of a terraced living room. I am waiting, with open arms and solace.

I am Death.

Traditionally, in literature, art, songs, I am depicted as a man in a shabby, hooded cloak with my scythe poised to cut you down. I am to be feared, run from. But that's not the truth, that is not my *raison d'être*. How are you to know the real me, after all? You only find that out in your closing seconds, when you're searching for your final embrace, your final act of love.

At the point of death, when the physical body grunts and pants, when it seeps and oozes, when it screams and sighs, my presence brings calm. Eyes clear and wounds heal. Pain dulls and the fog lifts and in those final moments there is an undreamed-of peace. For I am there to carry you through those last moments, through the screaming and the seeping, through the fog, and deposit you softly, gently on the other side. And when you get there, with few exceptions, you are glad to see me. As you fall into the deepest and most dreamless of sleeps, and slowly, quietly, you fade to black.

As for the real me, I am fat, thin, dark, fair. I am tall. I am short. I have a plump welcoming bosom and the gnarled, age-spotted hand of an eighty-year-old. I am the woman you most want to see in those final seconds you live on this earth. I have been wives, daughters, best friends. I have been a beloved nurse, a primary school teacher. Your first love. I am the ultimate mother.

I am Death.

Lives are given to me – I never take them. Never. Even in the most accidental situations, in those final seconds you give yourselves up to me. But there are the exceptions – the murdered few who are taken deliberately and agonisingly. Too early for their short lives. And those, those my friends, are the ones selected painstakingly and ruthlessly by Him. And if it's you, if you're the chosen one, it's always the same. I can only stand and watch as He spins the wheel of chance and picks their fate. I can only watch as He pulls the trigger, holds His long fingers around your throat, twists the knife in the wound, etches your name on the bullet in the chamber. I stand by, ready to pick up the pieces, and I come for you when He is spent. You claw at me, scream, sob. Desperation takes hold of you and I am helpless. I hold you, whisper what words of comfort I can. I cradle you, rock you, gently shush and hush you until you realise the inevitability of your position and succumb to me. Cosset you while you calm yourselves and wait to face that which is unavoidable. Until eventually, slowly, quietly, you fade to black.

And who is He?

He is the Devil.

In 1590, I sold my soul to the Devil. I was twenty-three.

2

I WAS BORN IN 1567 IN THE TINY VILLAGE OF Tranent, clinging to the fraying skirt hems of Scotland as they dragged into the icy waters of the North Sea. My name was Elizabeth. Elizabeth Murray. Lizzy, Lilibet, Bess. The Devil was all around us in that remote spot, lashing the shores with whipped-up tempests and slicing us to the bone with the Arctic winds. But while the others could wrap up, turn their backs to Him over the whistling winds, He had chosen me and from that there was no escape. Where I went, He would undoubtedly follow. I was marked – a livid red birthmark scoring the soft skin below my right ear and curling into my neck. A question mark etched into my skin. I found refuge in the dark – when the flickering light from open fires disguised my disfigurement and I could hide in the shadows. Refuge in the dark, and among the women of my family.

We'd gather on the kirk green late into the long summer evenings, huddled in the shadows of the squat, thick-set stone church, backs turned to the wind and driving rain. The walls were at least six feet thick and when we were there we were safe. Me, my sisters, my mother, my aunts. It started small – just we six – before more women from the village joined us and we would gather nightly to swap tips and exchange advice, gossip about the local men, offer a friendly ear in a hostile world.

I had a talent for a poultice. Bring me a lame horse and he would walk; an infected finger would soften and bend under my care. I heard the whispers from the village – we all did. 'Witchcraft', 'Devil's Child', 'Dark magic', flitting past our ears and floating in the air to be netted and pinned like fragile butterflies by those who believed. And we'd laugh – laugh at those men who feared and revered us in equal measure. Who had their own meetings by firelight to 'free their midst of evil', flames dancing in their eyes, shadows carving canyons into weathered faces. Only a day later they would appear at our doors, heads hanging, eyes cast to the floor and feet scuffing the dirt as they mumbled out requests. A lame mule; an angry, red, swollen eye, weeping and oozing; a third stillbirth in the family in as many years. They were torn between their contempt for us and their need. And that made them despise us all the more.

So when the King's men came to rid the country of witchcraft and magic, there those same men stood. Eyes once more turned to the floor. Toes once more scuffing the dirt. Names mumbled, fingers pointed towards crofts, and faces turned away from women bundled and pushed ahead of men dressed in metal, their rich fabrics saturated with colour in the harsh light bouncing from the sea. Faces turned away from me and the women who would join me on those long, late nights on the kirk green. Faces turned away as we were bundled and pushed into dank dungeons dripping with slimy moss to await a trial – accused of nothing more than helping and healing. Accused of a know-ledge the men would never understand. Accused of witchcraft and a devotion to the Devil.

I am strung up in that freezing cell. Shackled to the wall and strapped into a witch's bridle – the metal prongs jabbing into my cheeks and the spiked iron bit tearing welts into my tongue. For days I hang there. When my body sags under its own weight, under the exhaustion of night after night without sleep, the spikes bite into my tongue and pain jerks me upright and awake. The whistles and whispers of the wind begin to sound like voices. Until, after an eternity hanging in the dark and cold, those whistles and whispers become a voice. His voice. Charming and cajoling; curt and cold. Chipping away at me amid the drips of my prison. Chip, chip, chip. Drip, drip, drip.

I first see Him through the gloom, sitting in the corner of my cell. Long legs stretched out in front of Him, head leaning back against the cold stone wall.

His skin is alabaster white, creating a soft halo that shines unnaturally clean in the midst of the squalor. His nose is turned up at the smell of stale excrement, at the faecal streaks that smear my legs. His clothes are those of a gentleman: well-cut, rich fabrics, with a long dark cloak wrapped around His thin shoulders to keep the cold and the damp at bay. Even the rats that use that wall as a channel between their nests and the outside world give that incongruous figure a wide berth. Though we've never met before, I recognise Him as soon as I see Him. As soon as I hear that voice.

'You know they've said it for years, don't you?' He examines His fingernails, blunting the torn edge of one against the rough fabric of His woollen trousers. 'Jem Porter says you sold your soul to me when you were ten. Thomas Mortimer says you came out of the womb with the Devil in your eye.'

I know what Jem Porter says. And Thomas Mortimer. And Francis Miller. I know what they all said. The hushed whispers when I was small, rising to sideways comments in the street as I grew into a woman, became open jeers and shouts in the street in these last few years. Open jeers and shouts echoing down empty lanes, sly jabs in dark alleys, mucus hawked from the back of throats to land in globs at my feet. I know what they say for I have heard it since birth.

He stands, then crosses my cell to peer out of the tiny barred window level with the street outside. He steps back as the stinking piss of a passing horse splashes through the gaps, keeps His distance as the cartwheels that follow closely behind churn urine and dirt into mud to send it splattering into my hole. 'Listen to them out there. Calling your name. "Bring us the Witch!" "Death to the Witch!" "Devil Woman!" That's you, Lizzy – you're the one they've come to see. And they won't be happy until you're dead.'

I know that too. I know I am going to die, and I know my death is the one thing that will sate those men. I have heard the cries, the hoots of a crowd baying for blood. Smelled the stench of burning human flesh long after the screams for mercy have died down. Sensed the crowd whipping themselves into a bloodthirsty frenzy of death.

'It's a shame to die so young, isn't it, Lizzy? What are you? Sixteen? Seventeen?'

I try to answer but my tongue is pinned by metal spikes, and all I can manage in reply is a long spool of drool that drips to the floor.

'Where are my manners?' He draws up to His full height and strides across the cell towards me. 'Asking you questions when you have no hope of answering?' He draws one long finger down my cheek then cups my chin and raises my eyes to meet His. Wipes away the saliva that leaks from the corner of my mouth with a cold thumb. 'And, without even explaining why I'm here.'

He tuts to himself, before standing back to fold His

arms across his chest and contemplate me, His head cocked to one side.

'It's simple, Lizzy. Quite simple. All I want is your soul. What's the harm in that, eh? If you're going to die anyway? And you are going to die, Lizzy, make no mistake.'

I don't hear any more. Once more pain overwhelms me and my mind closes itself to the horror around. The cell fades to darkness as I lose consciousness, and hang lifeless from my shackles once more.

I have no idea how much time passes in that tiny cell. It could be hours, days, weeks. Time has lost all meaning. Jarring my head against the metal frame as I come round suddenly. The first few seconds always, always unexpected. Happy moments of innocence before my vision clears and the clarity of my situation swims into focus.

When I do wake, it is to the sound of names being called. Eliza. Agnes. Mary. Margaret. Names of the women of my childhood who are being summoned to their end. Alice. Jane. Katherine. Names that are called first by the warders, to be echoed by the guards who accompany them to the marketplace. Names that are picked up by the waiting crowd and cheered and whooped as shrunken figures shuffle past. Names that fade to wisps on the air, replaced by animal yowls and guttural howls as flames lick skywards and the Devil is chased from within. And when I wake, He is there.

Sometimes He sits. Sometimes He paces the smooth flags. Biding His time and waiting for me to wake. Sometimes I see Him standing at the barred window of my cell. Breathing in deeply to savour the smell of burning wood, the stench of burning flesh. And when He senses my body rallying, my mind awakening, He is there to continue His pursuit, His relentless pursuit, of my soul. He can be charming, wheedling when He wants to be. Dropping His voice and smoothing my hair back from my face. Soothing the ache as the damp from the sodden walls seeps deep into my bones.

But for every ounce of charm, He can be curt. Petulant. Pulling on the chains that bind my hands, my feet. Making me shriek with pain, whimper with fear. Squeezing my cheeks in His hands until the metal of the hood scrapes against my teeth. Hissing into my ears, spitting my name. 'You can make this stop, Lizzy. It doesn't have to be this way, Lizzy.'

This is done to break my spirit, to tatter my will, to exhaust my body, to win my soul. And it works, let me tell you. It works. When He is kind, I want nothing more than to make Him happy, to win Him round. And when He is not, well, I would do anything to once more make Him so.

As those names are called, those names as familiar to me as my own, as I drift in and out of consciousness, dragged sharply back to reality by the searing pain, I notice some changes in Him. With each name called, a graze. With each breath of acrid smoke, a bruise blooms hyacinth blue on that pale cheek. With each scream from the funeral pyre, a wince and a clutch at ribs. These deaths are affecting Him. Physically hurting Him. For although He is the Devil Himself, He is somehow not immune.

Darkness sweeps through the cell, plunging me once more into a night of the deepest black. My head nods, sending spasms of pain through my ravaged body, and I tumble into blackness once more. Safe from pain, safe from the reality of my surroundings.

When I wake, He is there. A new day, a new start. He is renewed, refreshed. His skin shines alabaster white, with not a trace of a graze to betray the pain He has suffered. And His pursuit of my soul begins again with relish. 'Where is the harm, Lizzy? What loss is it to you?' He chips. 'It is all I ask, Lizzy. One soul when you have your very life to thank me for.' And I listen to His beseechings, I acknowledge what He says. But His questions raise some of my own. Where is the harm? What loss would it be? Do I really have my life to thank Him for? For He is the Devil, and surely things cannot be as simple as He suggests.

With the rising sun, the names come flitting through the window as more of my family and friends are led to their fate. And as the screams reach us, so the pain they inflict upon Him becomes ever more evident. A ruby drop of blood weeps down a sharp cheekbone. The white of an eye bleeds red. Breathing becomes laboured.

I cannot be sure, but these deaths and their proximity to Him have a profound effect.

Mid-afternoon and I awake from my pain-induced slumber with a start. I am numb. Pain has softened. My body is rallying. He is standing by the barred window to the cell, shoulders straight, body pulled upright. Without turning He speaks.

'I need you, Lizzy.' He leans forward to peer into the street. 'I sensed you wake. I felt you rally. And I knew.'

'What?' I breathe, through crushed lung and bloodied tongue. 'Knew what?'

'We are one, you and me. You have seen the damage these deaths inflict upon me. You have seen the pain I suffer.' He turns to face me. A shaft of sunlight highlights His glowing skin. Skin that is white, clean, unblemished. His breathing is steady, no longer labouring under the cracked ribs suffered by this morning's cull. 'When I sensed you rally, when I felt your strength giving me strength of my own. I knew. We are linked, you and me. We are one.'

'But I will die. Maybe not today, maybe not tomorrow. But I will leave. And you cannot save me from that.'

'Oh, but Lizzy, I can. You will die, as you say. A mortal death. But give me your soul, Lizzy, and I can reward you with eternal life. And, what's more, an occupation for that life. To fill those endless years, that yawning eternity of life without life.'

'What will this entail?' I stammer. I feel my body weakening, and as it does I see the ruby tear once more track its way down smooth skin.

'Allow me to show you, Lizzy. Tomorrow. For tomorrow is her time, isn't it, Lizzy? Your mother's? Tomorrow I will show you your role and you can agree or disagree with what you feel. But please note, Lizzy, I need you. And we are for ever to be linked. From that you cannot escape.'

With that, pain floods my body and I collapse against the unforgiving upright of the iron form that holds me. He shrieks as a gash opens on His chest and blood seeps through the rich brocade. The darkest black of the subconscious takes over to support me and soothe me until once more wakefulness will take hold with its inescapable pain.

Behind closed lids I hear Him speak. Soft. A whisper on the stagnant air. Warm hands cup freezing feet where they hang above the cold stone floor.

'It's her turn today, Lizzy.'

Long fingers gently pull at numb toes.

'The crowds have gathered. She has left her cell. Can you hear them, Lizzy?' Thumbs smooth calloused pads.

'You can see her, Lizzy. One last time.' His grip on my feet tightens. 'All I want, all I'm asking for, is the soul of one girl who will shortly herself be at that stake. You give me your soul and I give you employment and an eternal life. Can't say fairer than that.'

I'm exhausted. I'm in pain. I can't even cry for fear of jarring my head against this metal frame and sending more spasms of agony through my body. I gag. A sob of acquiescence chokes out from behind a restricted tongue.

'Go out there. Go out to your mother. She's at the stake now. Go out there. They won't see you. Not while I'm with you.'

I have lost reason, lost the will to argue, to question. It makes no sense, but such is the force of His presence that whatever He says, I accept.

He stands, stretches long arms high above His head. Entwines His fingers to stretch the joints, stiffened in the damp air. They crack loudly, echoing against the cold stone. Reaches up to unclip the iron frame of the brutal headpiece. Cups my chin with His hand as He eases the bars over my head and slips a finger into my mouth to lift the bit from my tongue. Unhooks my arms from the shackles and cradles me against His chest to lower me, slowly, gently, to the floor.

A jumble of dark clouds muffles the mumble of thunder on this tumbledown day. Even the dim light of an autumn afternoon is too bright for eyes accustomed to darkness, making me blink and shrink back into the cocoon of my cell. He grips my arm, steadying me on my feet, supporting and guiding as we step out into the marketplace. He was right – no one can see us. No one is paying any attention to a tall, pale man and a blood-caked, shit-caked girl pushing their way through a howling crowd.

We reach the front, where feet line up against the circle of stones that mark the edge of the fire pit. They've turned up in their hundreds, from the towns and villages scattered in the surrounding hills. Turned up to jostle for position, climbing on to one another, pushing each other out of the way to vie for the best view. Clambering on to the central market cross to get a better view. To watch the witch burn.

She stands, back to the stake, straight-shouldered and head held high. Not for her the begging, the admission of guilt, the hair-tearing of her contemporaries. She stands proud, content in the knowledge she has done nothing wrong. Faith in her God and belief in herself hold her body straight and true. Her refusal to bend, to bow, to break, infuriates this crowd. Blackened cabbages are launched in her direction, globules of spit land at her feet. Still she does not flinch.

I pull forward, trying to struggle free from His grip. To get to her. To free her wrists and pull her down from that pyre before the flames can take hold. But He is strong. Stronger than I could ever be. He grips my upper arms and pins them to my sides. 'Lizzy. No. Not yet.'

Four men step forward, holding lit torches they dip to kindling and tease the hay wisps beneath. Flames curl and lick, enveloping the tinder that leans up against her. And still her face is set. Lips pressed together, eyes turned to the sky above, seeing through and past the smoke that spirals ever higher to the heavens.

A flame takes hold of her woollen dress. Sweeps upwards to cloak her body in fire. And then, the screams begin. Long, drawn out, moaning screams. Screams that turn the ravens to wing, and my blood to ice. She can hold back no longer. The heat, the fire, squeezes the air from her lungs in a high-pitched shriek. But still she will not beg. She will not give them the satisfaction.

The screams get louder, shriller. The jeers of the crowd fall to silence as they watch, open-mouthed. Bodies shrink back from the searing heat of the fire. As skin melts and hair burns away from her scalp. As clothes burn to nothing and the smell of cooking meat and singed tresses conspire to offend the nostrils of all who stand and watch. They've seen it before, this crowd. And they'll see it again. But still they retch. Choke on the thick smoke that weaves its way between them, shrink back from the fierce heat of the fire that licks out of the inner circle in its search for fuel. Bile rises in my throat. An irrepressible urge to vomit.

The screams quieten, the pain so all-consuming that she can do nothing but wait for death to come. I feel a nudge in the small of my back. Him.

'Go to her. See her off safely.' His cheek oozes with droplets of blood.

I resist Him. Push back with my shoulders and turn my head away from the sight of a broken woman, stripped back to the very bones that held her so upright in her final moments.

'You won't feel a thing. Go on. She doesn't have much time left.' The nudge becomes a shove. 'If you don't go to her now, you'll never get to say goodbye'.

Deep breath. In. Out. I step over the crude stone circle marking the boundary of the fire. In. Out. Step onto white-hot embers that crunch and crumble beneath my feet. Again, He's right – there's no pain, I can't feel the heat that should be burning through my skin. Through the haze, I can see the shrivelled, burnt figure has been replaced by the woman I know and love. Skin replenished, hair hanging about her face, shoulders drawn up and back.

'I thought He'd come.' Her face is peaceful, calm. Her voice soft. None of the rasping shriek that only moments before filled the crowded square.

I grab at her. Wrap my arms around her and bury my face in her neck. 'What do you mean?'

I pull back to look her in the eye, to tuck a tendril of hair behind her ear. The skin of her forehead is smooth, unlined, cool to the touch. Not a bead of sweat betrays the previous moment's torment.

The restraints have fallen away. Hand holding elbow, we two sit amid the dying flames, the white embers that crumble to the softest ash.

She smiles. 'Call it a mother's intuition. Maybe it's years of seeing Him in the shadows, watching you at every turn. Feeling Him in the wind. He's always kept his distance, but I knew He wouldn't need much encouragement when the time came.'

'Why did you never tell me?'

'You heard them, Lizzy, their whispers about you, about your grandmother. Binding you to the Devil Himself. What good would it have done to tell you the truth, to open you to their hatred? Your ignorance was your innocence, Lizzy, your protection. If you didn't know, how could anyone else be sure?'

'But what is the truth? Why does He want me? What have I ever done?'

'Not you, Lizzy. You've done nothing. He wanted you from the very moment you were sown into my belly. For the long months you were cosseted in my womb. He's wily. A deceptive Reynard – He slips in unwanted and takes what He wants. Night after night in my dreams He taunted me until I knew not what was a nightmare and what was true. For months I fought Him – waking in the dead of night and keeping myself awake until the first fingers of light crept over the sea – for when I was awake He couldn't get to me, He couldn't get at you. But my fighting was punished, with pain and fear and the threat of losing my unborn child. With blood staining the matting on the floor of our home. And as the seasons passed and as you grew in my belly, I could fight no longer. Night after night

I would succumb to sleep, the safety of hours free from pain no match for the sound in my dreams of His voice chipping at my resolve. And when you were born, marked as you were, with that red scar from throat to ear, I knew that He had won. That you were His.'

'But I am not His! I am yours, I am Father's, I am—'

'You are His, my darling. There are a chosen few. Those He seeks out when they are but seeds in a fertile soil. Those He watches over and protects, whom He furnishes with talents and skills that elude we mortal folk. Your talent for herbs, your healing hands – He gave you those, much as He gave them to your grandmother, and to her grandmother before her. And in return for that protection, that patronage, when the time comes He requires one thing from you, Lizzy. He requires your soul. For it is the souls of His children, willingly given, that nourish Him, that help Him to thrive, that will enable Him to live for generations to come. You can turn from Him, you can die here, alone in this market square. You can reject whatever it is He has in mind. But you must listen to Him. Listen to what He has to offer you. If you reject Him, a certain eternity in Hell awaits. And the road to Hell is not what the scriptures would have us believe, Lizzy. It is not the final resting place for those who have sinned, bubbling with brimstone. It is His final resting place for those by whom He has been shunned. It is a place of longing and of loss. Of sadness. Of desperation. Of wondering eternally what could have been and what might have passed.'

'But if I do sell Him my soul? I die without the threat of Hell awaiting me? Then I prove everyone around us right, prove that their years of jeers were correct. That I am nothing but the Devil's Child.'

'Your existence proves them right, Lizzy. The knowledge you hold in your hands will always mark you as His in the eyes of those around you. Whether you give Him your soul, or whether you condemn yourself to an eternity in Hell, these men will never know for certain, and they will never think differently of you. What is He asking you to do? Will it hurt people? Harm them? You must follow your conscience, Lizzy. If you feel it is wrong, if it is more unbearable than Hell itself, you must come here, to the stake. Accept your fate as I have done and have hope that you can lessen His anger, that He will soften to you. Only you can decide what path you should choose – the road to Hell, or towards whatever He is offering in return for your soul. For they are the only paths open to you, my dearest. As His chosen subject, the path to Heaven is blocked.'

Head bows on weary neck. Shoulders slump against the rigid iron pole. Fingers toy with the soft ashes beneath me. My mother reaches over. Clasps my filthy hand in hers. Clean. Smooth. Soft. 'Has He told you? What awaits?'

'Not yet.' His weeks of visits, of relentless persuasion have taught me nothing other than His obsession with gaining my soul. 'He hasn't elaborated. Only to say that in return for my soul He'll give me employment and an eternal life. That in return for my soul I can avoid the end that's been written for me.'

I look over to where He stands, leaning the full length of His slim body against the stone cross in the centre of the square. The bitter wind has chased up the tunics of the crowd, skittering them back to shelter, to safety. He stands alone in the ebbing mass, unruffled, unfettered. His eyes haven't left me since I stepped into that sacred circle and now they bore in to my own. Black. Bottomless. But now, the droplets of blood on that pale cheek have cleared, and He stands before me unblemished.

'Ask Him, Lizzy. Give Him the chance to explain. You have a choice. You have a way out of this.' She gestures around her at the smoking, charred wood, at the cracked bones of the previous occupants of this sacred circle. 'At least consider that. Even if you don't agree to go ahead with whatever He has in store for you. Think of the alternative. I know what that end point is. I know the pain, the searing heat, the feeling of your skin peeling from your body, bit by bit, of hair melting into flesh. Today, I have truly visited the hell of mortals, Lizzy. And you can avoid that.'

I look back at Him. Arms crossed. Cloak heavy with

gold. I nod. A barely perceptible acknowledgement that I'm willing to discuss His offer.

At my nod, He finally breaks His gaze, steps down from the cross and strides across the empty square to the stone building that has held me these past few weeks. Just before He passes through the open doorway, He turns to me, and once more locks His eyes to mine. A breath. A pause. Before ducking His head and being swallowed within.

'We don't have much time, my dearest. He won't wait for ever.'

We have been sitting in silence, we two, in that cold market square as clouds scud overhead. The only sound the stark cawing of the ravens that perch high above us. Our only companions are the two guards who stand either side of the pit, waiting for the heat to die down. And as long as we are here, it won't. He'll make sure of it, I know. They'll keep their distance.

'You were such a good daughter. Loyal and kind. Loving. I couldn't have wished for a better daughter. And with that talent. Just like my mother. I never understood her feeling for the herbs, never knew until He came to me that I would never be able to under-stand it. Do you remember when you used to sit with her and crush the leaves? A tiny little thing perched beside her with a bowl between your knees.'

I nod. I do. I do remember. The heady punch of cropleek crushed with garlic in the mortar. The days spent scouring the hills for milkthistle and dandelion. The musty, dusty, metallic tang of copper bowls and dried wormwood.

'I have worried for you for my whole life, Lizzy. I have known this day would come – I knew not when, or where, or how. But He brought those men here, Lizzy – He decided to summon you to Him, He is in need of your nourishment, and the lives of the other women are of little consequence. I want you to consider this, Lizzy. I really do. I can't bear the thought of you suffering the pain I've just endured, and to suffer that pain for evermore. But you will be careful, won't you? Promise me you won't agree to anything unless you know exactly what you will have to do. You must promise me, Lizzy. He's the Devil, Lizzy. Promise me you'll look after yourself.'

She grips my hands between hers. Brings them to her lips to kiss my blood-stained fingers.

'I promise. If I don't like the sound of it, I'll walk away. Walk into the flames with my head held high and your name on my lips. And I can grit my teeth and face Hell in the knowledge that I have not caused yet more suffering. But if I can avoid it? If I can live a life away from them . . .' I jerk my head in the direction of the Jem Porters and the Thomas Mortimers of the world, no doubt leering and jeering, cheering themselves with tankards of ale. They can watch me as I burn, watch as they hurl His name in my direction. But I'll watch them through the saffron haze of flames, knowing that if Jem Porter were able to tear his eyes away, to glance over his shoulder, he would come face to face with that fabled being Himself.

'Be careful, my love. You must do the right thing. You must do what you believe.'

I wrap my arm around her shoulder, gently pulling her into a hug and rocking her as she rests her head against mine.

'I will. I promise.'

'Goodbye, my dearest girl. And good luck.'

And as we rock, I feel her slipping away. I feel her fading in my arms until finally, gently, she breathes her final breath, and while her bones settle in the embers, the mother I know, the woman I love, gently fades to black.

I don't know how long I sit there in the embers and the ashes in the centre of the market square. When I look up I can see Him across the square, the outline of His body against the black doorway of the prison building. Waiting for me to return. And eventually, pushing myself to my feet and wiping my tear-smeared, blood-stained face with a hand filthy with ash and dirt, I do.

It's a long, solitary walk across the cobbles. I stare resolutely ahead. Focused on Him. I can't turn, can't look back to see the charred and broken remains of my mother's body. He watches my every step wordlessly. Looks down at me as I stop in front of Him.

'So what is it that you want me to do if I sell you my soul? An eternal life and . . . ?'

'You've just done it.'

I squint up at Him. 'Done what? I've just said goodbye to my mother.'

'You've ushered her on. Everyone has to die, Lizzy. Every soul has to pass on somewhere. And that will be your role. You will attend every death however you so choose, and you will see them through and past their final breath. Mind you, you should be prepared. You will be feared. You will be hated. For no one will know the real you until they are in a position in which they cannot avoid but to meet you. But all that is a small price to pay for an eternal life, isn't it?'

'Well, yes . . . But, I don't really understand. What do you get out of this? Why do you care that souls pass on?'

And why should He want me of all people to do it?

He sighs a deep sigh. I wait in silence for Him to explain. When it comes, it's with an air of impatience, and a spelling out of each syllable as if explaining to a child.

'You have seen the effects these deaths have on me, Lizzy. The physical pain I endure when lives end. And the link we have, Lizzy, enables you to act as my cypher. To soothe those deaths, to support those souls in their final moments, takes away the pain that I have been suffering for an eternity. A pain that is becoming unbearable. I did not become who I am by chance, Lizzy, I have had to make sacrifices of my own. And in addition, for me to survive I need untarnished souls. They are my nutrients. My lifeblood, my night, my day. They keep me warm in the winter and shade me from the burning sun of summer. Simply put, Lizzy, they are my everything. An untarnished soul, given willingly, can nourish me for years, for decades, even. I can supplement that with the lives I take – with those I poison, strangle, stab. If I take a life, yes, I get that soul. But it's a snack. A mere titbit to keep me going before I can next feast. It's the pure souls I'm after – the ones given to me consensually with a full under-standing of consequence, the ones in which I'm invested, the ones to whom I have given years of my life. And if you give me your soul, if you maintain my life in that way, so I should give you something in return. Every action must have a reaction.'

He pauses in his soliloquy, watching the men as they grab my mother's bones. Kick them to one side. Trample on them and leave them to crunch under foot as they lay fresh tinder at the stake. Fresh tinder for their next victim. Fresh tinder for me.

And then He's off and running again. 'What kind of eternal life would it be with no purpose, Lizzy? And so, if you are to do me this favour, this gracious favour I might add, I must provide a job for you. Keep you happy. Eternity quickly becomes a very long time with nothing to fill it – you mark my words. And acting as my cypher is the perfect job for both you and me.'

I look over at the pile of firewood, the men milling around for the first sniff of new blood, to the white shards of my mother's bones scattered over soft ashes. Why not? It doesn't sound that bad – eternal life and a chance to help people die with someone they love at their side, right to the very end. I think of the chance my mother just had – to spend her very final moments with her daughter, wrapped in a love to protect her from the pain of reality. Why couldn't I give everyone that chance? If I can do this in any way I choose, why not do that for everyone? Allow them to spend their last moments with their mother, daughter, sister, wife. Offer what comfort I can until they too, like my mother, fade to black.

'You must bear this in mind, Lizzy. If you take me up on this, if you accept this work and the eternity that lies before you, if you sell me your soul, I will own you. If you change your mind, have second thoughts, if the thought of eternal life weighs too heavy to bear and you find the task of death too burdensome, you can't just run, Lizzy. For every action, remember, there must be a reaction. And you must, must remember this: I. Will. Own. You.'

He gets up, pulling me by the hand and leads me back to my cell. As we approach the door and prepare to step back into the darkness, He turns to me. 'Well?'

I can hear the men down the stone passageway

heading my way. 'Elizabeth Murray', 'Ha ha ha – burn her, the Witch Bitch!', 'Jem! Bet you can't wait to see this one go up!', 'Fix that with your potions!' Jeers and shouts echoing towards me, bouncing off granite walls, ringing with contempt.

'I'll do it.'

'Good girl. My Little Death. My Little D. Now, let's get you back to where you belong.'

Back in the cell, the iron bridle hanging from the wall, Lucifer takes my hand. Kisses the back of it as if I'm a lady stepping into a carriage. Fixes the straps over my head and slips the cold metal bit into my mouth. But there's no pain now. No discomfort. I feel nothing. He lifts first one hand, then the other to fix them into the shackles against the wall. Steps back to leave me hanging, to await my fate, as the men burst forth into the room.

I'm led back to the market square by a chain attached to my iron head-dress. Paraded for the townspeople to see. Sly kicks at my legs from the people leading me. The dull thud of vegetables thrown from the crowd and hitting my shoulders, my back, the side of my head. Hands push me forward, jerking me back when I stumble, over-balanced by the weight of the iron frame around my head.

Whenever I look up He is there, an island of calm in a surging sea of hatred and vitriol. A sea of looming, angry red faces, mouths wide open in a communal death chant. The sun is setting and my path is lit by flaming torches carried overhead.

They lead me over to the stake, tie each hand behind my back. Stack the firewood around my feet. Make their final pronouncements of my status as witch and set light to the kindling with one of the procession of torches. The flames curl and dance, licking up my legs and catching my sacking dress while the waiting crowd cover their mouths and noses as the smell of burning human flesh billows out across their eager mass. They laugh and point as tendrils of smoke entwine with my hair. Cheer as sparks catch and flare, as fabric falls away and skin is exposed to melt like wax. I feel nothing. He is leaning against the stone cross, arms folded across his chest, eyes boring into mine, a twisted smile on his lips as He stands head and shoulders above the seething swell. As the flames grow, enveloping my head in a gossamer cloak of smoke, as the scene before me warps and distorts through the heat haze, as my mortal bones crack and groan in the blaze, I don't take my eyes from His. And as my body dies in that Scottish market square, I am born as Death.

3

IT WAS OVER FOUR HUNDRED YEARS AGO, THAT cold day in that exposed market square. Four hundred years since I took that offer, since I sealed my fate. Four hundred years of this, my new life. This life of Death. Day after day. Year upon year. Each second lived a mirror flash of the reflected life of the women I embody. Each second lived as someone else. Me and not me. Them and not them. For four hundred years.

In the early days, I flew with pride from one death to the next. Held my head high as death followed life and souls swept by me to their final conclusion. But in these latter years, I have found it cold, this life without life. While I move from one to the next, basking in reflected love and a shared history, my core remains cold. My fingertips have no feeling for the skin beneath them; there is no need for sustenance, so in all of these years I haven't tasted a morsel to make the mouth water, to make the stomach rumble.

Do you know how monotonous endless life can become? Incessantly shifting, never-ending, never-pausing? A constant whirl from bedside to battlefield, from a lonely kitchen table to the plastic incubator on the hospital ward. The death itself becomes inconsequential, meaningless as seconds pass in hours and I whirl, morphing from one woman to the next, to the next. And the brief moments between these deaths, when I pause to catch my breath and float unbidden in the darkness before being tugged to attention and summoned to the next bedside, roadside, homicide . . . Well, those brief moments serve as the most painful reminder. That while I tend to a death I am everything to the person with whom I sit, with whom I reminisce, but in the intervening moments when I float alone in this world, I have no one. No one, and nothing. I keep my previous life at arm's length – a haze, a blur. A mirage in my memory that shimmers and shines, that lures me in only to disappear when I get too close. And so on I whirl, from one death to the next, never stopping to think of the pain of my missed life, so consumed am I with death.

Until one day, everything I know, everything I hold dear, it changes. Changes overnight. I'm caught unawares, knocked off my feet and spun around until up is down and right is wrong. More than four hundred years on from that cold market square, the constant whirl slows abruptly in a ubiquitous hospital room. I am pulled up short, brought to a halt as time sweeps around me in lazy arcs. And in the centre of this storm, calm, oblivious . . . Tom. The eye at the centre of my storm. Tom. Four hundred years on from that cold market square I fall in love.

Four hundred years pass and I find myself, as I often do these days, in a hospital ward. Hunched shoulders shelter the bed. A cold, dead hand clasped in huge paw and crushed against creased brow. It's her I've come to see. Tubes masking a pale face. It's her I'm here for, but it's him I can't tear my eyes from.

Although he can't see me, it feels as though he's watching my every move. As I clamber onto the bed, raised high on its haunches to facilitate access, as I whisper into her ear and press my lips against a clammy forehead to murmur and soothe, as I plump the cushions behind her head, he watches.

Around us nurses bustle and fuss, hooking up saline drips, smoothing down sheets. There are no windows in this room, no way of knowing the time of day, the state of the world outside. Only the rolled-up sleeves of the consultant when he arrives, the damp patch of cotton clinging wetly to the small of his back and the fine mist of sweat on his brow betray the heat of an unseasonably warm late October day somewhere outside.

She fades in and out. The whitened knuckles of a clutching hand betray the innate fear she's hiding from the man sitting by her bedside as the clinical beep of the respirator jabs into her skull with every mechanised breath. The rush of a forced inhalation chased by the hush of an outward sigh.

Ever since her diagnosis as a teeny tot, Kate has known this day would come. That the daily physiotherapy and dietary supplements would only keep the cystic fibrosis under control for so long. She knew it when she met Tom that first day in the Student Union, when he chased her down the length of the corridor at the Freshers' Fayre to get her to agree to come and watch his rugby team's first game. It's why she resisted him for so long. Didn't want him to get attached to a broken girl who was going to have to leave him one day through no choice of her own. Didn't want to have to explain to a complete stranger about the strange bruises on her chest and back and the gritty powders in her food. But he persevered, young Tom. Walking her home from lectures and turning up after training for a cup of tea and a biscuit in her tiny room in halls. He persevered until the two of them had fused together and there was never one without the other. Until she realised that although she might not live long, she couldn't live what life she had without him.

And he too has known, since she explained her illness, way back when. He too has known this day would come. As he has pummelled her chest daily to loosen the phlegm and mucus that churns in her lungs and clogs her airways. He has known that the complications would crop up more and more frequently. That their time together could be all too short.

Knowing doesn't make it any easier though, does it?

We've been lying side by side for half an hour before she speaks.

'He was so bloody persistent – remember?' She nods her head towards Tom, lips moving in silent prayer to a God he's never previously believed in. A last-ditch attempt to reverse the inevitable.

I have climbed onto Kate's hospital bed as her mother. Ash-blonde hair perfectly bobbed and tucked around tiny gold earrings. A cashmere sweater paired with tailored flannel trousers. The papery skin on the back of my hands is dusted with the tell-tale signs of summers in the sun. I curl myself next to her, stroke her hair as she rests her head against my shoulder.

As we lie there, I do remember. That persistence of first love. I remember the eager twenty-year-old being brought home for the first time, nervously shaking hands with Kate's dad and chucking a ball around the back garden with little brothers and a yapping Jack Russell, the only breed whose hair didn't induce bubbling coughs. I can see him turning to check she's there, check she's OK. And she was at her happiest – the final piece of a jigsaw had slotted into place to complete the picture of the people she loves.

'I'm glad he was, though. Glad he was so bloody stubborn. Do you think I've been selfish? If I'd left him years ago he'd be happily married now, wouldn't he? Two point four children and a black lab.'

'Not the tiniest bit.' How could she even think that? 'He wouldn't have let you go for a start. And you've had seventeen wonderful years together. No one and nothing can ever take that away from either of you.'

'But no one wants to be a widower by the age of thirty-seven do they? That's what I've given him – pitying looks on the street and a label that belongs to an eighty-year-old. That's my legacy.'

'Oh Kate . . . Katie K . . . Don't you ever, ever think that. He wouldn't have changed it for a second. Not one second.'

'I want him to be happy. I want you to let him know that it's OK. That I know he loved me. That it's OK for him to meet someone else. To fall in love. I want you to tell him that. I don't want him to ever forget me, what we had. But I want him to live his life. Find a nice girl. Have the kids and the dog and the wife who will take him through to the end of his days, not leave him floundering alone like I have at the end of mine.' Her voice breaks through the tears. 'You will tell him, won't you?'

I look over the top of her head at the man crumpled by her side. At lightly freckled forearms and a curly mop-top of hair standing up at angles from being raked through by desperate fingers. And I fight an urge to calm those fingers, to twist my own into soft, dark curls. To lean over and kiss eyelids screwed tight shut in silent prayer.

'I'll tell him.'

'Thank you.' A whisper.

She closes her eyes, squeezes Tom's hand gently in her own one last time, and to the unbroken monotone trill of the heart-rate monitor, Kate Olivia Sanderson fades to black.

As the alarm sounds, the room is submerged in a flurry of activity. Nurses run in to surround the bed, lifting lids to shine bright lights into dead eyes. Tom shoves his chair away from the bed, backs himself into the corner, never taking his eyes from the body lying in front of him. Gulps. Gags. Sags to the floor. He can't hear the voices that implore him to 'Get up please, Tom. Come with me, Tom.' Can't feel the hands that take him by the elbow to lead him out of the room. Steering his shoulders as his body corkscrews to turn to her. To call her name.

They lead him out into the corridor. Press a plastic cup of hot, sweet tea into his hand and settle him into the hard-backed chair where he slumps, eyes closed against the beep-thud of the defibrillator. He's shaking. Shivering despite the warmth of the corridor. He takes a sip of the tea, but he can't force it past the ball of tension in his throat and he gags, spluttering hot liquid against the back of his hand, pressed hard against his lips.

I slip out of the room. Leave the nurses to their fruitless task. She's gone now. I should leave.

But I don't. I can't.

In the corridor, he looks straight at me, grief and disbelief in his navy-blue eyes fringed with lashes saturated with tears. And reflected in his eyes I can see it. See everything that I want. See everything that he thinks he has lost. It hits me full in the stomach, like a punch. There is no gradual dawning, no gentle awakening to the thought. It's as though a floodlight has swept across my vision, and where there was darkness, now all is clear.

I want to live. I need to live. I want a love so overwhelming that life is meaningless without it. I am desperate to feel the love of a family, the woozy headiness of a day spent drinking red wine in front of a fire, hot breath against my neck in a semi-dark room. The giddiness of laughing till I lose my breath, the great racking sobs that exhaust even the strongest. I want to smell freshly baked bread and cram it into my mouth, oozing with melted butter. I want to roll in freshly mown grass. I want to live, and I want all that life brings with it. I see it all, exposed in stark relief. Everything that I crave. Everything I've missed.

And I know. I know in that longest of seconds. There is only one way for me to grasp life and all that living brings. My time has come to end this monotony – this never-ending task of ending. To bring about the death, you might say, of Death.

And there is one man alone who can help me – one man with the power to give me what I can only dream of. He is my nemesis and my colleague.

I must go and see the Devil.

4

THE POPPIES AND BALSA WOOD CROSSES OF THE
Westminster Abbey Field of Remembrance stand out
blood red and bone white against the grass. It's dank,
drizzly, a typical November afternoon in London – fog
hanging in the air and dusk peeking his head around
the corner no matter what the time of day.

I enter through the West Door – brought up short
by the Tomb of the Unknown Soldier. Carpeted in
poppies, the gold lettering of melted ammunition plain
against the polished black marble. I knew him of
course, the Unknown Soldier. I knew them all.
Gathered together on those cold, wet, claggy trenches
in those most final of moments – sharing smokes,
singing – always singing – about packing up your
troubles in an old kit bag while smiling all the time.

Those were busy days, I can tell you. I'd sit with
them for hours, those men. Battered and bruised,
tattered and torn. To each of them I was someone

different – sweethearts from back home, mothers and sisters. I sat with them in those French fields, wiped the caked mud from their faces, laid my head against the death rattle of mustard gas clogging their lungs. They cried on me, they laughed. Ruffled my hair and showed me their letters from home. And then one by one, with their hands in mine, they would fade to black. Some in a matter of moments, some lasting hours, days. The Unknown Soldier was one of the last.

Now, on to the task in hand. As ever, I have to search for Him – I have requested an audience and it has been granted – but He's never one to make things easy. I keep going, down the central aisle, through the Quire Screen with its gilt-adorned carvings and golden stars picked out against a cerulean blue sky. Past the heavy oak choir stalls and down towards the altar. Round the back of the Shrine of Edward the Confessor, whipping round the Chapel of Henry VII and into Poets' Corner. This is not a sight-seeing visit. I am not a tourist – this is a means to an end.

Up ahead and tucked off to the side, a heavy wooden door. Chances are if He's not perched in the rafters or lounging in the Coronation Chair, taunting the vergers with His invisible presence, He'll be tucked away, hidden, waiting for me to find Him, His own little game of cat and mouse. I slip through the door into the darkened corridors of the Cloisters.

I see Him immediately. Sleek and feline in an impeccably cut suit, His hair slicked back from His angular face. He's lounging against the wall on a stone bench running the length of the corridor. One slim ankle hooked over its opposite knee. Above Him, a simple plaque in the rough stone walls – Jane Lister, dear childe, 1688. (Tuberculosis. Feverish embraces in a room on Cheapside. Poor little thing. She clung to me as if she'd never let go.) He stands, stretches to His full height.

The winter light struggles through the columns of the arcade, fighting through the stained glass at the apex of each arch. The individually lit vaults do nothing to warm or welcome.

When He speaks, it is with a sneer of indifference. His voice is cold, clinical, clipped. Ringing off flagstones worn smooth by centuries of feet.

'You wanted to see me?'

I know no one can hear Him but me, I know that no one is even aware of our being there, but I wince. I try to encourage Him into an alcove. Somewhere less open. Who do I think I am? He's the Devil. We're staying right where He wants us. Years of experience have told me exactly who holds the reins in this relationship.

'I . . .'

A pause. Silence in that cold, stone corridor.

'I . . .'

Try. Again. Fail. Again.

'Get on with it,' He snaps. 'You wanted to see me.' He can't abide having His time wasted. 'After all this time – you don't write, you don't call. And now you demand a meeting and all you can do is stand there and splutter.'

'I've had enough.' I've said it, it's out there. I wait for the explosion – for the 800-year-old walls around us to crumble and fall. For the shriek of His disapproval. But, nothing. He's nothing if not unpredictable.

'I need this to end. I want my life.' I feel like one of the sulky, monosyllabic teenagers who populate the modern-day streets with their moodiness.

Still nothing.

In a small voice, I continue: 'I want my soul back. Please.' A little courtesy can't hurt.

He smiles. A smile cold, pitying, contemplative, oddly paternal, all at once.

'Oh, Little D, Little, Little D . . .'

I hate it when He calls me that. He may as well team it with a ruffle of my hair and a chuck under the chin.

'And what do you propose I do about this? About your having "had enough"? Shall I pat you on the back, wave you on your way, wish you a merry life? Perhaps we could have a yearly get-together? Reminisce about the old times over a cheese board and a glass of the finest port?' He laughs, a mirthless, derisory snort. Contemplates me down the length of His long, thin nose.

I open my mouth to speak, to explain.

'Don't.'

One word, a gunshot. I stay silent.

'Why now, Little D? Why now, after all these years . . . ?' Looking down at me through narrowed eyes, long finger stroking His chin. He reaches to cup my own in His other hand, forcing my face to tilt towards His. Forcing my eyes to make contact with His own. He stares into them. Blue eyes freeze the air between us.

'You idiot.' He sighs. 'You foolish, stupid girl. You've fallen in love. Haven't you? Haven't you?'

My eyes drop, look off to the wall beside him, to the polished flags, to the long stone bench. I need not speak, He has answer enough.

His hand releases my chin. 'Fool.'

He takes my arm, hustling me along the corridor, round the central garden and back into the body of the church. Although the throngs of tourists can't see us, they sense the menace in their midst – an impercept-ible shiver as we pass, a votive candle breathing its last and sending a plume of smoke spiralling above it.

As we enter the church, His pace slows. Deliberate. Thoughtful. Pausing to admire the odd carving, stopping to frown at the memorials of the people who have defied Him. I'm not the only one who knows the inhabitants of the Abbey inside and out.

Eventually, He speaks.

'So. That's it, is it? You want your life? Your soul? You do know I can't just hand that to you on a plate, don't you? You do know that if I am to give you what you are asking for, I need to know that you deserve it? You do know that I am going to have to make you earn it? You do know that, don't you, Little D?'

I do. I do know that. But it's been too long. I have served this role for an eternity and I can't do it any more. I know the stakes are high, but the thought of another yawning expanse with no escape is almost too much to bear. Now it's out there, and now He's even contemplating it, this is my chance. If I don't take it now, He certainly won't give me another.

'Do you remember what I said to you? Back in that cell?' He studies my face through narrowed eyes, chews on His lip while He considers His options. A woman passes – brushing His coat with her handbag. He doesn't flinch. She pulls her cardigan tighter around herself and hurries off in the direction of Poets' Corner.

'You do remember, don't you, Little D?' He asks, cocking His head to one side. 'Back in that squalid little cell of yours all those years ago? Foul place . . .' A muttered aside. 'What did I say? What did I tell you? Hmm?'

He doesn't even bother to wait for an answer. He's taken centre stage, is throwing himself into the role. And all I can do is watch and wait.

'For every action, Little D, there must be a reaction. Yes? You remember that?' He stops in front of the Isaac Newton memorial, looking up at the golden globe heralding the heavens hanging above his head.

'D'you know, I mentioned that very thing to Sir Isaac once. Every action having a reaction . . . I think he might've seen something in it . . . Anyhow, I digress. There was more, wasn't there? Hang on, let me think . . .'

He taps a long finger against His chin. I hear Him muttering under His breath, playing for time, ever the showman. 'For every action . . . a reaction . . . Yes! There was more, wasn't there, Little D. I do remember what else I said. Yes, I distinctly remember this bit. If you take me up on this, I said, if you take me up on this, I will own you. If you wanted to get out of our little arrangement, there must, by the very nature of your wishing to abandon me, be consequences. Yes, that's it. For every action, there must be a reaction.'

The pacing continues. Finger tapping against cheek, face turned to the ceiling in contemplation.

'After all, Little D, if you're depriving me of the nourishment of your soul, I'm going to need something to fill the gap, aren't I? Until I find myself another willing volunteer. So, what do you say to a challenge? How do you feel about that, my little one? I shall set you a challenge, and if you pass with flying colours, you shall have your life. This "soul" of yours will be back intact and unharmed. And you can live your life. Live your life, love your man. And then die like the rest of them.' His nose wrinkles in distaste at the word 'die'.

I nod. I was expecting nothing less. When I offered up my soul to Him all those hundreds of years ago, I should have known getting it back wouldn't be so easy.

'What do you propose?' My voice cracks and I clear my throat – He always has this effect on me. I try to be strong, to stand up to Him, but He terrifies me.

'Five deaths. That is all, Little D. Relatively easy I would think, given your . . . what shall we call it . . . ? Speciality . . . ? Your field of expertise . . . ? You will bring about five deaths. Five deaths of my choosing. If you do them well, if I am satisfied with the way you handle yourself, with the way you kill these chosen five, then what you desire will come to pass. God knows I can't abide the idea of mortality and I have very little idea why you would want such a thing, but if you want your precious soul, these five deaths will be your price.'

I stand facing Him, the chequerboard of the tiled aisle between us.

'Your move, Little D.'

A deep breath. I accept. It sounds too easy to be true. Of course it does.

'So, our first candidate . . . Now, where shall we start? No time like the present, eh?' He's almost avuncular. It's unnerving.

He strides off to the North Aisle, leaving me running to catch up. Along its length glass-topped wooden desks are laid out, strewn with the scarlet poppies of remembrance. In each one a huge book, neatly engraved with the names of the fallen. Hundreds upon hundreds of names, meticulously listed. I know them all. I have met them all.

He leans against one, casual, indifferent.

'There's a gap, Little D. The one that got away, you might say.' He runs His fingers down the Ws – Wall, Walters, Weatherby, West, Weston, Williams. He stops. Between Williams, F. R. and Williams, J. P. A gap. Not something the casual observer would ever see, but a gap sure enough, an infinitesimal gap.

'He outsmarted me, that one. All his life he's been getting the better of me. And I think it's time we put a stop to that, don't you, Little D?'

Williams, H. I.

Number 1.

5

I'VE MET HYWEL IFOR WILLIAMS BEFORE. QUITE A
few times, in fact. And my friend the Devil is right:
Hywel has 'cheated death', as they say. I've been there,
ready and waiting, and each time he's slipped away,
righted himself, taken that lungful of air that blows
me out of the room. And good for him, I've always
said – I've never wanted to be where I'm not wanted.
Until now.

Tuesday, 16 February 1926.

It's a cold day. A freezing, bitter, cold day in a Welsh
mining village in the Rhondda Valley. Frost blurs the
cobbles on the main street and a scream rings out.
A guttural, base, animal scream. A sob. A groan. A
whimper. Whispered voices reassuring, calming. 'Good
girl,' I hear them soothe. 'Just one more push.'

The voices slip through the small gap of an open
sash window on the first floor of a mid-terrace house.

A tiny opening despite the cold of the day outside. But where frost blooms in spiky petals on the windows of the houses either side, here condensation runs in streams down the panes to collect in a puddle on the cracked-paint windowsill.

Despite the freezing day, the air inside the bedroom is thick, stifling. The fire in the hearth is ablaze. Logs hiss and crackle in the grate, throwing out sparks that chase each other up the chimney bright as fireflies before burning out to nothing.

A woman in bed, shivering and convulsing but with sweat pouring from her brow. Her nightdress is soaked with sweat and blood. Sweat and blood, smeared with mucus and tears. Naked knees drawn up to her chest, every sinew in her neck straining. She screams again, grunting, head thrown back – the animal yowl of a fighting mother.

More whispers. Shadowy figures move around the room. She hears snippets. Glimpses of what these figures know, of what they can see.

'Wrong way round.'

'Cord wrapped round his neck.'

'Losing blood.'

Her scream turns to a whimper. A moan. A soundless sob. Her head sags against her shoulder. Exhaustion is taking over. She's been doing this for hours. Blood is flowing freely on to the sheets. Her face is pale, waxy. Hair plastered in strands to her cheek. The shadowy figures take their positions around her bed –

one holding her shoulders, murmuring words of encouragement into her ear, the other reaching between her legs, rearranging the unborn child, trying to turn him, free his head from the cord encircling his tiny throat. She can see me now, standing in the corner, fading in and out – now lit by the flare of the fire, now imperceptible in the shadows. As the seconds tick by, as her breath becomes laboured, rasping, I become clearer to her – she can see my face. The face of her mother, so very like her own. The black dress and high collar of turn-of-the-century fashions. I move to the edge of her bed. Sit to take her head in my lap, smoothing her sodden hair away from her forehead, plaiting the sweat-soaked strands between my fingers. Humming her favourite song from when she was a tiny girl. She is ready now – she can't fight any longer, she knows that this life has done for her. But she can't go yet, can't move on without seeing her son. So we sit and we wait. And we rock gently to and fro, to and fro as the midwife works around us to extricate him from his slippery noose. As they pull him out and his first squawking, mewling cries rend the cold February afternoon, she rests her exhausted head on my shoulder, and with a whispered murmur of love to her tiny son, Dorothea Maeve Williams slowly, quietly, fades to black.

And so, from the very beginning his life, from those very first seconds, I knew Hywel Ifor Williams. And he knew me.

*

I didn't see him for a few years. If truth be told, I forgot all about that tiny child who'd fought his way into the world. I had other things to worry about. When I saw him again he was a man.

Tuesday, 6 June 1944.

Well, I say a man. More like an eighteen-year-old boy who had seen too much, who already knew too much of the hellish way of the world. An eighteen-year-old boy who had seen more than any man twice, three times his age should see. An eighteen-year-old boy with death in his eye.

He shouldn't even have been there, shouldn't have made it this far. He should have been turned away in that community hall in Swansea. Drawing himself up to full height and presenting his forged documents to the recruiting officer. Smooth cheek ignored in favour of broad shoulders and a body accustomed to hard work. He was enlisted into the 2nd Battalion South Wales Borderers that day in October 1941. A fifteen-year-old boy gifted three extra years in a single handshake.

Leaving home meant leaving Angharad. They were inseparable, those two. Clambering up coal heaps together, lying for hours in the meadows pointing out shapes in the clouds floating through the cornflower-blue skies of a Welsh summer. She'd hated him for signing up. As much as she could bring herself to hate him. Shouted at him again and again that he was too young to die, too young to fight. But he was convinced that he had to do his duty and go and join the thousands of others on the front line. And he made her promise that she wouldn't say anything, wouldn't tell his Da what he'd done until he was far away. Far, far away and the ham-sized fists and deep baritone ring of a furious father were left well behind. So she promised, and she hated herself, but she kept her promise and didn't say a word.

And now, tonight. Two and a half years of training, fighting, watching friends die, helping friends live. Two and a half years to bring Hywel here, to the Normandy coast. To bring him here, for this night of nights.

I'm sitting in the dunes – waiting for the distant drone, the hum and whirr of planes crossing the Channel, troops swallowed in their bellies. The sky is black, heavy with thunderous clouds and midnight. I've been waiting. Their arrival has been delayed by the weather, but I know they're coming. I know they'll be coming to me in their hundreds. Boys, mere boys, all of them.

The first wave passes overhead, parachutes like a swarm of jellyfish bells against the blackened sky. If I didn't know how this ended I would think it almost beautiful. And with this swarm, so my work begins. In fields and dunes, forests and villages. Time is of no consequence to me – this night is endless and there is much to be done. A second can last a minute, an hour, a day. Each of those following days lasts a month, each month a year – a gritty, cold, harrowing year. A minute, a day, a month of tears and helplessness and laughter and songs and heaving, racking sobs. Minutes, days, months when boys become men, and where those men come to me to die.

I am everywhere and nowhere. Ushering souls from the cold wet sand, lying low as bullets whistle overhead. Cradling bodies in blood-churned mud. Collecting those boys as they lie strewn across the fields, blood bubbling on their lips, choking from their lungs. Some are calm in the face of inevitability – they smile at me as we hold hands, kiss me as their bodies slump. They're expecting me – they've seen me in the faces of the friends who have gone before them, in those other boys who never made it this far. Grateful for the solid warmth of a comforting breast and a final reminder of their humanity in all this hatred and waste. Happy, most of them, to see the girl they love for the very last time. To be scolded by a mother who's not seen them for months and who arrives armed with a freshly baked cake for one last feed.

Then, of course, there are the others, the ones who haven't prepared for this, who weren't expecting the savage hand of fate to hit. The ones who had blithely refused to countenance the very real truth that it could be them. They run from me, shove at my chest, hit at my face, rip at my clothes. Push me with all of their dwindling strength. Bite at hands that try to embrace weary bodies.

Then, when they can hit out no more, they collapse against me, sobbing and shuddering in the dark of the Normandy dawn. The pain lasts longer that way – the searing heat of the bullet in their chest pulses as long as they fight, until that too fades. And one by one, over the seconds, minutes, days, they fade to black. This is no place for a woman, I've heard it said. I've never seen a place a woman was more needed.

Hywel comes from the sea – the second wave. Ships loom on the horizon in the gun-metal Atlantic, 'Men of Harlech' singing in their veins. I see him from a distance, hauling himself out of the surf, the shock of the freezing water causing him to check himself for the briefest of moments. Heavy wool trousers cling wetly to his massive frame. That child, who had such a rocky start in life, has grown into a mountain of a man. He stands six foot two, broad-shouldered and straight-backed. His movement is solid, assured – he looks around for his fellow men, dragging one forward, checking over his shoulder for another. Head low in his tin hat, running up the beach for cover. Shots fire out around us, men fall as bullets zing and ping. From somewhere in this melee, the reedy notes of a bagpipe dance on the cold air. Mines explode, showering sand, wood, scorching metal that burns into young skin. He has magic in his feet, young Hywel, missing missiles by millimetres. He runs on through the confusion and desolation, past the bodies lain prostrate, the severed limbs lying ownerless. Right past me. He sees me, he recognises me. Pauses for a second, a look of confusion on his face. He rights himself, shaking his head and runs on. Passes a friend in my direction. He has no interest in me, now is not his time.

Tuesday, 8 October 1963.

Fast forward nineteen years and the boy is well and truly a man. Back from the hell and the hatred to the open arms and unquestioning love of Angharad. Not a day goes by when he doesn't think about me, doesn't wonder if he was going mad all those years ago when he saw his mother in the middle of the mayhem and the mines. I have no way of explaining, you see, until that final day when we meet and everything falls into place.

Angharad was waiting when he returned – the fourteen-year-old girl was an eighteen-year-old woman at the end of the war, petite and pretty, warm and witty. Gleaming conker-brown hair impeccably set, cobalt-blue eyes twinkling. She always knew he'd come home and she would have waited until the end of time for him to do so. Sometimes, in that awful war, it felt like she would have to. They were bound, the two of them – she, a tiny acorn inextricably linked to her oak. They started planning the wedding as soon as he arrived back from France. Not another second to lose.

Not another moment to waste. A simple ceremony in the local chapel, photographs on the steps outside. Angharad, traditional in the hand-stitched lace of her mother and her mother's mother before her, Hywel in his father's old Sunday suit worn to a shine at the elbow and knee, but he has a new shirt for the occasion – crisp, white collar starched and stiff.

Their marriage is a happy one. He's a man of few words – he's never had much to say – but since the war his desire to speak has waned even further. Angharad makes up for it, chirruping and singing her way through the day as she waits for her boy to come home. She loves being a wife, loves looking after their simple terraced home and waiting for him to come home at the end of every long day at the mine. Even now, seventeen years on, she still gets butterflies at ten past five knowing he'll be back in twenty minutes. Her love. Her *cariad bach*. And when she sees his massive frame looming through the pane of glass in the kitchen door she is happy. Her man is home and she is content.

They've never had children. They've tried – Lord knows they were desperate. And it nearly happened more than once. But then the cramps and the pain and the blood. Every time, the cramps and the pain and the blood. The agony as their babies were taken in the darkest of nights by the local doctor. Barely more than a bundle of cells. Limbs partially formed. Thin, pink skin translucent. I watched as they cried – Angharad's head tucked into the crook of his shoulder as he strokes her hair and whispers and lulls. Anything to take the pain away. But he can't. He's helpless. And then finally, after years of dashed hopes and sleepless nights, they accept their fate. They are two and they are strong.

And then one day, Hywel doesn't come home. The butterflies flit, as they do every day at ten past five. At twenty past, Angharad pops the kettle on the hob. At half past, the boiling water purses its lips to whistle, ready for a well-deserved cup of tea to welcome Hywel through the door and slake the coal-dust-parched throat. But today there's no figure looming at the back door. No boots kicked off on the kitchen step and no dirty kiss, smearing her face with black marks as she laughs and chides.

Today, Hywel doesn't come home.

She sits and waits for him at the kitchen table. Sits and waits. The butterflies have settled to a hardened knot in the pit of her stomach. The cup of tea she's made for his home-coming sits cold and forgotten on the dresser, a skin forming on its surface. Every tick of the grandmother clock in the kitchen passage a whip crack. Tick. Tock. Tick. Tock. Filling her ears and mind with every second he doesn't return. As the minutes pass into hours, the fire in the range dies down and she sits, cold and alone in the dim light. And still the clock, it ticks and it tocks.

And finally, finally at a quarter to eleven, there's a

knock at the front door. Nobody ever knocks at the front door.

On that same cold October night, I'm up the hill. Up at the coal face both literally and metaphorically. While Angharad was baking, the mine was falling in. Collapsing in on the heads of the men below. And we all know that Hywel was in there.

I've crawled inside, deep into the gut of the earth. To the ten men huddled there. Splintered wooden struts bar their way, the sound of coal settling slithers and snakes into their ears. I have seen to three of the men – wrapping them tightly in their coats and kissing their eyelids closed, their heads nestled one by one into my lap. I extract their crushed and crumbled limbs, right their heads on broken necks. But Hywel, Hywel holds me at arm's length. Although he can't see me in the darkness, he can smell me in the air – the musky scent Angharad sprays on the nape of her neck, that tangles in her hair as it drapes across his cheek. He pushes me out of the way. Just a nudge. Just enough to let me know I have no place here. Move on please, nothing to see. But the air is getting thin and it's only a matter of time. I only need to sit and wait.

A trickle of blood runs down his forehead and his body is twisted unnaturally, uncomfortably. He rests his head against the sheer face of coal and thinks of Angharad. Only of her. He knows she'll be waiting, from the second the clock ticks past half past the hour and he doesn't walk through the door. Knows she won't leave the house until he's back, until order is restored and he's come back for her. He can see her sitting there at the kitchen table, small hands clasped in front of her, eyes fixed on the clock. Refusing to think the worst. She's a stubborn one, his Angharad. He thinks of their wedding day. Of the home-made quilt on their bed, stitched together square by square in front of the fire in the parlour on cosy evenings spent in companionable silence. He thinks of the stew and potatoes waiting for him in the slow cooker and his stomach rumbles in the darkness.

Up on the surface, an air of panic hangs over the scene. Rescue workers divide into groups. The task at hand is slow and laborious, success balancing on a knife edge. Too long and the little air they have will run out, a suffocating carbon dioxide build-up to tempt each of them into a final sleep. Too quick and the roof falls in to crush and break the men below into a million little pieces.

They work in silence. Lips tight in grim faces, skin grey in the fading light. Although the sky above is still showing vestiges of the crisp blue of an autumn afternoon, the shadow of the mountain has thrown the operation into a premature darkness. Lamps light the entrance to the mine, casting an amber glow across the hillside. The metallic ring of shovel against stone echoes out in the cold afternoon air, bouncing off the exposed rock faces on all sides. They work for hours. Painstaking, tiny advances. One shovel at a time.

Down below the men can hear the movement above. Tiny chips of coal rain down on them, breath held with every flurry, anticipating a landslide. An eerie sense of calm pervades the space – these are hardened men in both body and mind, and they know the risks of the mine. They know that each day could be their last.

As the hours pass, breathing becomes harder. Oxygen is running out and those still clinging to life are getting light-headed. Their eyes have become accustomed to the darkness and one by one they begin to see me. I am Martha, wife of Thomas. I am Dilys, mother of Gareth and Dylan. They've done everything together those boys – eighteen years of Dylan following Gareth's every move. So when Gareth said he wanted to look for work at the mine, it was inevitable Dylan would be right behind him. And finally, I am Bethany, three years old and cuddling my father in that cold, dark and scary place. The only person I still haven't appeared to, who still won't even entertain the idea of my presence, is Hywel.

'Whaaa . . . ?'

A bright light shining in his face shocks him awake. A plastic mask bundled over his face floods his lungs with oxygen. He jerks his head back, knocking it against the cold, hard rock and wincing as a shooting pain slices through his neck where it's bent in a most unorthodox fashion.

'We've got one!' Big hands work quickly to free limbs. Big hands, surprisingly gentle in their efficiency. The pain from a dislocated shoulder makes him pass out again. But not before Angharad flits across his mind's eye – alone and cold at the kitchen table.

At the surface, the first fingers of dawn are reaching out across the mountain peaks. The crews have worked tirelessly and relentlessly. And only Hywel has made it this far. The others follow him lifeless on stretchers out of the rubble of the mine entrance – a solemn procession shrouded in pink blankets blackened with coal.

The first ambulance takes Hywel – blue light flashing, bell ringing, bouncing back louder against the hard lines of slate and slag heap. Behind this first vehicle, his colleagues are carried in a silent cortege of flashing blue.

More lights – fluorescent tubes shuttle overhead as the hospital trolley sweeps along pea-green corridors and faces crowd above him.

'Fluids.'
'Oxygen.'
'Nasty bump to the head.'
'Angharad . . . ?'
'Ward 6B.'
'Fracture of the right tibia.'
'Administer chloroform.'

'Angharad . . . ?'

He passes in and out of sleep. So very, very tired. Coughing up thick, black phlegm. Lids heavy, eyes gritty. Mouth dry, teeth furred. His limbs feel like they've been set in concrete, his head as though he's been abandoned in a February fog. I watch him through the window to the ward. Watch as the nurses in their white peaked caps, with their starched bosoms, change his drip. As catheters are changed and slowly, slowly the colour returns to his cheeks. I watch as Angharad huddles close and grips his hand, chattering away as if he's listening to every word. And he is. Deep through the opiate fug he can hear her chirp. Deep under that chloroform blanket he smiles to himself. Don't worry, Angharad. He's not going anywhere.

And he doesn't. For three days I watch and wait, wait and watch. As he clambers out from his drug-induced sleep and returns the grip on Angharad's hand. As his lungs clear and broken bones begin to knit. When he wakes, Angharad's stream of chatter stills to a calm pool of silence as she tucks him in and fetches his water. The hours between visits are interminable in their silence, and yet the silence of her attendance whistles past in minutes.

And so the days pass and I leave them be. Leave them to each other. Don't worry, Angharad. He's not going anywhere.

*

Tuesday, 23 September 1997.

I've been checking in on Angharad for two years now. An ugly tumour loitering silently in her right lung, crouching over her days and waiting until it's too strong to be ignored, too big to fight. Reaching its fingers through delicate tissue to grasp at each breath she struggles to take.

She's even more shrunken than usual today – a tiny figure, hollow-cheeked and bald-headed, bundled beneath the blankets. Even the cocktail of steroids designed to keep up her appetite has done nothing to strengthen her and the little weight she carried on her bones has dropped off. Now it's Hywel who chatters – the man of few words has found them now, and they all come at once. A constant stream to ease and appease. With a countdown looming over them now he's desperate to cram every word into whatever time they have left.

She's had good days and she's had bad. The aching bones and nausea flood over her one day to be nowhere in sight the next. She shivers through the nights under clouds of duck-down before throwing the covers to one side to endure the unpredictable hot sweats. She doesn't want to leave him, knows he's got so many years left in him. But she's tired. Tired of fighting her way through every day. Tired of fearing what the next day will offer up. Tired of the effort it takes just to open her eyes every morning. Tired of seeing doctor after doctor to be told of yet another encampment set up by rogue cells to mutate and repli-cate and kill.

Hywel hovers over her, clucking like a mother hen. He'd give anything to take away the pain, to comfort her during those long, dark hours when even the feel of a cotton blouse against her skin is unbearable, and when sleep just won't come. But he can't. And without his power to protect, he feels useless.

He is with her, as he always is, when I come to meet her. Sitting in the armchair next to the bed – a high-backed upright upholstered in deep red brocade, brought up from the lounge so she need never be alone. He sits and reads out choice pieces from the day's papers. Never about death, or pain, or suffering. Never about the subjects on which she is now a quali-fied expert. But she loves the space fillers. The little stories that raise a smile and warm the cockles. The dog who's learned to surf. The man who saw the face of Jesus in a slice of toast and proclaimed the Second Coming. The tiger weaning six piglets.

As she lies and listens, so she coughs. This latest one started a few days ago, bubbling and gurgling in weakened lungs. Flecks of blood hidden in hankies. Wheezing breaths disrupting an already fractured sleep.

Hywel eases himself up out of the chair to go and make another cup of tea. 'Back in a jiffy, *cariad*. Don't you go anywhere.' She laughs, tears welling as the effort induces yet another racking, hacking cough.

As he leaves, I brush past him in the doorway, a breeze from an unopened window. Settle myself into his chair, the sister she lost aged seventeen. A mirror image of the younger Angharad, conker-brown hair curled atop my head in victory rolls. The cat stares straight at me with wide, green, unblinking eyes. Leaps from the arm of the chair to the bed to settle next to her owner and fix me with a hostile gaze.

'Angharad?' I ask, a whisper. She's settled back into the cushions, eyes closed against the glare of weak morning sunlight. As I speak, she can already feel the weight lifting from her chest, feel the lumps in her kidneys, in her liver, in her lungs, begin to dissipate and dissolve.

'Marianne . . .' She opens her eyes. Knows me straight away. 'I always loved your hair like that . . . Could never do it myself . . .' She reaches out a hand to wrap a curl gently around one finger. Looks down at her wedding ring and bites back a sob. 'I don't want to leave him, you know.' Tears swim in her eyes to brim at the rim without falling.

'I know.' I reach forward to take her hand. Wrap her tiny fist in mine. 'He'll be all right, won't he? By himself?'

'He'll miss you. Of course he'll miss you. But he loves you so very, very much. He knows he can't keep watching you go through this.'

'I'm sorry I couldn't give him children. There's no one to look after him now. Who's going to know how he likes his eggs? Who's going to remind him that he needs to leave out the milk bottles?' The first tear falls, snaking down her cheek into the crook of her neck. 'But I'm so tired. And I hurt. Every day I hurt. A little bit more. Every day.'

'I know. But it's time to go now. One last sleep.' I cup her cheek in my hand, soft as silk. Brush away tears with my thumb.

'Look after him for me.'

'Always . . .'

And as Hywel comes back into the room, balancing tea and gingersnaps, the final pain seeps away and Angharad Williams fades to black.

6

STRAIGHT BACKS AND STIFF UPPER LIPS LINE THE graveside. In the murky light of an overcast morning, faces are as grey as the clouds above. With the first fat drops of rain comes a morbid bloom of black umbrellas. Even the birds don't sing today, the only sound accompanying the minister's words the low moan of a distant lawnmower.

Tom stands towards the head of the grave, slightly apart from the throng. No umbrella. Dark hair studded with diamond droplets of rain. He stands close to the vicar, tucked in to shelter in his reassuring calm. His eyes stare intently at his shoes, shining black against the unnatural green of the astroturf that edges the grave. He counts the fringes of turf, the tiny holes stamped into the leather of his brogues. Anything to avoid looking at that box in the ground. The vicar speaks in a low hum, and with every word, as ash meets ash and dust becomes dust, Tom sags. The sags are barely perceptible, until it's unclear how he's managing to stay upright.

But though his body sags, though his lips move with unspoken words, though his breath shudders and exhausted eyes are rimmed red, still there are no tears.

They walk from the grave in silence, the mourning few. And still, in the distance, the lawnmower moans.

Back at Kate's mother's house, Tom stands apart from the groups of people who huddle together for support and cast sympathetic glances in his direction. Through the fog, he can hear them exchanging their whispered concerns.

'He's lost weight. Is he eating?'

'He's not answered any of my calls.'

'Do you think we should go over? You know? Say something?'

He leans against the mantelpiece, next to a silver-framed picture of his wedding day, and stares into the middle distance. Unblinking. Knocks back a tot of whisky, wincing at the burn at the back of his throat. He can hear the whispers. Can see the reluctance of each of those little groups to intrude on his grief.

Friends of his, friends of Kate's, who, despite years of inconsequential, mindless chat, are now unable to find the words. He lets the crystal tumbler hang loosely by his side – he'd give anything for one last inconsequential, mindless chat.

A tall girl breaks from the ranks, comes over to lay her hand on his arm. Leans in to briefly rest her cheek against his and kiss the air by his right ear. He tries to fight the automatic flinch as skin meets skin, but she felt him go rigid and she blushes at the perceived intrusion. As she pulls back, his eyes are closed and Kate's face dances beneath lowered lids as he breathes in the familiar perfume. Coco Mademoiselle. 'A girl always needs a little Chanel in her life,' Kate used to say.

'Tom.' The tall girl reaches up to tuck a strand of long, blonde hair behind her ear. 'How are you, darling?'

He smiles a tight, bitter smile that shows no teeth. Knocks back another tot of whisky. Watches the long earring that dangles to her shoulders swing against her neck. It was one of Kate's. She'd asked Kath to wear them to the funeral, so a part of her was there. But Tom can't take his eyes from it. Can't forget how it felt when she used to lower her face above his late at night and the soft gold brushed his cheek.

'Me? Oh, you know, Kath. Life's pretty rosy at the moment. Couldn't be better!' Inside he's screaming at himself. 'Stop it! Stop being such a bastard!' But the voice inside can't connect to the mouth that forms the words.

'Tom . . . I just . . . well . . .' She's lost for words. Kate's best friend and even she doesn't know what to say. 'We're all here for you. That's all I can say, I guess.

When you need us, when you want to see us . . . we're all here.' She nods her head towards the group she's broken free from. A small gaggle of their uni friends who are watching the exchange warily, assessing his reaction to Kath before they make moves of their own.

'Look, Kath. I . . . I've just got to go and talk to Kate's mum, yeah? I'll see you all later.'

He pushes past her and skirts the watching group who gather round Kath to console her in her failed bid to bridge the gap. Ducks through the doorway into the kitchen and the bottle of Glenmorangie Kate's mum thinks she's hidden behind the brown rice and plain flour in the pantry. He shuts himself in there, crouched on the floor to take quick swigs through tight lips, while I sit high above, legs dangling over the edge of the shelf, and watch.

7

TUESDAY, 8 JANUARY 2013.

It's always a Tuesday with Hywel – always a Tuesday when I see him. Funny that. I like a pattern.

It's cold. Grey and cold. Bleak and grey and cold. A dank wet fog hangs over the town, swept in from the hills to tuck the residents up for winter. I'm spending the day with him, with Hywel. I want to be with him for every minute of today.

Because I know today is going to be his last.

He is a ghost of the man I know of old. His hair bleached white with age and his huge frame is stooped, shrunken. Once cobalt eyes are pale and watery, the whites yellowing and the drooping pips in the corner standing out fleshy and red. I accompany him as he goes about his business, spending the day in companionable silence. Shuffling to the corner shop. Fumbling with the papers. Stumbling up the steps. Everything an effort, everything taking an age. His breath huffs and puffs with every step, a cloud billowing out to hang momentarily in the damp air. Everything hurts now. He can barely remember what it felt like to run down the pitch, tossing a rugby ball to the lads without a thought. Now, when his legs do manage to do what he asks of them, it's with a creak and a groan. An ache. A jab.

His clothes are neat. His shirt ironed, his tie – always a tie – straight and full at the knot. Even the tie takes longer now, as fingers whose knuckles are swollen with arthritis fumble with the slippery fabric. But he can't bring himself to wear one of those ready-made ones on their skinny strip of elastic. Angharad would be horrified.

We get home. At least the place he calls home. A drab little council flat in a low rise block on the outskirts of Merthyr Tydfil. It's not where his heart is, though.

Muted greys and browns, flaking paint and rucking lino. Carpets stained by tenants before him, having been chosen by the occupants before them. Net curtains soak up condensation behind ill-fitting windows. It's all on one floor – all he could possibly need and all he can possibly manage – hallway, living room, bedroom, bathroom. All no more than five steps from each other. It's not a home. When he moved here he knew that. It's the place he came to die. He just didn't know when that would be.

He moved here five long and lonely months after Angharad died. The terrace got too big for him, you see, and in every corner there was a whiff of her. A whisper. An overwhelming feeling that at any minute she was going to walk through the door, singing away to herself and popping the kettle on. Unbearable. The mattress they had shared for years still bearing the imprint of her body to remind him of her absence every time he woke in those long and lonely nights. Unbearable.

And here, he has everything he needs. He's got his things in a glass cabinet – his 'bits', he calls them. The cherry wood frame meticulously waxed and polished, the shelves packed with the ceramic birds that he's been collecting for years, perched on their ceramic branches among pictures of Angharad.

We sit, together, on the sofa. A cup of tea. Gulps and slurps break the silence. The rattle of an unsteady hand settling cup into saucer. A worn gold wedding ring on a swollen, gnarled finger clinks against china. We sit together, in silence. Staring into space, lost in years, decades. Lips wet and slack. Lost in a million moments.

I don't know how long we sit there. It could be minutes, it could be hours. The only indication of time passing is the light outside as afternoon turns to dusk turns to the blackest of nights. Darkness punctuated by the flickering on of sodium lights as they one by one come to life. Time lasts so much longer these days. It's not unusual for him to wonder, as the carriage clock on the mantel strikes three, if it can still be Tuesday. When Tuesday feels like it started three days ago. Sometimes, he has no idea how long he sits here, while buses sweep past the window and tea goes cold in a china cup.

Finally, time for bed. Another day over. Another long day endless in its emptiness.

We get up slowly – knees creaking as he straightens at the hip, at the knee, finally drawing his back and shoulders upright. Checks over his bits one last time before he goes to bed – ceramic birds with heads cocked, Angharad's face over and over. Forever twenty-one, thirty-six, forty-five, seventy in her wooden frames. '*Nos da cariad.*' Night night, sweetheart. Every night the same. Every night the ritual.

He switches off the living room light. Into the bathroom, avoiding the inevitable truth of the mirror under the bare strip light. Dentures into the glass by the sink. Through to the bedroom – throwing back the quilt Angharad stitched all those years ago. Nylon sheets crackling with static. Feet easing out of slippers, weight easing backwards to lift each leg up on to the bed, slowly, slowly, joints cracking. Everything takes so long these days.

His mind's going – they've been telling him that he should move into a home, that he should think about who's going to look after him for the rest of his days. Gwen from down the road comes round every so often – checks he's been paying his bills, that he's got food in the cupboards, isn't making his tea with stale milk, white flecks floating. She's noticed more and more that he's starting to forget things – leaving the two-bar gas fire on when he goes out, or forgetting to open the curtains in his bedroom. Going to the shop with his slippers on. Picking up yesterday's newspaper and not remembering the stories he'd read the day before.

And tonight, tonight dear reader, he forgets to check the bathroom window. And I've opened it. I've opened up his house to the outside world.

Glasses on the bedside table. Lamp off. Sleep.

I watch and wait while he settles. Brow furrowed in the concentrated sleep of babies and the old. Even sleep seems to be an effort nowadays. Eventually, I can leave him to his gentle snores. I have a job to do.

Heading outside I see a boy, down by the garages. twenty-two, twenty-three years old – looks younger. Pale, spotty complexion. Yellowing teeth. Thin, so terribly, painfully thin. He's trying to jimmy the lock of a Ford Mondeo. Darren Matthews. I've seen him before – laying out the tools of his trade in a dirty back room.

Needles, spoon, citric. Belt wrapped round his upper arm, biting into young skin. Veins standing to attention desperate for the rush of the opiates on that spoon, for the euphoria to wash over, for the cramps and the sweats and the chills to subside. I'm always there, in the shadows of these grubby little rooms. Watching, waiting for the last hit. Waiting for the pulse to slow and the breathing to become shallow, for their shoulders to slump and their eyes to glaze. Waiting for the look of guilt when I crouch over the stiffening body and they see their mother, grandmother, their tiny, toddling daughter. Always, always the look of guilt.

Darren Matthews. He'll do.

He can't see me – he doesn't know I'm there. Doesn't know the path I'm going to lead him down. A stringless puppet with which to do my bidding. A noise spurs him to spin round, leaning casually against the car. Metal strip tucked into the back pocket of his jeans – nothing to see here. It's a fox rifling through bins, eyes like mirrors in the moonlight.

He turns back to the car, and with a flick of the wrist and a flash of steel, locks pop open and he's in. Pops open the glove compartment to find an Elizabeth Duke watch and some scratched CDs. It won't be worth much, the watch, but you never know with these things. Beggars can't be choosers, as they say. And he's buggered if he'll let them see him begging.

As quick as he's in, he gets out, slamming the door and slipping the watch into his back pocket. Walks quickly, smartly in the direction of the flats with a quick glance over either shoulder to check he hasn't been seen.

And as he walks, I trot by his side to keep up. Gently take his elbow to steer him towards the walkway running down the front of the flats. The sodium glow of the streetlights reflects off the open window – leading the way, beckoning him in.

Darren knows the place, knows the little old guy who lives there. Always banging on about the war. He had no kids – must be minted. Kids cost a fortune, so if you've never had any, you must have loads of cash. Stands to reason.

A glance over our shoulders and quickly, noiselessly we're in. Over the sill and dropping down lightly onto the cracked linoleum floor. Damp creeps up the wall, reaching its black fingers out between candy pink tiles around an enamel tub. A rubber hose hangs limply from a mixer tap. Drip, drip, drip. A single toothbrush in a toothpaste-stained glass on the sink.

I'm right behind him, pushing him forward. Easing open the bathroom door. Slowly. Slowly. Into the hallway. A creak underfoot. He pauses. Three doors in front of him – seventies wood veneer, aluminium door handles. To the left, Hywel is sleeping – Darren can hear the snores. He takes the central door – opening with a hushed brush over the thick pile of the pink carpet. Flicks on the light with the smallest of clicks – if the old bloke can sleep through that bloody snoring, he's not going to notice the light. Looks round the room – small TV, worth nothing.

Loads of bloody knick-knacks. Knick-knacks every-where. A glass cupboard – full of birds and cups and little china vases. Birds and cups and little china vases and pictures of some bird. The same blue eyes smile out at us from wooden frames on every shelf.

Angharad.

I need Hywel in here. Need him to wake up and find us. I leave Darren to comb the room – opening drawers and rifling through their contents like that fox in those bins. Feral. Desperate. Nervous sweat exudes a musty stench.

Into Hywel's room. I bump into the bedside table, give him a bit of a shake. I see his eyes open in the gloom. Confused. Closes his eyes. Then he hears it, hears someone in the room next door. Darren's done away with any subtlety and finesse – he's ransacking and desperate. He knows there must something in there – now he's in, he knows that he can't leave with nothing.

Hywel sits up. Leans against me as he stuffs gnarled toes into sheepskin slipper. Shuffles to the door – light from the living room peeking through the frosted window above the bedroom door. He's sure he turned the light off.

Out into the hall. More noises. The telephone sits on the table in the hallway by the front door. As he gets to it we bump into the table. A vase of plastic flowers rocks in the slowest of slow motion, it rocks to and fro, to and fro on its base and falls, tumbling through the air to land with a thud on the cold laminate floor.

Darren hears the vase hit the floor, he's out of the lounge and we're working as one – my hands are his as we grab Hywel by the shoulders, push him up against the wall.

'What the fuck are you doing, old man? Calling the fucking police? Not likely . . .'

Together, we shake him. Our hands move to his throat – pin him into place. He's weak, but he pushes back.

'Get out of my house. Leave me alone. I don't have anything worth taking. I won't report you, just go. Leave me alone.' His speech is muffled – missing dentures and the hangover of sleep make it hard for words to form.

We grab his wrist, twisting his arm behind his back. His skin is paper to the touch. Force him down the hallway to the lounge. Five small steps, no more. Shove him into the room. Head makes contact with the glass cabinet. A bruise forms on his temple, swelling to close one eye. A thin trickle of mucus runs down his face from one nostril, spit dribbles out of his mouth onto my hand. He's lying back, trying to lean up on his elbow to push up on to his knees. His aching, arthritic elbow. His aching, arthritic knees. To Hywel, Darren is gone. Fading in front of him as the oxygen seeps from his blood. All he can see is me. My face – his mother's face. My hands – twenty-five-year-old hands from eighty-six years ago wrapped around his throat. Pushing, squeezing against windpipe and gullet. Cracking and grating.

'It was you, wasn't it?' His voice, strained against the force of my grip, stops me. 'It was you I saw. In France. All those years ago. I thought I was going mad.'

I nod. Tears well in my eyes. I let go of his throat as a lump forms in my own. 'Yes.' A whisper. We lean back, together. Resting against the glass cabinet, catching our breath.

'I've thought about that for years. Wondered how my mother could be there. I thought my mind was playing tricks on me. Angharad used to tell me I was a daft bugger, seeing my mam on the battlefield.'

'It was me.' My head rests on his shoulder.

'And it was you I saw in the hospital after the mine went down. All those nurses I thought looked like Mam . . . All you?'

I nod.

'I wouldn't look at them, you know. Wouldn't look at you, I suppose. I didn't want to go then.'

'I know.'

'I wish I'd known her, you know. Wish Angharad had had the chance to meet her. Mam would've loved Angharad. I just wish she hadn't had to die for me to live, you know? I had one picture of her and my Da. All upright and proper like photographs used to be back in the day. Used to look at it all the time. But even though it was all upright and proper like, you could see it, in their eyes, that they loved each other. And I took that away. I'd've given anything not to have taken her away.' His voice breaks with a dry sob.

'I know.'

'Every time I saw her, you, I thought it was my mind playing tricks. That I was so desperate to know her that I would convince myself she was there. Like she was looking over me like a guardian angel. Silly really. But it was just you wasn't it? Waiting for me to die.'

'I'm sorry. I'm sorry things have to end like this. But they do have to end and I don't have a choice. I'm sorry. I'm so very, very sorry.'

'Don't be.' The words stop me in my tracks and I twist my head up to look at him, eyes narrowed in confusion under a scrunched brow. Why?

'I've never wanted to live without her, you know? Without Angharad. When she died a little bit of me died with her. And since then, not a day has gone past when I haven't wished I was with her, wherever she is. Will I see her now, do you think? After you've gone?'

The hope in his eyes hits me full in the face like a punch. 'I don't know, Hywel. I would love to say yes, but I just don't know for sure. I can only take you so far.'

I move round to kneel in front of him. Look into

those eyes, those watery, yellowing eyes and put my hands back around his neck. A deep-seated survival instinct prompts him to reach up to pull them away but I'm resolute, determined, and we both know he hasn't a hope. Fingers scrabble at my fists as I push and I squeeze and a crushed windpipe cracks and grates. Legs kick against air trying to get some footing to push against. Choking noises, straining against my grip. Eyes looking straight at me – burning into me. Choking, choking. The hands fall away, flapping helplessly. His body goes limp, the fight gone. I lay him down, cheek on the thick pile of the pink carpet, eyes staring up vacantly at the cabinet. I hope you find her, Hywel. I really hope you find her.

'I'm sorry I'm sorry I'm sorry I'm sorry . . .'

I stare down at him, my hand cupped over my mouth. I can't believe quite what I've done. Move myself to curl on the floor beside him, wrapping my arms around his lifeless body and gently rocking him. Smoothing his thin hair, yellow with age and hair-oil, drawing his eyelids closed to the scene that has unfolded around him. 'I'm sorry I'm sorry I'm sorry . . .' Repeating myself over and over again as we lie on the floor until the words run into each other in a never-ending hush and shush of regret. As we lie on the floor, my face buried in his neck, tears falling unchecked. And as Angharad watches us from her glass shelf, forever twenty-one, thirty-six, forty-five, seventy in her wooden frames, as Darren Matthews steps over a cooling body with a muttered expletive, Hywel Ifor Williams slowly, quietly fades to black.

8

SOLES SLIP AND SLIDE ON SMOOTH PEBBLES AS I make my way across the beach, each footstep sinking backwards in loose scree. It's early morning on the south coast and the bay is deserted, but for a dog walker high up on the cliffs and a lone figure in the far distance.

Him.

When I finally get there, I find Him settled into a low-slung folding chair, suit trousers rolled up to the knee to expose slim, white calves and feet snug in the finest cashmere socks and Italian calfskin loafers. He's got an ice cream from somewhere and I watch as He tilts his head to dab His tongue at synthetic swirls. On this cold January morning on the Sussex coast He cuts an incongruous figure.

I sink into the identical chair to His right, rusting metal frame shifting and settling into shingle and shale. Wait while He finishes this early morning treat, nibbling His way through wafer cone and chocolate flake. Watch as He brushes the crumbs from a well-tailored lap.

Finally he speaks. 'Well?'

'Done. One down.'

'I know, Little D.' He sighs, already exasperated with my reluctance to be forthcoming about having just killed a man. A defenceless old man who's done nothing more than spend his life surviving. 'Did you think I would just let you crack on and not bother to check? Oh, Little D, you are a charming little thing, aren't you?'

He leans His head back against his chair, stretching His legs out in front of Him and closing His eyes against the morning sun. Settling in for a story.

'Come along. How do you feel? How did it go?'

So this is the way it's going to be. I might have known. Living and reliving. Analysing and assessing. I might have known He'd want to the gory details, want to hear an account straight from the horse's mouth.

And so I give Him what He wants. A step by step, blow by blow account of how, after eighty-six years, Hywel was no longer going to get away, to slip the net. Of how my hands still spasm and twitch at the thought of being wrapped around his throat. Of how I stood back and watched over him for the four days he lay alone in the lounge, with only pictures of Angharad and tiny ceramic birds for company and day turned to night turned to day turned to night in the world outside. How I stood and watched over him until Gwen popped her head round the door after umpteen unanswered phone calls. Listened as the stream of her chatter, her calls of 'Cooee, only me!' on entry were stifled by the rising stench of a stiffened body and the sight of an upturned hallway table lying abandoned next to an upended vase of plastic flowers. How I sat on the sofa, as drips of condensation chased themselves down the window and an ambulance was called from a cordless phone, huge buttons handy for arthritis-laced fingers and dwindling eyesight. How I watched with Angharad, held captive in her numerous frames, as police and paramedics arrived to remove the shrunken body and reveal the fingerprints of a local heroin addict dusted liberally across mantel and sill.

And I tell Him how I went into the bathroom on that day and vomited self-loathing and disgust until my shoulders heaved with empty retches and I struggled to raise my head from the cushion of a black plastic toilet seat. How the memory of the crunch and crack of a crushed windpipe still makes the bile rise in my throat. My voice is a monotone. Devoid of emotion. Distanced from my acts.

All the while He sits, eyes closed, head leaning back, a small smile playing on thin lips. Sits in silence but for the occasional murmur of encouragement when words fail and tears threaten. The occasional prompt when my mind sweeps me back to that council flat living room and my mouth hangs dry and speechless in the memory.

'Well done, I must say. Well done, Little D. You're going to have to toughen up, though. If you're going to make it through all five unscathed. You're terribly . . . emotional . . . Reckon you can do it?'

I don't know if I can. Every time I close my eyes I see the bulging eyes and desperation of a dying man. Hear the strained and whispered scream of a constrained throat. It can only get worse. Not one dying man looming behind closed lids, but five. Five of who knows what shape and size.

He senses the reluctance in my silence. The reticence evident in the lack of a reply.

'You don't have to, you know. We can call it all off now. It's much easier for me if we just stay as we are – you carry on doing what you do, and we abandon this rigmarole in aid of your soul. Silly idea anyway. Should've known you wouldn't have the strength for it. Ah well . . .' He sighs, presses bony hands against metal frame to push himself up and out of the chair.

'No. Wait.'

Bulging eyes have been replaced with a broken figure next to a hospital bed. A forehead resting on strong forearm, fingers entwined in soft, dark curls. The musky smell of sandalwood aftershave and the memory of navy eyes rimmed red with grief. If I stop now, there's no hope of ever getting what I want, and the thought of eking out a miserable existence for an eternity with his memory vivid in my mind's eye is unbearable.

He settles back into the chair. Turns to watch me struggle with what I want to say. In the end the arguments, the reasoning, the justifications fail me and I shrug my shoulders in defeat.

'Who's next?'

'Well, Little D. I'm glad you asked.' Rubs His hands together and grins that wolfish grin. Reaches underneath His chair to pull out a thick leather-bound photo album, scuffed at the edges, snapshots spilling from between well-thumbed pages. The early pages crammed with the faded, rounded edge photographs of a Truprint era, twin girls squinting up at the camera from a pebble beach, ice creams smeared across tanned little faces.

'She's one of the lucky ones, this one. Lived a life too easy. Let's put a stop to that shall we, Little D?'

Rose Charlotte Harrison.

Number 2.

9

NOW ROSE, ROSE IS A TRICKY ONE . . . SHE'S ONE
of those girls. Comes from one of those families. To
say she's lived a charmed life is nothing short of under-
statement. I've never had much reason to see her over
the past thirty-two years – never had to wait patiently
for the breathing to slow, for limbs to stiffen and eyes
to glaze. Never had to avoid her eye for fear of being
seen too soon.

My friend the Devil finds these people as infuriating
as the ones who get away – the Hywels of the world.
Because these people have the audacity to go blithely
through life unharmed. Without even chucking Him a
cursory glance, let alone considering the harm and
hatred that He might inflict. And so, revenge must be
taken.

I am sorry, Rose, for what I am about to do.

I look back over the years – a scrapbook of snapshots

that, seen from a distance, blend into one huge picture of the woman as she is now.

Life was blessed from the off. Even her birth was an easy passage. Slipping into the world with barely a murmur, fist sleepily rubbing her eye as with a yawn and a stretch she butted her tiny head against her mother and nestled in. Twin sister Hannah followed closely behind – irascible and hot-tempered, headstrong from the word go. Healthy bouncing bairns the two of them – identical twins adorable in matching dresses. Rose is the older by ten minutes and from the very start she's the reliable one, the responsible one. Even in the cot she'd throw one arm over Hannah to calm fractious cries, curled up together against the outside world.

Flick through the pages – past summers on French beaches, winters clad in woolly scarves and bright red wellies. Past the early eighties perm of Mum and the bushy sideburns of Dad. Aged three, a brother appears – sealing the Harrison family unit. Christopher. Chubby frame propped up against the proudest of older sisters. He's a screeching bundle who the girls adore – they coddle and mother him, clucking around, watching his tiny chest breathe in and out, holding their ears close to a tiny, snuffling nose. They hold books upside down and recite favourite stories. Puréed carrots are messily shovelled into a gaping mouth, the yellow lino of the kitchen floor flecked in orange goo. He becomes their third wheel, their life-sized doll – as soon as he can walk he follows them wherever they go, toddling after them, desperate to keep up. Patiently sitting with eyes closed while Hannah paints his lids with crumbling green eyeshadow and his cheeks with stubs of old lipstick and Rose drapes him with bracelets and necklaces from a successful raid on Mum's bottom drawer. He's a willing and adoring accomplice.

The girls' first day at school. They stand in front of a red-brick semi on the outskirts of Manchester – paintwork freshly touched up, garden well tended. Rose's left fist clutches Hannah's right while free hands grip brand-new stiff leather satchels. Blue eyes squint into the sun, gappy smiles proclaiming a recent visit from the tooth fairy. Blonde bunches curl into ringlets – Rose's tied with a pink ribbon, Hannah's blue. It's the only discernible difference to those who don't know them. But look a little closer and the peas in a pod are as different as night and day. Rose is neat, impeccably dressed, brilliant white socks pulled up to the knee. By contrast, one of Hannah's socks is already gathering around her ankle and the burgundy and gold striped tie is askew. Day one of school and already a white smear on her grey polyester V-neck where milk has splashed out of her cereal bowl and dribbled down her front to be wiped away by a grubby hand.

These things never happen to Rose.

It's these little things, these tiny markers that people will eventually use to distinguish between them in the absence of any obvious physical differences. But for now, with a new career at school lying ahead, a whole new world of mischief opens up to two girls whom no one can tell apart.

There's a roll of cinetape tucked into a curling envelope between the pages. A flickering square of light projected onto the wall of a darkened room takes us to a kids' party. Two home-made birthday cakes sit in pride of place in the middle of a table crammed with sweet treats and paper plates stacked with egg sandwiches and miniature Swiss rolls. A princess castle smothered in pink buttercream icing and jelly sweets for Rose sits next to Hannah's lopsided, smiling Mr Bump. A small arm stretches across the table to scoop a glob of sugary confection onto a finger and the camera moves left to show two giggling girls in their party dresses being shooed from the dining room by their mother.

Guests start to arrive and the games begin. Newspaper flies around the room and Opal Fruits are shovelled into small mouths as the parcel is passed. When the music stops a room full of dancing, prancing party-goers freeze into wobbly statues, casting surreptitious sideways glances at the all-seeing eye of Mr Harrison in his capacity as judge. With the last guest to leave the tape runs out and we are left with the jumping and juddering of a pure white square of light against the shadows.

The school years whip by – punctuated by parties, tinselled with trips to the zoo and summer weekends spent with cousins. Rolling down hills of freshly mown grass and playing in pub gardens fortified by a glass of Coke and a packet of crisps as the grown-ups finish warm pints of bitter and flat gin and tonics in the bar, shafts of late afternoon sun cutting through the smoke-hazed air. There are sprinklers to run through, dens to build and ransack. Rabbits, hamsters and guinea pigs to feed and a grouchy old tomcat who's best left alone if you know what's good for you. In the summer holidays that stretch for an eternity they camp out in the back garden, stocking up on supplies for midnight feasts that will be eaten, without fail, before the sun sets.

Late teens and it becomes easier to tell who's who. Rose's hair falls thick and straight, the cornfield blonde of her childhood has petered into a mousy brown that shines red in the right light. Her make-up, if she ever wears any, is clean and fresh. Her clothes simple, tailored, classic. By contrast, Hannah's hair changes with every photo – blue streaks here, back-combed and wild there. Six months of deepest gothic black sliced into an asymmetric bob. Eyes ringed in thick, black kohl and a tiny silver stud glinting in her nose.

At seventeen, the first boyfriends appear for both girls. It's a cliché – for Rose, the captain of the school cricket team. They're the golden couple of the sixth form and each thinks they've found 'The One', with the whole-hearted undiluted certainty of first love. Straight As for Rose as Jamie hits six after six over the boundary of the school playing fields and the school ooh and ahh, whoop and cheer.

For Hannah, needless to say, the local bad lad. Sleepless nights for Mum and Dad waiting for the guttural roar of his motorbike to pull up outside the house and Doc Martens to scuff and clump down the drive and into the hall. Whispered nights sitting together at the end of Rose's bed to dissect and discuss the furtive fumblings of the evening. Hannah's the first of the two to have sex and for the first time Rose feels alone, left behind. She giggles when Hannah laughs, and winces in all the right places, but for the first time in her life she feels awkward and shy around her little sister. For the first time in their life they've not done the same thing and for a few weeks it confuses her. In the photos, Hannah's eyes adopt a knowing look, the hint of a smile playing on full lips. In response, Rose's are wider, unsure. Naive and unnerved.

At eighteen the inseparable twins go in different directions. For two such diverse characters, they've never clashed and have certainly never spent more than two nights apart. Rose ventures north, to an English and journalism degree at the University of Newcastle. Hannah couldn't be further away – an Art Foundation at Brighton. The two are poles apart, Rose feels like a single entity. She misses her sister every day – glimpsing her from the corner of her eye and turning to point something out only to find she's talking to a complete stranger. But every day apart is easier and gradually, imperceptibly, she begins to feel lighter. For years she's been the responsible one 'Rose'll know what to do . . .' they say. 'Rose'll make sure Hannah gets there on time . . .'. The weight of expectancy and duty is no longer hanging heavy and God, is she going to have fun.

By the second year of university, the cricketer has disappeared, the weight of a long-distance relationship throwing the two off balance. He's replaced in picture after picture by groups of friends huddled in scruffy student living rooms, film posters on the wall and half-drunk cups of tea and dirty plates scattered across every surface. It's her first taste of freedom and she loves it. Three years pass in a blur of parties and lectures. Nights drinking vodka and Red Bull in a sticky-carpeted club, before stumbling to seminars in cold studies, last night's make-up smudged under tired eyes, mouth glued with the residue of the morning after. Six of them cram into what should be a three-bedroomed terraced house – the attic has been converted into two bedrooms and the lounge and dining room a further two. They squash themselves into the kitchen-cum-lounge-cum-dining-room every night, worn furniture and carpets disguised under patterned throws and rugs.

It's a happy, dysfunctional, kids-playing-at-adults home away from their homes. From what I can see, it hasn't seen a Hoover since they moved in.

After three years, graduation photos of the twins standing straight-backed and proud against the ubiquitous mottled blue-brown background of official photography. Mortar boards firmly in place to be later thrown into the air in homage to the US college movies they have grown up with. Though their ceremonies are at either end of the country, the formula is the same. In both photographs, fingers are tightly wrapped around fake scrolls and shoulders shrouded in black gowns. The only difference the brightly coloured university colours draped around their necks. Rose has done it: secured a 2:1 and a highly sought-after job on the lower rungs of a busy weekly magazine in London.

She throws herself into work with glee, revelling in the bright lights of the big city, the morning commute, jostling for space on the Tube with coffee cup in hand and headphone buds plugged into her ears. She works her way up through the ranks, long hours and tight deadlines made bearable by the knowledge that she's doing a job she loves and that she has a natural talent for.

The pictures through her twenties are filled with old friends and new. The same faces from cramped university digs take on a certain maturity as they move into white-walled modern apartments in East London. New faces from the office crowd around city centre bars to chew over the gossip on the pages of their beloved mag. Boyfriends come and go through these years –

work and friends the focal point. And throughout, flitting between family and friendship groups, there's Hannah.

We thumb through to her late twenties, and finally, we meet Dom. Tall, shy, reliable Dom. City breaks and skiing holidays begin to dot themselves among the festivals and theatre trips. Eyes lock together as bodies mould to each other in laughing embraces. The love between them is palpable, bathing everyone who bears witness in its warm glow.

Finally, moving day and a new flat. Just the two of them. The two of them and an old ginger tom rescued from the local cats' home. Boxes piled high as Rose fills shelf after shelf with books. A toast to their first night together – grinning faces over plastic glasses brimming with wine. Where the wineglasses are is anybody's guess. But they are happy here. It is a home together. A home for the heart.

And there, the pictures run out. We have reached the present day. Empty buff pages lie waiting for a future life not yet lived. A future life that won't be lived. Not if I'm to succeed. And here we join Rose for her last night with her nearest and very dearest.

10

I LEFT HIM FOR A WHILE. WALKED AWAY FROM that pantry in Surrey to leave him to get on with his life. But I couldn't shake him. He was always with me. Loitering in the back of my mind, bottomless eyes staring back at me every time I closed my own. And whoever I was, whoever's life I was living, I took him with me. The brightest pinprick of light in the corner of my mind as those around me faded into their darkness. I tried to forget him, tried to get on with business, get on with death. But that light, floating, shimmering, it couldn't be doused.

When I saw him next, he'd made it back to work. Going through the motions at his desk in a windowless office in Farringdon. I found him sitting at his desk, staring blankly at the screensaver on his computer screen as it bounced and flipped and morphed. Tapping the hard plastic of a biro against his teeth. Eyes drawn, again and again, to the digital clock stuck to the fabric partition separating his world from the others.

I meandered around the office. Took my time getting to him. Peered over shoulders at screenfuls of incomprehensible numbers. Trailed my fingers along desks scattered with papers and smudged with ink. Hooked a fallen bauble back onto the drooping arms of the fake Christmas tree forcing false jollity into air thick with apathy. In the corner, a man in his fifties choked back a hacking cough, swallowing thick mucus metallic with blood. His body doubled over with the force. I'd be seeing him again within weeks.

As I approach Tom's desk, the girl at the desk next to him pops her head up over the partition. Emma. Flips long blonde hair from side to side and starts the nervous chit-chat of the unsure. Fiddles with her nails and begins to chatter in an unnaturally bright voice. He can't hear the words. Can only see the hair. The perfectly polished nails. The curve of her breast as she leans forward against their shared wall. Her cheeks are flushed – so many times in the past few weeks she's wanted to open up a conversation, and so many times courage has failed her and she's found herself crouched over her seat – not standing, not sitting. The no-man's-land between launching into a chat and losing her nerve. They used to flirt, back in the day. Harmless banter between colleagues. Nothing that ever meant anything, nothing that would ever give Kate any reason to worry. But flirting nevertheless. A not unpleasant way to pass the monotony of a working day. And she's missed it. Missed him. So today, she ploughs ahead. Leans forward, encroaching on his space. Leans in close. So close he can smell the fruit cocktail perfume of her shampoo. Can see a smudge of ink on bitten lips. Pre-vomit saliva floods his mouth. Breath comes in short, sharp bursts, catching in his chest. Blood rushes to flush his face and a bead of sweat traces a long course down his spine. Hot. So hot. He has to get away. He stands abruptly. Trips over his words and tips over his chair in his bid to get away.

She stares after him. Her cheeks redden and she brings a hand to cover her open mouth. Looks desperately across the office to her best friend Rachel, who's been watching events unfold from across the room. Rachel shrugs. Mouths 'You OK?' Emma shakes her head. Sits back at her desk and rests her forehead in her hands, allowing long blonde hair to draw curtains between her and staring faces as tears prick eyelids screwed tight in mortification. Three weeks. It's only been three weeks. Too soon, Emma.

I find him in the bathroom. Breathing heavily. Panting. Loosening the tie that binds. Patting sweat from his forehead before sluicing a clammy face with cold water. He stops. Stands still. Chokes back yet another retch. Stares himself out in the cracked mirror above the chipped sink. I move behind him. Thread my arm around his waist and prop my chin on his shoulder to watch his face in the glass. Drop a feather-light kiss on to the back of his neck. Soft lips held to hot skin. He calms. Breathing slows. Shoulders drop back to where they belong. Deep breath in. Long breath out. Deep breath in. Long breath out.

'Mate,' he mutters at his reflection. 'Pull yourself together.'

I release my arm from around his waist. Trace the line between my lips and his skin with light fingers. He reaches up. Rubs that very spot on his neck with a warm hand.

He has me trapped. And he has no idea. In the mirror we're entwined, fingers threaded together, eyes locked. And he has no idea.

Back in the office, he passes behind Emma's desk and pauses. She keeps her head turned to the computer screen, studiously not noticing the shape hovering behind her desk. 'Emma . . .'

She turns. 'Tom, I'm sorry, I just . . .'

He waves her words away. Looks down at his feet. 'Don't. Please. I'm sorry. It's not you . . . It's . . .' He trails off, winces at the cliché. Squeezes past the back of her chair to grab his jacket from the back of his own, pulling his stomach in and chest up to avoid any part of his body touching hers. Head down, through the maze of desks, past colleagues with their eyes fixed to flickering screens, resolutely not watching him go. Through the maze and out into the cold.

And so we walk home together through the streets, Tom and I. Kicking leaves that gather soggily on the pavements as breath blooms in dewy clouds in front of us. Despite the aimless appearance of this stroll, despite the wandering pace, it is anything but. Every junction presents a decision. Every junction warrants an evaluation of which direction offers the lesser of two evils. Turn left here and we pass the school where she taught, eager hands held in the air through windows bright and shiny in the fading afternoon light. Continue ahead and eventually we will pass the restaurant where he asked her to marry him.

It doesn't matter though. Doesn't matter how circuitous a route we take. How many landmarks we bypass, how many streets we determinedly avoid. Because the end point is always the same. On this street corner I'll leave him. Here, by the red postbox shifted away from the upright by roots buckling the pavement below. I'll leave him here to walk the final stretch alone. To an empty flat on a tree-lined street. An empty flat that echoes with the sound of her silence.

II

AND NOW, IT'S TIME. ROSE'S FINAL DAY HAS arrived. I loiter in the dark garden, peeping in through a condensation-fogged window to the warmth within.

They're both there, Rose and Dom. Pottering around in the kitchen. She's standing by the hob frying onions and mince while he opens a bottle of wine, twisting screw into cork. He mutters something under his breath – makes her laugh as fat spits out of the pan, sending her backwards into him. He wraps her in a hug, kisses the top of her head. Tugs on her ponytail to pull her face to his.

She's thirty-two today. Thirty-two for ever. Not that either of them knows that yet. Fine features, blonde hair always hastily pulled together in a ponytail, a laugh always on the verge of bursting over and out.

Dom is three years older. Altogether more serious, his brow has a permanent furrow – a slight frown where he parcels up his innermost thoughts and worries. She lightens his darkest thoughts and he is there to ensure she doesn't waste her entire life on reality shows and red wine. They've been together for three years and I find them today in their basement flat in Highgate, a huge, ginger cat weaving around their feet.

There's a knock at the door backed up by a ring on the bell. An identical blonde enters the room – hair plaited into a floral scarf, nose ring glinting, lips a blur of constant chatter. Hands animated into a whirl to emphasise points made and moved on from. Hannah has come over for dinner, as she does three, even four times a week. Left to her own devices she survives on a diet of take-aways and ready meals. It's not unusual for a pint and a packet of cheese and onion in front of the television to replace five a day and exercise. And so, the older sister by ten minutes looks after the younger. Cooking dinner and proffering words of wisdom as the latest crisis engulfs her twin. A cheating boyfriend, an amorous boss. A job that requires too much of her time, a job that asks too little of her talent. Life is never straightforward for Hannah.

Three bodies bundle round the kitchen table. Red wine sloshed into beakers leaves ruby rings on a patterned tablecloth sprinkled with crusty crumbs from a baguette broken off and passed on. A vast lasagne bubbles and oozes in the middle of the table to be heaped on to mismatched plates and devoured between mouthfuls of chat and gulps of Merlot. Rose sits back cosy and content while Hannah and Dom spar and joke, both revelling in having found the older brother, the younger sister they never expected to have.

Dinner eaten and they move through to the lounge. Feet curled onto sofas to delve into some reality show – the lives of a bunch of posh twenty-somethings conveniently packaged into half-hour bites of gossip and scandal. The girls love it, love the supposedly unscripted storylines engineered to astonish and delight, love to watch as loves and lives tangle and fuse. Dom, sitting on the old leather armchair in the corner, struggles to understand the fascination and buries his head in *Private Eye* for gossip and scandal of his own.

The yawns set in and Hannah wraps up to head out into the cold. She grabs her sister in a hug and with a 'I'll give you a bell tomorrow' and a wave goodbye, she heads off to the Tube and home. And so Dom and Rose head to bed. Grinning at each other in the mirror through toothpaste-foamed smiles. Tossing clothes onto the easy chair to scurry under the duvet and slot into place. Rose falls asleep with a heavy leg thrown over her hip and Dom's gentle snores purring in her ear. Cosy. Cosy and content.

In north-west London, John Barrow slumps in his armchair. Another long day at the wheel, another long evening to spend chasing the bottom of a bottle. He stares blankly at a muted TV in the corner of the lounge, seeing but not watching brightly lit contestants vie for the holiday of a lifetime. Since Sheila left last year the drinking has gone from bad to worse. A day at the wheel is torture while the cravings for a drink gnaw at his stomach and thoughts of her crowd into his head. A few more glasses before bed and the gnawing will dull and the chatter of what could have been will quieten. A few more glasses before bed and he can find solace in a deep and dreamless sleep. Without the booze she haunts his dreams – from a mundane nagging about the washing-up to bitter taunts about his failures. He drinks to obliterate the problems the drink has caused, sucked into a twisting downward spiral from which there is no escape.

Eventually, in a darkened room lit only by the flickering television screen, with tears drying on his cheeks and Scotch wet on his lips, still in the clothes he's been wearing all day, head bows on neck and John sleeps.

It's an early start for us the following morning. Got to be at the bus depot by five. Blearily wiping sleep from his eyes and shaking his head to try and clear the hangover fog, John and I make our way out of the front door into the pouring rain. Get to the yard to stand in the cold, hands wrapped round steaming mugs of tea to try and inject a little warmth against the damp seeping through to his core.

He stands apart from the other drivers – men he's known for years but who have given up trying to involve him after months of countless knockbacks. They worry about him. Go home and tell their wives about the help they think he should be getting. But it's not so easy to bridge the gap when he's lost in thought and any opening gambits are shut down to leave unfinished sentences hanging in the morning air. There are only so many times people will see their invites rejected before they're no longer forthcoming. And John has long since passed that threshold.

Together, we climb into the cab of the double decker, settling into the worn seat, adjusting mirrors. Preparing for a long day in the saddle. I perch on his lap like a child, feet resting lightly atop his. We lace our fingers together and wrap them around the steering wheel as the motor chug chug chugs into life with a cough and wheeze and a cloud of acrid smoke.

Drops drip from amber leaves to swish under the tyres of passing cars on the Archway Road. Rose's fingers are freezing, gripped around the handlebars of her trusty old bike. The morning commute. Back-to-back traffic for her to weave and dodge. Horns blaring, thick exhaust fumes billowing from buses choking the legions of cyclists. They wait at red lights in their droves, poised to leap out of the gates at the first opportunity.

Down the Archway Road, under Suicide Bridge.

Creeping and crawling slowly, slowly around Archway roundabout: cars, bikes, buses, trucks vying for a spot. I scan the road ahead of us, ahead of John and me. Tens of cyclists jostle in their neon jackets, balancing straight-legged on their pedals as they wait for lights to change, for gaps to emerge.

Straight down onto Holloway Road. The packed bus groans under the weight of a Monday morning commute. Standing room only, steaming bodies pressed against fogged windows. The combined maraca shake beat of commuters' headphones ticks and spits, punctuated by the rhythmic squeak-swoosh-thud of wiper rubbers against glass.

I see her up ahead, head down, legs pumping. Caught in the stream of cyclists flowing into the turn of Highbury Corner. I have to be careful – to pick her out of the bunch, to separate her from the swarm. Split the prey from the pack. We stop at a red light, cyclists ahead poised for the jump. Rose on the extreme left, tight against the kerb and boxed in by a City type, grey flannel trousers tucked into luridly striped purple socks. The sun has broken through the dense blanket of cloud, casting Rose and her fellow drones into deep shadow.

There's a left turn ahead, for the bus anyway. Poor Rose will be continuing straight ahead. For a nanosecond longer than she really should.

Together we accelerate, John and me. My foot presses down on his, our hands entwined at the wheel.

We push forward, easing past Rose, trapping her against the kerb as she wobbles over a pothole. I yank the wheel, a lurching leap forward to take the corner too early. John tries to resist. I can smell his panic, the tang of sweat as he loses control and the wheel slips through his grasp. He'll think there was a fault with the steering column. Think that something got trapped under the wheels. Think that tyres skidding on wet leaves have pulled this beast of a bus out of his control. He'll think anything over the next weeks and months. Anything to avoid thinking that he did it. That a muddled mind and blood muddied with Scotch caused this to happen. That he killed her.

It's over in moments. A thud and a crunch as flesh and bone hit the side of the bus full on and fold to the floor. A bump as the back wheel drags body along asphalt and tries to roll over her inert frame before nonchalantly giving up and rolling backwards to rest. The half-hearted roll is the final insult. The final nail in a roadside coffin. Enough to finish the job. The spokes of her bike wheel glitter and glisten as it spins, unchecked, in the gutter. Drops of rainwater twinkle and shine like diamonds in the half-light.

Silence on the bus, broken only by that tinny tick of commuting headphones. And then a groan, ripping through the air, dragged from the very gut of John. He fumbles with the cab door, nerves and fear numbing his fingers and making a simple task a mountain to climb. Silent, disbelieving faces watch him the length of the bus. Blank and uncomprehending. Upstairs passengers peer down the stairwell. He forces the doors open, falls into the gutter, grazes his hands on rough paving slabs. Runs to Rose. To the girl lying bent and broken under the wheels of his bus.

But I'm there already, crawling under the hot chassis to take her hand in mine.

She turns her head to see me. 'Hann . . . ?', breathed through bruised ribs and a lung filling with fluid. 'What . . . ?' Brows knitted, face creased in confusion.

'Hang on, you're not . . . Who are you?' A shriek. Confusion morphs into panic morphs into fear. Eyes widen into dawning realisation. I don't know how they know, but when the time comes they always recognise me.

I reach forward to reassure. 'Get AWAY from me!' Feet scrabble against tarmac in a futile effort to move out of my reach. 'Get OFF me! Get your hands OFF me!'

'It's OK,' I whisper into hair matted with blood. 'I'm here, I'm here. Shushushush.' Lips pressed against her head. My hand reaches for her fist, twisted under her. Blood oozes from underneath her torso, trickles from her ear. Her face is unharmed – if it wasn't for the mangled body below you'd never know that life was seeping away, minute by minute, second by second. She pulls back, body rigid in my arms.

'No. No no no. No!' Short, sharp punches aimed at my face punctuate her words. She pushes against my chest, straining with the effort. The harder she fights, the calmer I am. Wrapping her scraped and bloodied fists in mine. Stilling the fight. Waiting for the acceptance to come. It will come. It always does.

Her hand works free and claws at my face, hooking fingers into my cheek in the scramble. 'Get AWAY from me! I swear . . .' Words choked out of a collapsing chest.

'No.' The shriek is now a whisper.

She begins to cry. Softly, silently. Her chest heaves and gasps, judders and rasps as she battles against punctured lung to summon enough air. Tears run down the side of her face, pooling with rainwater on asphalt. She can no longer feel the damp and cold soaking through her clothes, no longer feel the dull pain threading through her core.

The world around moves in slow motion, immersed in the thickest of treacle. Blue lights approaching. On . . . off . . . on . . . off . . . They come too late, the wailing sirens. Too late for Rose. Whooping and screaming as they get louder and louder and closer and closer. John's face looms overhead, a picture of anguish that blurs in and out of focus. His lips are moving but we can't hear the words. We lie together on that wet tarmac, bodies spooned as they were in the womb, my arm enveloping Rose in a protective hug.

'Is this it? Am I . . .' Disbelief.

I nod silently. A choked cough of accession. I can't speak. Can't even begin to explain that I have done this. That if it wasn't for me she'd be turning into the office courtyard round about now. Running up the metal steps to put the kettle on for a morning cup of tea. Laughing at the text from Dom that flashes, unread, on the phone lying in the road next to her.

I start to hum. Songs they used to sing when they were kids, songs they used to hear on the radio in the car. Red, red robins bob bob bobbing while 'Money for Nothing' stirs a 'Bat Out of Hell'. She joins me. We sing together, out of tune, out of time. Her on drums, me on lead guitar, arms flailing in the drizzled air. Talking over each other to laugh at the silliest things. Words flip and fly, dip and dance as we compete to remember the best bits – the ubiquitous reality-show montage at the end of a life well lived. As the end approaches, pain lessens and mangled limbs straighten and unfold. People work around us, lifting the bus out of the way, setting up screens to prevent the gawking of the passers-by, necks craning to see what they are so glad to have avoided. As the day passes, rescue crews finish their work and leave. Lift the shell of a body into the back of an ambulance, face covered in a sheet, before driving away, blue lights flashing silently in reverence. Screens are dismantled, police tape cut down. A plastic A-frame proclaiming an accident the only marker of a life cut short. So quick, so efficient. They don't see us. Still there. Still singing. Hours pass on the wet tarmac as we watch day turn to night and the world carries on around us. But we can't stay for ever.

'I think it's time.' We're lying on our backs watching the stars overhead. 'Are you ready?'

A squeak from the back of her throat the only sign that she's heard me. Lips pressed together to hold back tears. A deep breath in to be blown out shakily. 'I don't have a choice really do I?'

It doesn't warrant an answer. 'Tell Dom I love him.'

And we lie hand in hand, and we watch the stars, and as Orion's belt dips low above the mansion blocks, slowly, quietly, Rose Charlotte Harrison fades to black.

12

I'VE BEEN HERE BEFORE, IN THIS HIGH-CEILINGED room. Nineteen twenty . . . three. No, two . . . Nineteen twenty-two. Back when it wasn't a living room. When this was the master bedroom of a masterful house, and Gordon Lyons, businessman and philanthropist lay in a huge bed swathed in red velvet and gold brocade. I came to him then as his first love – a young Indian girl from his early days as an officer in the Raj. Wrapped in silks, jingling my way around his bedside. Smoothing hair from his fevered brow while his wife sat to one side of the bed, rigid with grief, forgotten.

But now, the William Morris wallpaper and turn-of-the-century furniture are gone. The grand house has been converted into flats, the des-res of thirty-something locals. In floor-to-ceiling alcoves either side of a massive fireplace, books in their hundreds line the walls – contemporary blockbusters jostle with first editions dug out of antique book dealers on the Charing Cross Road. I slip one out from its nest, open it to bury my nose in lignin-scented pages yellowed by the years.

And today, in this room that stands in darkness, lit only by the flickering blue of the TV screen and a shattered shard of orange light that jabs through the blinds from the street-lamp outside, I can't sense the sniff, the whiff that usually accompanies my work. The hum, the breath that hangs in the air when death is so close. The air is still. Stale. Quiet. Discarded clothes dot the room – a T-shirt tossed over the back of an armchair, a hooded sweatshirt reaching its long arms to the floor from where it's been chucked on the sofa. Empty cups and crumb-covered plates litter the floor and a regiment of mugs lines the edge of the sofa, milky films forming on the surface of undrunk tea.

From the kitchen, a noise. Pans clattering in a sink already piled high with dirty dishes. A hissed 'bugger' as a lid falls to the floor with a clang. A soft sob of helplessness seeps through the crack in the door. A slump-shouldered figure pushes its way through into the living room. Dead eyes, red-rimmed and staring. He wants to cry, God knows he wants to cry. Wants to open the floodgates and release that pressure that sits at the base of his throat, behind his eyes. The pressure that strangles swallows in its vice-like grip. But the tears won't come. His dark hair curls lankly, greasy with neglect. He's empty – the living embodiment of heartbreak and loss. Tom. For this is the inside of that empty flat on that tree-lined street.

At the sight of him, I feel as though I've been punched in the stomach. I can offer no solace, cannot take him in my arms to soothe his hurt, to calm his fears. All I can do is creep on to the sofa next to him. Sit, a silent companion, while he stares vacantly at a TV screen, barely seeing the chiffons and sequins of swirling, twirling dancers. He used to refuse to watch this programme. Told Kate it was a load of old rubbish. But she loved it, and he loved her and now he will watch. Every Saturday. He will watch for her. Tell her what's happened when the judges score and the crowd roar. When the credits roll and two minor celebrities stand, alone together in pools of light to await their fate, to find out who will live to dance another day.

On the arm of the chair, Tom's phone flashes, unanswered, in a silent ring. He stares blankly at the TV, the satin swish and salsa shimmy unseen. Eyes are dry and red from lack of sleep. He yawns. Stretches. Head begins to nod on his shoulders. Sleep is desperately needed. As his head droops, he wakes with a start. Gets up and goes to the bathroom to clean his teeth. Her toothbrush still sits in the mug by the sink. Her shampoo still stands by the taps in the bath, a sticky rim of dust forming on its lip.

He gets into bed. Lies there, open-eyed. Resolutely, determinedly sticking to his side. Won't encroach on her space. Can't encroach. The duvet to his left is untouched, unruffled. Waiting. Ready. In case – just in case – she comes back. Within that confined side, with its invisible walls, he tosses and turns, turns and tosses. Flat on his back, pillow balled beneath his head. Leg thrust out from beneath the 12-tog before cold toes are bundled back in. The outline of his body highlighted by the single lamp that shines through from the hallway. He can't stand darkness now. The suffocating, all-enveloping, blinding darkness. That lamp will shine through the night.

On the bedside table luminous green figures have an ethereal glow: 02:47, 04:12, 05:39. So, so tired but sleep won't come. Not for any length of time. Not for the past couple of months. During the day he can barely keep his eyes open, but at night the fear of seeing her in his dreams and losing her over and over and over keeps eyes wide and mind whirring. The numbers click through the minutes, flick through the hours, and all he can do is watch and wait until they tick around to 7 a.m. and his day starts again.

And as he tosses and turns, turns and tosses, I settle into the battered old armchair in the corner of the bedroom to watch over him. I can't go near him, can't touch him. Not with the deaths of Hywel and Rose hanging fresh in my mind's eye. Even sitting in the same room as Tom seems wrong, voyeuristic almost, intruding on life when so recently I brought death. I can't go near him, but try as I might, I can't tear myself away. I have to stay close in the hope that somewhere, somehow, he can feel my presence. Feel that he's not alone, not abandoned, not left to face the world on his own. My eyes follow the outline of his face. Straight nose, downturned mouth. Stubble darkening cheeks hollowed by a month of eating nothing but the bare minimum needed for the basic act of survival. Eyes staring, unblinking, at the ceiling. And I feel an overwhelming urge to love him, to cherish him. To protect him from the world out there that has so cruelly let him down. And that is why. Why there's no sniff, no whiff. No hum, no breath. I've not been brought here for death. Here, on the inside of that empty flat on that tree-lined street. I've not been brought here for death. What I'm doing is right. Hywel, Rose, whoever is thrown in my path at random next. Their sacrifices, their deaths are bringing me ever closer to this, to where I've been brought and where I belong. For I have been led here, to this echoingly silent flat on this tree-lined street, by the heart.

13

THE PULSING ROAR OF THE CROWD HITS US LIKE A passing freight train. A mushroom cloud of sound billowing up and over the high walls of the stands. He leads me through the old-fashioned turnstile beneath stacked seats, His usual suit today offset by a red and white scarf jauntily looped around His neck. The pitch opens out before us as we emerge into the baying crowd – an emerald island in a cheering, swaying sea of cherry red.

'Hot-dog?' He asks over His shoulder.

'No. Thanks. I'm fine.'

Hot-dog?

He shrugs. 'Your funeral.'

'I think I'll survive.'

We're here to talk about people dying. However he wants to dress it up. Hot-dog indeed.

He looks down at me with an arched eyebrow. 'Suit yourself. It gets cold out here – you'll be glad of it later.'

I ignore Him, follow Him to the concession in moody silence. Wait as He squeezes behind the melamine counter to help Himself to the processed meat rotating on a rolling grill, squirts a meticulously precise thin stripe of ketchup down the length of the orange sausage. The spotty kid behind the counter is oblivious to the presence behind his station. He stares, slack-jawed and gum-chewing, and waits for the half-time whistle to release the floods of fans for pies and pints.

Hot-dog in hand, He leads me high into the stands to two unoccupied seats. Chants swirl and surge below us, ebbing and flowing from end to end to crash against the opposing fans in their isolated corner of royal blue.

'So then. Rose.'

Rose. And John. Let's not forget John. He may still have his life, but what a life to lead. Overshadowed at every turn by the whispers and stares, by the screeching of brakes scored as clear as tyre marks on tarmac through his mind. Dream after dream, night after night, in which he tries in vain to straighten the steering wheel, tries to stop the sickening lurch to the left.

They arrested him on a charge of manslaughter. They breathalysed him on the roadside, slumped against his bus, bathed in the flashing blue lights. Led him to a waiting police car when the digital numbers clicked up and up and the flashing red light blurred in front of his face, spurred by sylph-like wisps of alcohol dancing in an exhaled breath. Cautioned him and chucked him into a cell to stare dazedly into the corner from the thin, plastic-coated mattress on a concrete ledge for a bed. Bailed him and sent him home to await trial and sink deeper and deeper into another bottle of Scotch.

His one call was to Sheila. Sheila, who didn't even try to disguise the disgust in her voice. Who could barely bring herself to speak to him when she came to collect him from the station in Barry's car. Barry. That bloody bastard who's been sleeping with his wife. The love of his life. That was the final straw. Being picked up in that bastard's car, by his own wife. The final straw that broke the camel's back and left him sobbing and exhausted in the front seat, unwashed hair leaving a greasy smear on the passenger window.

I hadn't even thought how this would affect my unwitting assistants. After Hywel, I cast not a thought for young Darren Matthews. The knowledge that he'd soon be residing at Her Majesty's pleasure regardless and the inevitability of a heroinic demise had presented me with the most perfect of accomplices. I shed not a tear for hurrying nature on her way. Didn't even join the flock of net curtain twitchers watching from every side when the police knocked on his mother's door and led him away head hanging, hands shackled.

But John. With John I took a broken man and I crushed and I crumbled him into a gritty dust of his former self. There is nothing left from which to rebuild himself. Nothing left that he can salvage. He has died his very own death and yet life refuses to give him up.

And so, to Rose. Somehow she was easier than Hywel. I don't know why. Maybe because I didn't physically kill her with my bare hands. Didn't feel the crack and the crunch of cartilage under my fingers. Didn't have to look into pleading eyes and fight against the superhuman strength these people summon from their very depths to just bloody well survive. I was removed and so unmoved. When I got to her, in those following seconds, it was nothing I hadn't seen before. Just another death like all of the thousands, the millions, that have gone before. The look of horror. The look of fear. Each smudged at their hard edges by the softening dawn light of realisation. By a slow and gradual acceptance of inevitability and helplessness.

'Well, Little D? Rose? Done and, shall we say, "dust to dusted"? Ha! "Dust to dusted"!' He chuckles to himself.

'Done.' I refuse to get dragged into His comic asides. He really is vile.

'I must say, I think it was a little remiss of you. To run her over just like that.'

'Remiss? Why? She's dead, isn't she? Isn't that what I'm supposed to do?'

'Yes, yes. Strictly speaking, that's exactly what you're supposed to do. But, you know . . .' He pauses, jiggles a perfectly shod foot crossed over a perfectly clad knee. 'Bit of a cop-out, don't you think?'

'No! No I don't think.' I look up at Him in disbelief. 'I killed her, didn't I? I did what you wanted. There were no rules. You didn't tell me how you wanted them to die. Christ . . .'

'Don't bring him into it. For God's sake . . .'

We stand with the crowd as a goal is scored and a wave of euphoria sweeps whooping fans to their feet. He waits for the swell to recede before speaking again.

'I seem to remember, Little D, saying that you could have your soul back if I was happy with the way you went about these tasks. And, let's just say I thought you would take on a more, shall we say, hands-on approach. Can't make this too easy for you, can I?'

I hate Him.

'So, what? The goalposts change and I just have to keep playing the game?'

'My game, Little D, my rules. And if you want to play it, you're just going to have to follow them, aren't you?'

His voice is level, entirely reasoned, unfairly reasonable. As if arguing with Him wasn't hard enough. But He's right. If one's foolish enough to make a deal with the Devil, one can only expect to have to dance to His tune.

'So . . .' A bite of hot-dog, carefully chewed. Washed down with a swig of a saccharine-sweet bright-orange fizzy drink. 'Let's pull our socks up for number three shall we? Make a real effort.'

'Fine. Who is it? One of them?' I reply petulantly, gesturing at the sleek, thoroughbred boys of modern-day football racing from one end of the pitch to the other.

'No, no. Don't be silly.' He pauses, cocks His head in contemplation. 'Although . . . Hmm . . . Yes. Now you mention it . . .' Shakes His head. 'No, no, Little D. Let's stick to the plan, shall we?'

I don't answer. As He pointed out only moments before, this is His game. These are His rules. And there's no way I'm getting sucked into picking my next victim.

He reaches into His breast pocket. Pulls out two season tickets for a couple of seats twenty or so rows in front of us. 'Best seats in the house, Little D. Right on the halfway line. Halfway up the stands. Lovely view of the pitch. Lovely . . .' He drifts off, lost in thought. 'Sorry, I digress. Couple of weeks' time, it's the derby. Let's give him a last day to remember, eh?'

'Sure. Who is he?' What's the point in a day to remember when all you leave behind is a day the people in his life will never forget?

'He's a family man. An average Joe you might say. Loving wife and two point four kids at home. Loves the football, loves it. Been supporting this lot since he was a kid – used to come quite a bit with his dad. But he can't come so much any more. You know what these family types are like, Little D – ballet lessons and tap-dancing and horse-riding and all that other gumph parents shovel into their little darlings. Means he doesn't get to do what he wants to do. Why on earth people want families is beyond me . . . Even you, Little D. Even you want that, don't you? Oh, look at that! Lovely! Lovely work . . .' He tails off, distracted by the fairy-tale footwork of a young Brazilian lad on the field below.

'Why him though?' There's been a reason for the other two. Tenuous at best, but at least the merest hint of reason. 'Why've you picked him? What's he done to deserve this?'

He turns to look at me quizzically. 'What's he done to deserve this? Nothing, Little D, nothing at all. Why should you think anyone "deserves" to die?'

They don't. No one deserves this. But somehow, that doesn't seem to be stopping me.

'We're going to use Rob as an example, that's all. It's not all going to be sweetness and light when you finish this little game of yours, you know. Life isn't all it's cracked up to be. And it can be taken away at a moment's notice. I think that's what Rob's death will show us, Little D. When you're alive, when all this has finished, the only certainty in your life will be death. However it may come to you, it will come. But, well. You know that better than anyone, don't you?'

His hand delves back into His breast pocket. Pulls out a tablet – one of those black, shiny rectangles so recently unheard of and yet so quickly omnipresent. What the hell am I supposed to do with that? I didn't even have a book when I was young, let alone this . . . thing.

'Might be good for a bit of background research.' He says, handing it over.

'Thanks. I'll take a look.' I turn it over and around in my hands, looking for some sort of clue as to how to use the bloody thing.

'Right then, you'd better get on with it. Enjoy the game won't you, Little D? It'll be a cracker. A real fight to the death.' And with that, he's up and off. Brushing hot-dog crumbs from His lap into the hair of the man on the row in front. Squeezing His way to the end of the row to jog down concrete steps and get lost amid the seething mass of a half-time crowd.

Robert Porter.

Number 3.

14

From: Joe Hatcher

To: Rob Porter

Subject: C'mon you Reds!

Mate. Two tickets on the halfway line next Saturday. You in????????

From: Rob Porter

To: Joe Hatcher

Subject: Re: C'mon you Reds!

Sorry, bud – can't. Going to see Beth's mum and dad – they haven't seen the kids in ages. What about Luke?

From: Joe Hatcher

To: Rob Porter

Subject: Re: Re: C'mon you Reds!

ROB! FFS man! Halfway line! The derby! Last

game of the season! Are you under the thumb
or what?!

From: Rob Porter
To: Joe Hatcher
Subject: Re: Re: Re: C'mon you Reds!
It's called being a good husband, my simple,
single friend. Thumbs ain't got nothing to do
with it . . .

From: Joe Hatcher
To: Rob Porter
Subject: Re: Re: Re: Re: C'mon you Reds!
Sorry, yeah . . . My mistake. Hen-pecked.
That's what I meant . . .

From: Rob Porter
To: Joe Hatcher
Subject: Re: Re: Re: Re: Re: C'mon you Reds!
Jeeeeeeez man! FINE. I'll ask her all right?!

From: Rob Porter
To: Beth Porter
Subject: Saturday
Hey baby,
Joe is NOT giving up. Driving me mental . . .
Any chance I can go to the match this
weekend? He's got these amazing tickets

somehow . . .
Loves you Xxx

From: Beth Porter
To: Rob Porter
Subject: Re: Saturday
Robbbbb – are you kidding me??? He's a
grown man, for God's sake – is there no one
else he can take?? What about Mark? You're
supposed to be coming to see Mum and Dad
. . . They haven't seen the kids for months.
Loves you too – most of the time ;-) Xx

From: Rob Porter
To: Beth Porter
Subject: Re: Re: Saturday
I know, I know. Don't worry . . . I'll tell him I
can't. (It IS the Derby though . . . . ;-))
xxx

From: Beth Porter
To: Rob Porter
Subject: Re: Re: Re: Saturday
Arrrrgh!! OK, OK. It's fine – you go. It's Billy
and Emily they want to see anyway . . . And
Joe already thinks I'm enough of a dragon. I'll
stay at theirs on Saturday night and drive back
in the morning.

You owe me BIG time, mister.
Xssss

From: Rob Porter
To: Beth Porter
Subject: Re: Re: Re: Re: Saturday
Have I ever told you how much I love you???
I'll make it up to you every night between now
and then, sugarlips! Promise! Xxxx

From: Beth Porter
To: Rob Porter
Subject: Re: Re: Re: Re: Re: Saturday
Yeah, yeah . . . Promises promises!
See you later. Loves you xxxxxx

From: Rob Porter
To: Beth Porter
Subject: Re: Re: Re: Re: Re: Re: Saturday
LOVES you. xxxxx

From: Rob Porter
To: Joe Hatcher
Subject Bad news . . .
Mate . . . I'M IN!!

From: Beth Porter
To: Rob Porter
Subject: Bed-head

I've just sat through an entire accounts meeting with the WORST bed-head ever! Ali just pointed it out to me as we were leaving . . . . Mortified!
Worth it though – you're a bad man, Mr P. . .
xxx

From: Rob Porter
To: Beth Porter
Subject: Re: Bed-head
Told you I'd make up for leaving you to it this weekend. Worth an early wake-up call, eh?
See you later, Mrs P. Xxx

From: Nick Turner
To: Rob Porter
Subject: Quarterly figures
Rob,
Can you swing by my office this afternoon? About 3-ish? Need to have a chat with you about this quarter's figures.
N

From: Rob Porter
To: Nick Turner
Subject: Re: Quarterly figures
Nick,
Sure – no problem. See you at three. Rob

From:	Rob Porter
To:	Beth Porter
Subject:	!!!!!!!!

Shit! Turner's just called me in for a meeting about quarterly figures. He never asks for meetings – he usually just ploughs in. Oh God. And I was late this morning as well . . . Wish me luck . . . :-/ How much is the dole nowadays??? Xxx

From:	Beth Porter
To:	Rob Porter
Subject:	Re: !!!!!!!!

Calm down, you daft old thing! Honestly, you'll be fine – he's got no reason to fire you! Has he . . . ??
And you were late for a perfectly good reason. Well . . . I thought so anyway . . . Good luck! Call me when you're out OK?
Loves you. Xx

From:	Jim Wright
To:	Rob Porter
Subject:	Turner??

Mate – just heard Turner asking his secretary to book you in for a 3 p.m.! What's going on??
Pint after work? Judging by Turner's face you might need it!

From: Rob Porter

To: Jim Wright

Subject: Re: Turner??

No idea – just mailed me and asked me to go in at three. F*ck's sake. Did he look like he was about to kick off??

Probably shouldn't be going for a pint after work – want to get home and see the kids before bed. And if this afternoon goes as badly as I think it's going to, I'll probably be checking out the job pages . . .

Laters.

From: Rob Porter

To: Beth Porter

Subject: Pack your bags!!

Where are you?? I've been trying to call you and I keep getting voicemail.

So . . . you're now officially married to the new Operational Manager for the North-west of England and North Wales!!! Apparently my team leadership in what has been a 'difficult financial quarter' (blah blah blah) has been 'incomparable' and with Geoff leaving last month, Turner can think of no one he'd rather have take on the role! BOOM!

I start a week on Monday. £10K pay rise. And a frigging company car! So . . . Maldives or

Seychelles this year . . . . ?
Call me!! Loves you Xxxxxx

From: Beth Porter
To: Rob Porter
Subject: Maldives please!!

I'm SO proud of you! (Sorry – was on the
phone to Mum about next weekend.)
Well done! Calls for a celebratory dinner, I
reckon. Chuck in a bottle of champagne and
you might get lucky when we get home too
. . . ;-)
What time will you be back? Shall I book La
Gioconda? 8-ish? I'll ask Debs if she can
come and watch the kids.
Loves you. So much. Xxxx

From: Rob Porter
To: Beth Porter
Subject: Re: Maldives please!!

Twice in one day, woman?? What's got into
you . . . ? I mean, don't get me wrong, I'm not
complaining . . .
Let's go to The Plough. I'll be home by seven
so we can take the kids too. Late night won't
hurt them once in a while right?
Xxx
(And don't worry, I'll book a cab – we'll still
get that bottle of champagne you're after :-))

From: Rob Porter

To: Jim Wright

Subject: Re: Re: Turner??

Bloody hell! Never known anything like it. I'm going to have to take a rain check on that pint, mate – got to go home to the wife and celebrate being made 'Operational Manager for the North-West of England and North Wales', don't you know. Don't know what's got into him, but Turner was like a different bloke. Turns out I've been doing something right for the past few months . . . Get in!

From: Jim Wright

To: Rob Porter

Subject: Re: Re: Re: Turner??

Get in! Blimey – wondered who was going to step in for old Geoff. Well played, mate. Well played. I'll keep that pint for you. Have a good one.

From: Rob Porter

To: Joe Hatcher

Subject: Saturday

Let's make it a big one on Saturday, my ginger friend. Just got a shit-hot promotion – start the Monday after the match. And Beth and the kids are away for the night. So let's do it in style, yeah??

15

AN INCESSANT BEEPING OUTSIDE THE HOUSE. THE impatient honking of a horn to hurry and harass. Joe's here – twelve on the dot and raring to go.

'I'll see you in the morning, beautiful. Have a good afternoon.' Rob leans in over Beth to drop a kiss on the top of her head. 'Bye, Bill! Bye, Emily! Have fun with Grandma and Grandpa! Be good, yeah? Go to bed when Mummy tells you . . .'

Beth rolls her eyes at him with a grin. 'I'm sure we'll be fine. Even if you are abandoning us . . .'

He goes back for another kiss. A proper one. A swift nip to the bottom lip. A squeeze around the waist and a pat on the bum. 'Be good. All of you. See you tomorrow. Loves you! Oh, and Beth . . . ? I will never abandon you. Not ever.'

Oh Rob, poor Rob. I'm sorry to have to break it to you, but you don't have much of a say in the matter.

In a few hours they'll be lost and alone, those three. Abandon them you certainly will.

He's out the door and down the path with a quick wave over his shoulder. Joe holds open the passenger door for him, radio blaring. 'Mate! C'mon! Let's get going! It's going to be EPIC! I've got to drop the car off at Sarah's first – said I'd go back to hers tonight. It's about fifteen minutes' walk to the ground. Today is going to be an amazing day, my friend, an amazing day!' He leans forward to wave at Beth out of the front window 'Don't worry, Beth! I'll look after him . . . Right then, Robert m'boy . . . Let's do this!'

As Joe witters on behind the wheel and Rob looks out of the window at the crowds streaming towards the ground in their red and white, I sit in the middle of the back seat. Look from one to the other. Lean in to catch every last drop of their conversation, not that Rob is saying much. He's happy to sit and let Joe chat while he watches the world go by. His world. The team colours he's followed since his dad first took him to the terraces on his fifth birthday flood the grey day with colour. Chants jostle on the breeze, the buzz of anticipation is tangible. Rob can taste it in the air. It mingles with the hot mustard, the battered fish, the fat spitting in burger vans. But it's always there. Nothing tastes like match day.

We park up outside a terraced house – the home of Joe's girlfriend for this week. Pull on thick coats and striped scarves. It may be nearing the end of the season, it'll be spring next week, but there's a nip in the air and until the third pint of lager insulates them from the wind blowing through the stands they'll need those extra layers.

And so, wrapped up and ready, we're off. Swept into the mass of bodies flooding the street and draining into the ground.

'Jesus Christ, Joe! Who did you sleep with to get these bad boys?'

'Funny you should say that, Roberto. Sarah's dad works for the sponsors. Think she might be a keeper, that one . . . Anyway, the guy who normally has them is on holiday or something, so yours truly stepped in to save the day. Couldn't let 'em go to waste, eh?'

The pitch lies beneath us – we're low enough to hear the managers chat to their leagues of coaches and physios, to count the blades of grass on the perfectly manicured pitch. But then we're high enough to see every second of the action. Slap bang on the halfway line. He was right, the old Devil. These seats are incredible.

Joe and Rob settle into their seats, beers tucked between their thighs. I perch on Rob's lap, arm lightly thrown around his shoulder, chin resting on the top of his head.

Three p.m. The whistle blows. Let the game begin.

*

The atmosphere in the ground is electric. Twice I've been thrown to my feet as the yelp of an anticipated goal has plummeted to the collective groan of a missed opportunity. All around me, the crowd lob words of advice, of insult, of despair in the direction of the pitch. All around me, the men, the boys, the women, the girls, urge their team onwards and upwards, carrying eleven men in their cherry red shirts on their shoulders to what must surely be a victory.

The home team score and the fans go wild. Joe and Rob leap to their feet, spilling beer to the floor. Wave arms high about their heads and grab each other in a bear hug. Turn to strangers either side and clap them on the backs. The goal-scorer's name flows up and around the stands again and again. 'There's only oooonne Johnny Mason! Only oooonne Johnny Mason!' The managers stand just yards apart on the touchline. Furiously chewing gum and shouting orders out to their legions battling on the pitch.

Minutes later and the away team equalise. Around the stadium, heads are held in hands and barbed comments tossed in the direction of the isolated few who dance and sing in their corner stand. Who taunt these proud fans in their cherry red. Remind them that they are fallible, that their invincibility is a transient beast, and what goes their way one minute can surely turn in the tide the next.

Half time: 1–1. The mood in the ground has dulled. Where once went arrogant chants of a certain win, now the fans seek to reassure, to recover, to regroup. There are forty-five minutes to pull this off, they say. Forty-five minutes to seal the win they need, for position and for pride.

Rob and Joe head off for a pie. Mouths water in anticipation of flaky pastry and rich meat filling. It's not gourmet by any stretch, but on match day, with Joe in tow, nothing else comes close.

Second half and the heavens open. The perfect pitch becomes a quagmire as sliding tackles score earthy brown rips in green velvet. Both play and players get dirty, lashing out with studded boots and clawing fingers. We huddle, the twelfth man, high above tightly choreographed combat. Songs and chants have given way to grim determination, to muttered words of advice mouthed in every seat creating a low hum that hovers in the air. Eyes fixed on the play below, not daring to miss a second.

A hiss echoes around us. A simultaneous sharp intake of breath from every member of that crowd. A late tackle from a defender on the opposing team has left a home player writhing in agony just yards from the goal. Necks crane to see whether he will make it to his feet. To play up, play on and play the game. But a stretcher is hurtling its way across the pitch to scoop him up and cart him off. Opposition players in their sky blue swarm round the ref to reason, to rebuke. But their protestations come to nothing as a red card is flourished high above his head and the offending defender walks from the pitch – head hanging, insults tossed from the crowd to bounce off slouched shoulders.

The penalty is lined up. Deep breaths from the chosen one as he paces backwards. One, two, three. A step to the right. A glance to the heavens. His rival dances on the line, jogs on the spot. Tries to anticipate the direction of the missile that will shortly be flying towards him. Breaths are held as leather makes contact with leather with a dull thud before the soft swish of a ball hitting the back of the net.

The rumble of the crowd thunders into a roar. 2–1 and only minutes left on the clock. Eyes turn in unison to the ticking red figures counting down in the far corner. To a linesman holding an electronic board above his head, proclaiming five minutes of extra time. The longest five minutes of the week. Endless seconds stretch ahead.

Finally, short and sharp. The final whistle.

'Mate! What a game!' A huge grin is plastered across Rob's face. 'That tackle – I mean, seriously, the man should be locked up for that. But, Christ, what a game. Thanks for the tickets, man – best game I've seen in ages.'

'You're welcome. What a joker, eh? Going in that high and that late. Jesus. Wouldn't want to meet him in a dark alley. You'd be a bloody dead man. Right. Now then, young Robert. I think it's time for a pint, don't you? I think those boys down there deserve nothing less than for us to drink to their collective health.'

Dark clouds hang full and heavy, throwing the red rivers flowing from the stadium into shadow.

'Mate, I said we'd meet Jim and Matt at the Red Lion? You good with that?' Joe always meets the same lads after the game. Same lads, same pub.

'Absolutely – lead the way.' It's not often he gets to the game, not often all the decisions are taken out of his hands, so when it happens, Rob revels in the long-standing tradition of Joe and his mates and habits that started with their dads before them.

And so they go to the pub. And they meet Jim and Matt. And they toast Rob's promotion with a couple of pints, toast the win with a couple more.

And after a few pints here, a couple of shots there, the cajoling starts, the convincing. It's the same every time.

'C'mon, Rob! Let's go into town!'

'Yeah, mate – come on! You're on a free pass aren't you?'

'Roberto! Don't leave us hanging, mate!'

And though he protests, those protests are futile, because that's all part of the dance. He'll laugh, and he'll argue, and he'll tell them he needs to be up early for the kids. But he knows, and they know, and we know that eventually he'll give in, and before long they'll be heading down Deansgate, that jubilant foursome, to the same old haunts, treading the same old path.

And because I know this, I'm already there. Tracking down a partner in crime.

It's not hard. In this city centre on Saturday night the streets are alive with potential cohorts. Thick-set men who spend their weeks in the gym and who've travelled in from the outskirts – from Moss Side, from Longsight, from Hulme. Who come into town to get drunk, get laid and get out. Thick-set men who are bristling with pent-up steroidal anger, primed to perceive even the most unintended slight.

But it can't just be any of them. I need to know that when I flick that switch, there's going to be no conciliatory backing down, no being led away by mates looking for a quiet night. I follow a few, ducking in and out of bars. But something always gives them away. A text message from a girlfriend that makes a granite face soften and smile. The glimpse of a small child clutching a huge teddy when a wallet is flipped open and twenties are slapped on the bar.

And then I see Reece. Reece Andrews. He's not terribly tall. Five ten at the very most. But he's wiry. And he's jittery. Eyes glitter and glisten from his last snort of low-grade coke off the back of his hand in the loo. On that very hand, a quincunx of blueish-black dots from time spent inside. What do they mean,

Reece, those dots? Find her, Follow her, Finger her, Fuck her, Forget her? Lovely. I can't think of a better man for the job ahead. I'm sure there are men who have those very same dots, who look at them every day and hold their heads in their hands in despair at a life lived wrong. Who scratch at them and try and burn them away so they can start a new life without that old one hanging over their heads. But you don't, do you, Reece? You wear them like a badge of bloody honour.

He stands slightly apart from his mates, all dressed in their Saturday night uniform of short-sleeved shirts and polished black shoes. No trainers, mate, not in here. Stands back and watches over them, swigging occasionally from a bottle of Beck's. He won't drink that Corona shit. With its bit of lime shoved in the top. It's gay, that. He stands back, watches over them all. Looking for the first signs of trouble. Not so he can avoid it, mind. Quite the opposite.

And while he's standing there, surveying the crowd, the boys on the other side of town are piling into a cab. Whooping and shoving each other, winking at a group of girls who are leaving the pub at the same time. All talking over each other to ask the cabbie to take them to Deansgate. To that stretch of bars down near the Arndale. You know, right? Next to Kendals?

So all Reece and I have to do is stay where we are. Stay right where we are. And wait.

*

The boys fall out of the cab and straight into the bar. A quick hello to the guy on the door – Joe's been coming here for years. Knows him well enough for a blind eye to be turned to a red football shirt peeking out from beneath the collar of a pale blue button-down. Jägerbombs all round – the heat of the spirit mingling with the sweetness of the Red Bull to deliver a direct punch to stomachs already swollen with fizzy lager. One round, two. Rob waves his hands in drunken helplessness, 'Mate, I can't do a third. Seriously . . .' before a third is plonked in front of him and he swallows back retches to see it off with the rest.

'Rob, I'm heading out for a fag? Want one?' Joe has to shout to be heard over the chatter of voices and pervasive thud of the bass of a nineties garage tune.

'Wah? Yeah, yeah. Fag. Good idea.' Rob follows him out of the front door. To the cordoned-off area in front of the windows where smokers huddle, bounce from one foot to the other and guzzle more booze to stay warm.

It stopped raining hours ago, but it's freezing outside. Despite the cold, the tiny smoking area is packed. Bodies herded together, gated in on all sides by metal barriers to allow passers-by to slip past untainted on the pavement beyond. Joe and Rob jostle through the throng. Hitch shoulders up to slide past groups of girls, legs in short skirts turning blue in the freezing night air.

And who should they end up next to in that squashed little space?

All it takes from me is a nudge in the small of his back. A gentle shove on that crowded pavement. A whispered insult dropped in the right ear. The wrong ear for Rob.

'What did you just say?' Reece spins round. Squares up to Joe who weaves on the spot behind him.

'Me? Nothing, mate, not a word.' Joe holds his hands up, gives Reece a lopsided grin. A smile of submission, conciliation.

'Do you think I'm a mug or something? I heard you.' Now his friends are turning round. Gathering behind him to fold arms over puffed chests and look over his shoulder at the guy who's been stupid enough to insult their friend.

'Mate, seriously, I didn't say a word. Honestly, just came out to have a fag. Must've been someone else.'

'Fucking prick. Typical United fan . . .' He's spotted the football shirt, revealed at an open neckline. 'Think you can slag someone off and then not bother backing it up. You're a fucking joke, mate.' His face is close to Joe's. He hisses the last sentence. 'A fucking joke . . .'

The fuse is lit. In fifteen years Joe has never missed the chance to avenge an insult, to wade into a fight. And Rob has never failed to step in to calm things down. On that I can rely.

'Look, why don't you just carry on back to wherever

you crawled out of and I'll carry on having a nice pint with my mates.' As he speaks, Joe's chest puffs up and out. He draws himself up to his full height. Spreads his fingers before balling them into fists to hang at his side. 'Dick . . .' He mutters, looking back over his shoulder where Rob stands, eyes drunkenly screwed up to take in the unfolding scene. This is where he steps in. This is where he always steps in.

'Joe . . . C'mon, mate. Leave it, yeah?' Rob grabs Joe's arm. Slips his taller frame between Joe and Reece.

'Did you just call me a dick?' Reece is furious. A cold, hard fury. Spit sprays in their faces from yellowing teeth in a snarling mouth. He shoves Joe in the shoulder.

'What if I did, eh? What are you going to do? Punch me?' Joe squares up. Butts back with his chest thrust forward. 'C'mon, then . . .'

'Joe, seriously. Back up, mate. He's not worth it.' But Rob's words are lost as a fist flies through the air and catches Joe on the cheekbone.

All hell breaks loose. Punches are being thrown in every direction. I hop off my vantage point on the metal railings. Squirm through the crowd to stand behind Reece. Slip a glass bottle just within reach. Hold his hand in mine to curl stubby fingers around a slim green glass neck. Jog his elbow so glass meets brick and shards shatter.

It's over in a matter of seconds. What will appear to

outsiders as an accidental lunge is, we know, a carefully choreographed *pas de deux*. Arms swing fluidly through the air in complete synchronisation. Jagged edges find resistance in soft skin before they puncture with the softest sigh. Hot blood pumps from a severed artery, puddling into a crimson pool on the concrete where Rob lies slumped after just one slash.

It takes Joe a second to realise what's happened. To turn and see his friend doubled up on the pavement. It doesn't register. It can't register. He was just stepping in to stop the two of them fighting. What the . . . ? It doesn't make sense. He stands over Rob and stares. Wordlessly mouthing his name again and again with a hand drawn up to a gaping mouth, slack and uncomprehending.

A bouncer pulls him out of the way. Lies Rob back on the pavement and bundles cloth at his neck to stem the flow of blood. The other has tackled Reece, one arm pinning down his neck as he sits astride his back. Holding his cheek to the cold concrete so he has no choice but to look at what he's done. But there's no remorse. No look of regret. He stares, defiantly. Short breaths huff and puff and he waits for the inevitable. He waits for the sirens.

And Rob, he just lies there. Skin fading to a porcelain white. I crouch over him, grab at arms lying lifeless and wipe away the trickle of blood that makes its way slowly from the corner of his mouth. His eyes, glassy and unfocused stare up at me, unseeing. As the night sky alternates blue and black in sync with approaching sirens, his head falls to one side and he breathes a word. A single name in a bubble of blood. 'Beth.'

We stand together in the corner of the operating theatre, Rob and I. Watching over the team of men and women in their blue tunics, mouths covered with surgical masks, eyes darting to the flashing, beeping machines that react to every change Rob's body makes. They work quickly, silently. Stemming the blood flow that has spurted continuously from the open wound. Three pints, four, five. As long as there's the faintest flicker of life, these men and women will do everything they can to bring him back.

Rob slides down the wall to crouch, hands cupped over his mouth as his eyes stare, disbelieving, at the lifeless body draped in blue and jacked up high on the operating table.

'I won't make it, will I?' He looks up at me, rubbing long fingers against stubble darkening his jawline. Reaches to wrap his fingers around mine where they rest on his shoulder.

'There's a chance, but . . .' I trail off. I feel like I owe him some sort of hope, however misplaced. However futile.

'God, Beth . . . What was I thinking? He always kicks off with someone . . . Why didn't I just leave it?'

Before I can answer, raised voices in the corridor are swept through swinging doors as a nurse comes in with yet more blood.

'Where is my husband? Where is he? I have to see him! Now! Rob! Rob! Rob Porter! Where IS he?' The voice is high-pitched and frantic, but there's no denying who it belongs to.

Rob looks up at me, standing over him. 'What the . . . ? That's Beth! What . . . Hang on . . . Who the fuck are you?' He scrambles to his feet, trainers wet with his own blood slip and squeak against the linoleum.

I close my eyes. Take a deep breath. Look him straight in the eye. 'I think you know, Rob. You know that you can't possibly be here talking to me and over there lying on that bed.'

He backs away from me, mouthing words that can't be spoken. Staggers backwards into a metal trolley with a clatter. Holds his hand up against me as I step forward to comfort.

'Stop. Don't touch me. What . . . ?' He looks desperately from me to the body lying on the bed, shrouded in blue. Back to me. Out to the voice in the corridor that cries his name. 'I don't get it. Who are you? What are you doing here?'

'I'm Death, Rob. Your death.' There's no other way to say it.

'No. No. You're not. You can't be.' He's still. Disbelief is written all over his face. He balls his fist into his hair. Pinches his brow between finger and thumb. 'What about . . . I dunno . . . You being a skeleton in a hood? What about that . . . scythe thing?'

'All made up.' I shrug my shoulders and hold my hand out to him. Slowly, gently so as not to startle. 'Most people who meet me don't live to tell the tale, Rob. So they make stuff up. They're scared of me, so they make me out to be this monster. But I'm not, Rob.' My voice is barely more than a whisper. 'I swear I'm not.

'If you saw me at the end of eighty years and you were old and you were ready, we wouldn't even be having this conversation. You'd know me from the very second I walked into the room – whoever I looked like. But you're not old, and you weren't ready. And so I have more to explain.'

While I speak my fingers have slowly breached the gap between us, until my palm can cup his cheek. He tilts his neck to rest his head in my hands. Nuzzles slightly into my palm to breathe in that perfume he bought her for Christmas that he can't smell without the familiar punch of longing.

'But you look exactly like her. Not, like, a bit of a resemblance. Exactly like her.'

'I know. That's what happens. You see me, everyone sees me, as the woman they most want me to be. And I am her, Rob. Right here and now, I am her. I know everything she knows. I know everything you've ever said to her. Everything you've ever done together. I know that you hate peas and love salt and vinegar crisps. I know that we were convinced Billy was a girl and called him Sophie for the nine months before he was born. I know that when you were sixteen and we first kissed you went home and told your nan that you knew exactly who you were going to marry. And I know that if this happened all over again, you'd still wade in and defend Joe. Even if you already knew what that guy was capable of.'

I've stepped forward now to wrap my arms around his waist in a hug. I can feel the body that's stiffened in shock relax as he presses his lips to my hair before resting his chin on the top of my head.

'Can I see her? I need to see her. I need to see the kids.' He wipes his nose on the heel of his hand. Takes deep breaths to bite back tears.

'She's outside. She's waiting for you. But you can only see her when your body is taken to her. Until you let your body go, and you have to do that yourself, you're tied to it. And once you let go, it's too late for goodbyes.'

He nods, silently. Begins to sob, quietly. Steps back to look at those bodies in the corner gathered under the operating light. 'I can't leave her. I won't leave her. I promised I wouldn't abandon her. This morning. This morning. I promised.' He stands. Punches the wall above my head. Lets out a yell of frustration from deep within. 'This is bullshit!' A guttural roar that coincides with a flurry of activity around the table as a heartbeat strengthens and pupils contract in response to bright light. He's not going to go without a fight.

For three days he veers between us. Identical twins bound in grief on either side of his bed. A flicker of an eyelid, the squeeze of a hand and he's hers. As organs fail, one by one, slowly but surely, he's mine. Swinging between lying motionless on the bed, swathed in tubes and monitors and plastic pipes, and railing at me. Shouting and yelling. Tearing at his hair. Upturning chairs. Kicking at walls.

He never once bemoans his own fate, not once. 'Look at her! Look. At. Her! Look what you've done to her!' He grabs my chin. Forces my head in her direction.

I can't. Can't look at her. All I see when I do look at her is Tom. A love that's been torn apart too soon. An emptiness in her eyes as she looks towards a future without him. While the act of stabbing Rob came easily, too easily, this is unbearable. To sit here, day after day and watch a life crumble and collapse. I've seen how this ends. Seen the sleepless nights and the vacant days and the turning to talk to someone who will never again be there. I've seen Tom doing it. See him living it every day. And now, I've subjected Beth to the very same.

When I do look, I have to fight the urge to throw up. Swallow back the bile that rises in my throat. The bile that rises because of what I've done. She is broken.

Greasy hair is slicked back from a face that yellows under the strip lighting.

Although her mum has brought clean clothes and arranged a room at a nearby hotel, she won't move from the bed to change, to rest. She sits, in the same clothes she was wearing on Saturday morning, when he kissed her on the top of the head, nipped her on the lip and told her he loved her. Now those same lips move in silent prayer to tell stories about the kids, about his parents, about their wedding day. Anything. Just in case he can hear. And he can. He can hear every word. It's the only thing that stops his ranting. When he walks round the bed and holds her hand and cocks his head to listen and laugh and press cold fingers to his lips.

But he can't fight for ever. The blood loss has caused irreparable brain damage. His body is slowly shutting down, like the lights being turned off at the end of a working day, one by one. Room by room. By the third day the anger has mellowed to acceptance of the inevitable. He perches on the chair next to me to regale me with stories, show me pictures of the kids. I know it all, because for these final precious days, although I am Death, also I am Beth. I have lived with him, I have loved him, and I must help him say goodbye.

The doctors come in to see her. Middle-aged men with wives at home, with children they've watched grow into adults. They come in to start the conversations about what more steps can be taken. To start the conversations about turning off the machine, about the quality of life he could expect if they were to continue pumping his heart on his behalf, to continue breathing air into his lungs with the artificial bellows by the bed.

Rob gets up from the chair beside me. Walks round the bed to wrap his arms around Beth one last time. To drop a kiss on the top of her head. He nods at me over his frozen body, and there's no need for any more conversation. I reach up to flick the switch on the life-support machine and watch as Robert Porter slowly, quietly, fades to black.

16

BANGING AT THE DOOR. A BANGING THAT PAUSES to allow a bellow. 'Tom? Tom. Mate. Open the door. It's me.' Alex.

We sit, side by side, backs against the door. An extra weight against the outside world in case the Chubb and the Yale and the chain all fail.

Our heads hang. Knees tuck up under our chins. Tom holds his hands flat against his ears. We wince, in unison, with every thump.

Silence. And then another voice. 'And me.' Higher pitched, softer. Janey. A pause. He can hear them out there, whispering to each other, deciding what tack to take next.

When Alex speaks again, it's a whisper. The softest of murmurs. His voice is level with Tom's ear, from his position hunkered down against the door in the outside world. 'Mate. Please. Just open the door.' There's a shuffle as Alex turns, leans his own back against his side of the door. Hangs his head and draws his knees up under his chin. And so they sit, back to back, bookends on either side of a door that won't budge.

Day after day his friends visit. Take it in turns to sit outside the door. Trying to time it so they bump into him on the way home from work, so he has no choice but to face them, to talk to them, to let them in. What they don't know is that he doesn't go to work, hasn't left the house for anything other than a pint of milk in weeks. So turning up at five, four, even earlier won't make a difference because they'll never catch him. But they can see the light shining through the crack beneath the door, hear the muffled sound of quiz show theme tunes wending their way from the lounge, and they know he's in there.

They adopt a daily shift of an hour or two, in pairs or alone. They call to him, cajole. Convince. Commiserate. Charm. Some sit in silence. Some relay news from their own lives. Throughout, Tom keeps quiet. He knows they're there and he knows they know he knows. But he can't bring himself to open the door. To see the cocked head and the look of pity. He can't trust himself not to react like he did to Emma. To snap like he did with Kath. If he doesn't open the door, he can't push them further away.

Finally, day after day, they accept defeat. Tell him through the door that they're going to go. To leave him to it. But they're there if he needs them. He hears that every day. That people are there if he needs them. But there's only one person he needs, and she's dead.

After each visit, he waits for the silence. Waits for heavy footsteps thudding down carpeted stairs and the chunky thunk of the communal door to the street swinging shut. He waits for half an hour. Waits for the coast to clear. And when it does, when he can lean his head out of the front window and see no one waiting below, he runs. Pounds down wet pavements, slick with leaves. When he runs, he can't hear her voice. Can't catch a whiff of her perfume. He can see her – he sees her on every corner. Sees her in the shadows cast by the trees outside his window. Sees her cross the road ahead, just out of reach. But as long as his mind is filled with the gritty scuff slap of trainers on tarmac, he can't hear her, and as long as his head is down and his legs are pumping, if he sees her, he can always run away.

17

A DESERTED PLAYGROUND ROUND THE BACK OF A
housing estate in the pouring rain. Huddled side by
side on the swings as the smell of rain-soaked tarmac
fills our noses and we watch the abandoned roundabout spin slowly of its own volition.

It goes without saying that He is, of course, perfectly
dressed for the weather. A skeletal, pale hand holds the
carved wooden handle of a huge black umbrella over
His head as He rocks His heels back and forth to
propel the swing beneath. I huddle in my pacamac –
the rain tip tapping on the peaked brim of my hood to
drip off the edge and drop onto my nose. My feet
dangle above black rubber matting laid to break the
fall of small bodies.

'So three down. Well done, Little D. I must say, I
never thought you'd get this far. Seems I underesti-
mated you.' He takes a long drag on a cigarette.

Breathes out a long sigh of smoke to mingle with exhaled breath in the damp air.

I hate it, hate myself, but there's an undeniable burst of pride. A burst of pride that shines bright to eclipse the memory of glass slicing skin. Of arterial blood spurting hot into my face and a metallic tang lingering on lips. It's a pride that fills me with a warmth where previously there has only been a cold, churning hate. With three down, I'm over halfway. With three down, I'm nearly there.

'It's getting easier,' I admit. 'I didn't think it would. I didn't think I'd be able to carry on after Hywel. I couldn't get that noise out of my head. Couldn't close my eyes without seeing his bulging eyes. I felt sick all the time at the thought that I'd done that to him. That he wouldn't be lying there if it wasn't for me. For what I wanted . . .'

'And now?'

'I don't know. Sitting in that hospital room with Beth was torture. Watching what I'd done to her . . . to them. The act of killing was, well, not easy, but . . . don't get me wrong, please don't get me wrong. I didn't enjoy doing it. I certainly don't want to have to do this more than absolutely necessary. But the act of killing him . . . I just didn't really feel anything. I know what I did and I know what I did was wrong, but I just didn't feel anything . . .'

I look down at my dangling feet. 'It was only when

I was sitting in that hospital room with Beth. That's when it hit home. That's when it matters. The ones that die, they find some sort of peace. Once they know what's happening, there's this . . . calm, I guess. It's the ones who are left behind that suffer. And I'm the one that causes that suffering. Me. And I hate myself for that.'

'Oh, Little D,' He sighs. 'You really are too soft for your own good. Do you think I sit around beating myself up every time I kill someone? Ha!' He laughs, a short bark of a laugh. 'Of course I don't! Honestly. You need to grow a backbone, my girl.'

No I don't. Not if it's at the expense of everyone else I don't. I'll stay soft, thanks.

'Well, regardless. I think we should crack on, eh? Step things up a little bit? What do you say, Little D? Ready for number four?'

'Why not? Go for it.' May as well get on with it. Only two more. How bad can it be?

The rain has stilled and slowed to a steady, fine drizzle. Across the playing fields a couple of kids ride their bikes, a dog chasing and barking. Leaping at spinning wheels and splashing into fresh puddles on the waterlogged field. Wet hair is plastered against their faces as they head for the gap in the fence backing on to identikit eighties Barratt houses, head for warm homes and tea on the table. Head for a motherly scolding and a clean pair of jeans.

'Ellie Morgan. Number four.' He nods in the direction of the kids on the far side of the field. 'They're her brothers. Her older brothers . . .'

Her brothers? But, they're young. Really young. The oldest one can only be, what, twelve? How old can this Ellie be?

'She's seven,' He lets the number float in the dank air between us.

'Are you kidding me?' My head whips round to look Him in the face, though His eyes are masked by the black curve of the umbrella. 'Seven? Seven years old? She's a kid! Surely there's someone else? Her mum? Dad? God, even one of the brothers – they're at least a little bit older, right? Come on. She's seven . . .' The desperate gabble trails off to a whisper. 'Surely you're not serious?'

'Deadly.' He smirks at His little joke. 'My choosing, Little D. Remember that bit? You end the lives of five people of my choosing.' His voice adopts a mocking tone '"My soul . . . I want my soul . . . I want to live . . . Please help me . . ."' Flips back to harsh reality. 'You asked for it. I told you it wouldn't be easy. But you asked for it. You've done this, Little D. With your selfishness, and this life you so desperately want. You've put a price on that little girl's head. You, Little D, no one else. You.'

I feel sick. This morning's bubbles of pride burst to seep bitter bile into my stomach. My mouth has filled with a cloying saliva and I'm fighting the urge to vomit right there. Right onto the rubber matting. Right onto His pristine loafers. A child. A bloody, bloody child.

'And what if I say no? What if I don't do it? For pity's sake – she's a child. I can't . . . No, I won't. There has to be someone else. Please . . .'

'You can, Little D, and you will. Because if you don't, well . . . If you don't then the deal's off, isn't it? It's no skin off my nose, you know, for you to head back to your old life. I don't really see what was wrong with that life in the first place. People would kill for that, you know, immortality. Eternal youth. You really do want to have your cake and eat it, don't you, Little D? I don't know why I bother . . .'

How can I do this? How can I sit here and accept that I'm going to have to kill this child. To hell with all that euphemistic 'ending a life' crap. I'm killing people. And now I'm supposed to kill this little girl. All for a life that holds no guarantee. All for a man who might not even want me.

I screw my eyes closed against the drizzle, rubbing cold fingers against the furrows in my brow as if pressing hard enough will smooth all of this away. 'I can't do it.' Barely a whisper. Breathed words don't even disturb the air around me. 'Not a child. Not a little girl. No. The deal's off.'

Before He can speak I'm up and walking. Putting as much distance as I can between me and His twisted, fucked-up games. Between me and the wheedling and cajoling that will convince me that this is all normal. That this is all justifiable.

I can hear Him shouting after me as I cross the field. 'Lizzy! Elizabeth!' No one has called me Elizabeth in four hundred years.

I walk for what seems like hours. It could be minutes. It could be days. The drizzle alights in tiny droplets on my hair and mists the world with an impressionist brush-stroke. Aimless wandering with no direction has brought me straight to one place. One place I feel safe and one place I have no right to be. Tom's flat.

I let myself in to the empty hallway. He's back at work now, and it's mid-afternoon on a Monday and I know he'll be staring blankly at a computer screen in his office while the hours tick away and he can come home to stare blankly at a TV screen before closing his eyes against the horror of another day without her.

I go straight through to the bedroom. To the battered old leather armchair in the corner strewn with yesterday's clothes. Grab a pillow from the bed on my way across the room and bury my face in it, wiping away tears and breathing in his smell. I've never met anyone who's smelled like him before. The faintest whiff prompts an involuntary pulse.

Behind scrunched lids I can see him as I left him last night. Head tucked into the crook of his elbow to blind eyes from the pervasive neon glow of a bedside alarm clock. Fingers curled to hold my hand so recently slipped free of his grasp. Closed eyelids kissed softly shut above soft lips slightly parted. He sleeps, intermittently. A disturbed sleep that he wakes from with a jump. A start of understanding that drags him into a cold consciousness when he reaches out an arm to find she's not there.

How can He even think I would do this? How could I take this little girl's life before it's even had a chance to be lived? Why is this one so much more difficult? Why should one life carry any more weight than another? The questions flit through my mind like moths on a summer's evening – as I register one, it's gone to be replaced by another and another and another, relentlessly bashing against the inside of my skull. And threaded through all of these thoughts, one that shouts louder than the rest. You got yourself here. You're the one who struck the deal. What were you thinking? Making a deal with the Devil. Stupid girl.

But then what happens if I don't follow through? If I don't at least try my every day from here to eternity will be overshadowed with what might have been. And if I thought it was unbearable before, God only knows how I will manage then. And if I don't carry on, then why did Hywel die? And Rose? And Rob? All dead. Because of me. All died in vain as part of a task that I can't bring myself to complete?

And I know. I know that I'll continue. That though the stakes were high and have just got higher, I have only myself to blame.

Without opening my eyes, I know He's there. Know He'll have followed me. Hell, He probably knew where I would end up before I did. Was probably sitting in the lounge waiting for me as I slipped through the front door. I can't look at Him.

'I don't like to be messed around, Little D.' His voice is surprisingly level. Calm. I know.

'I'm not doing this for me. You asked for this. You. I didn't seek you out for this game of yours. You did this. You came to me. Remember that, Little D. You came to me. Do you want this or not?'

I do.

'I don't like second chances, Little D. I'm not chasing you round waiting for you to complete this. If you want it, if you want to continue, it has to be your decision and you have to make it now.'

I take a deep breath in. Release a long breath out. A resigned sigh. 'OK.' I can barely hear myself, it comes out in the quietest of whispers.

'Sorry? What was that? I'm not sure I heard you.'

'OK. I'll do it. Ellie.'

'Well done. I knew you'd see sense.' He crosses the room from the sash window He's been gazing out of. Leans in close, face lowered level with mine. 'Don't cross me, Little D. Don't play games with me. You will always, always come off worse.'

I will. I know that.

'Two weeks, Little D. You have two weeks for this one. And if it doesn't happen in two weeks, that's it.

No more chances. Do you understand? I'll leave you to it. Let me know when you're done.'

He stands and sweeps out of the room, slamming the door in His wake. I grab the pillow I've been hugging and hurl it in His direction with a howl.

I've never hated Him more. I've never hated myself more. Ellie Morgan.

Number 4.

18

THE MEDIA CIRCUS HAS COME TO TOWN. HUGE Winnebagos line the streets, aerials jutting skyward as if hoping to snare a clue on the breeze, to catch a truth in the scudding clouds. The tweets have taken flight, to dip and dive through the evening air as a family's grief is parcelled into the bite-sized, gossipy chunks of a 140-character limit. From all around voices of different accents, different languages report the same news. A startling lack of information to warrant such numbers, but they wait, terriers at the edge of a rabbit hole, held static in time by the scent of a story.

'Ellie Morgan was last seen here, outside the Shipley's newsagent on Station Road at around six thirty on Tuesday evening. Nothing has been heard of her since. Local man, Ian Morris, has been helping with the search.

'Ian, did you know Ellie?'

'Only by sight. She seemed like such a lovely little thing. Always laughing. So sad. Horrid to think what could've happened to her.'

'And how have you been helping with the search?'

'Doing whatever I can really – we need as many people looking as we can. Checking your sheds and garages and cellars. There's a scared little girl out there – I'm sure of it. And we need to find her as soon as we can.'

'Thanks for talking to us, Ian. Good luck with the search.'

'Thanks.'

Come off it, Ian. You know, and I know, exactly where that little girl is, and searching sheds and garages and cellars isn't going to help, is it? Is it, Ian? As police search teams fan out across wasteland, an army on the march, as divers drag the depths and dogs sniff for a whiff of her, as Mum and Dad wipe away silent tears and gulp back deep, shuddering breaths, Ellie and I sit. Quietly in the darkness. And we wait.

Poor Ian. You see, he wouldn't have done it if it wasn't for me. He's had these thoughts for years, dark thoughts looming at the back of his mind in his late-night moments. Little voices chirruping in the darkness. He's sat at home, shoulders hunched over a glowing screen in a dimly lit room, looking at pictures that would horrify even the hardiest. Watched by Bella in the corner, resting a chin on crossed paws and raising a disdainful eyebrow in his direction. But he'd never act on these thoughts, never see these pictures brought to life. Would he? Turns out, with a gentle nudge in the wrong direction, he would. He'll never know what drove him to drive to the shop that day instead of walking, what prompted him to park in the alley while he let the dog out to snuffle in the grass. He'll never remember a figure in the front passenger seat, one hand guiding the wheel. A passenger who gave the dog a shove as they turned into the alley, causing her to whimper and whine and scrape at the door to be let out. But what he does know is that it was as easy as pie when he saw her, blonde and grubby in jeans and a pink T-shirt printed with princesses dancing a waltz in their floating ballgowns of blue and green. Thin arm thrown around Bella's neck to tug on her ear. It was easy as pie to tell her about the puppies at home. Did she want to see them? He only lived around the corner. Did she want to hop in? He'd drop her off home later – he had her mum's number so he'd give her a call and let her know. And he had fish fingers in for tea if she got hungry. So she hopped in, the lure of puppies too great to ignore. And the black thoughts were overwhelming. All those black, black thoughts, fought against for so long, crowded into his head. Chattering and yabbering and whispering suggestions into his ear.

And at the junction, where he could turn right to her home, to his home, to the estate where they both live, he pauses. Looks both ways. Checks his mirrors.

Drops hand to indicator. Turns left. Mirror, signal, manoeuvre.

They've been in the car five minutes before she speaks. 'What's your dog's name?'

'Betty.' Better safe than sorry.

'What's your name?'

'Michael.' No trace. Not if she gets away. Give him a chance to escape before anyone cottons on. Better safe than sorry.

Ellie pauses. Her dad's called Michael, but people call him Mike. And although she doesn't know exactly what this man's name is, she's heard her mum talk to him before and she's sure it's not Michael.

'You live near my house, don't you? I think you're going the wrong way. I think my house is back there.' She's bouncing round the back seat, trying to look out the back window, past the boxes stacked in the boot blocking a clear view through the glass. The roads are empty – it's a self-sufficient Peak District town, no commuters to drive in or out at the end of a day. No rush-hour drivers to recognise a small blonde accompanying a local man without a daughter.

'The puppies aren't at my house.' He clears his throat. Shifts in his seat. 'A friend of mine's looking after them. They don't live far. Don't worry – we'll see them quickly and then I'll get you home. Bel . . . Betty wants to see them. Check they're all OK. She is their mum, after all! Wants to make sure they're not missing her.'

But he said. He said they were at his house. He said.

'I think I should go home. I don't think my mummy will want me to see the puppies without her.'

He's speeding now – not too fast to draw attention, but subtly accelerating to put distance between him and a mother in a Derbyshire front room with a niggling feeling that all is not well.

'Nearly there!' Keep the tone light, Ian. No need to scare her.

Bugger. Traffic lights. He's going to have to slow down. Jumping them would only draw attention if there's anyone about. Are the child locks on in the back seat? Lock the doors in case she thinks about hopping out. Better safe than sorry. Who puts a set of traffic lights in the middle of bloody nowhere? He can feel a fine film of sweat forming on the nape of his neck. Knuckles white as he grips the wheel. But he's done it now. No going back. No unwinding the clock. If he takes her home now and she blabs – chatting away like little girls do. Blethering away to all and sundry. And they'll know there were no puppies. And they'll want to know why he said there were. So what could he possibly say to explain? No, he has to keep going. Better safe than sorry.

She's silent in the back. Arm looped around Bella, lifting her ear to whisper and chat. To soothe herself in the silence. He flips the switch on the central locking and the gears clunk into place – unmistakeable in the quiet car.

'What was that noise, Michael? Could I go home please? I don't think my mummy would like this.' He can hear the rising panic in her voice. Still so polite. So polite despite her fear.

'Sorry! Just knocked the switch by accident. Nearly there!'

Come on . . . Come on come on. The cherry red light shines for what seems like a lifetime. Without thinking his right foot pulses on the accelerator, revving the engine. He looks in the rear-view mirror – she's clambered over to the window and is tugging at the door release.

'Let me out! Let me out! I want to go home! I want my mummy!' She's starting to cry, wiping a snotty nose on a grubby sleeve and pulling and pushing at the door. 'I want my mummy!'

'SIT DOWN! You stupid little bitch. SIT DOWN!' His foot jabs on the accelerator, the car leaps forward on the black tarmac. 'Sit down and shut up.' His voice is lower now, a growled threat held in the very back of his throat.

She sits down. She shuts up. Only lets out the smallest of whimpers sneak out when she can't keep them in any longer. Clings onto Bella's warm fur, face buried into soft russet curls. Huge eyes turned to watch the face in the rear-view mirror. Breaths short, shuddering. 'Mummy, Mummy, Mummy . . .' A whisper. 'Mummy, Mummy, Mummy . . .'

*

Ten minutes later and we pull off the main road. Twenty-five minutes from pulling up in that alley, from invented puppies and a quick getaway. Twenty-five minutes from a mother starting to wonder where her daughter's got to. Twenty-five minutes from a local shopkeeper cursing the kids who just leave their bikes lying on the pavement to get under her customer's feet. Twenty-five minutes from changing all of their lives for ever.

Down a bumpy track, over an old red-brick bridge pebble-dashed with dried cow muck and rutted with mud. Headlights switched off to hide in the twilight. A derelict watermill off to the right, nestled into the trees. Windows bricked up with breeze blocks, heavy wooden door with the odd slat missing. Huge waterwheel decrepit and defunct, hanging from its axis, slats ground to a halt in thick mud, green with algae. He's been using this place for a few months now to store his tools. Belongs to a friend who had no use for it and was happy to hand over the keys for a bit of beer money every month. And in all the times he's been here to drop stuff off, all the times he's let Bella out of the car to sniff at rabbit holes and crouch against rotting tree stumps, he's never seen a soul.

The car pulls to a stop, surrounded by trees whispering into the night. He gets out, opens the boot to lift out some boxes. Watches Ellie through the grille he had put in place to stop Bella leaping around from boot to back seat. Watches her in her back-seat prison, eyes wide, body curled as small as possible. Bella gripped for warmth and comfort.

He heads in to check out the inside of this place. Eyes darting, blood pulsing. A fine sweat down his back and under his arms evaporates to chill him in the cold night air. What's he doing? What's he thinking? Too late now, got to get her in there, get her out of the way and then figure it out. He can't just take her home now. Oh God, oh God.

It's pitch black in there. The torch he carries sweeps a lighthouse beam across a sparse room. Couple of chairs. A chipped mug in a slime-stained sink. A few missing floorboards, bottomless black gaps. His tools piled in a corner. Out of harm's way.

He's a carpenter by trade, our Ian, and he sets to on the door – hammering loose boards over the missing slats, fixing an extra deadbolt to the outside. All reclaimed stuff, nothing shiny and bright and new. Nothing that will draw unwanted attention from the occasional dog walker who might pass through.

While he works he casts glances back at the car. Willing her silently to keep quiet. Praying that today isn't the day one of the locals decides to take a different path. He's never seen anyone, when he's been up here, but . . . Finally, he tacks a heavy blanket to the inside. Don't want any noise to get out. Muffle it. Muffle her. Better safe than sorry.

Back to the car and she's exactly where he left her. Good girl.

'We're getting out now, Ellie. Now you be a good girl. Stay quiet and it'll all be OK. OK? You can be a good girl, can't you?' He's back in control – his voice level, measured. Soothing a saddened girl. Why so sad, Ellie? Why so sad?

She nods. Sniffs back tears. Shrinks back against the door on the far side of the car.

'Come on, Ellie. Over here. Come on. Be a good girl, eh?'

She shuffles across the back seat, holding Bella on her lap like a shield.

'Up we go. Good girl.' Slowly, slowly. Don't scare her any more than you have already, Ian. He lifts her into his arms, feels her thin body tense at his touch. Knows she's wondering whether to scream. Whether to just give up. He gathers her up, warm and solid in his arms, breathes in the dirty smell of hair and fear. Backs out of the car. 'Good girl, that's the way. Good girl.'

She screams. Opens her mouth and really screams right into his ear, high-pitched and loud and ear-splitting in its clarity in the night air. Wriggles in his arms. Tries to bite him, kick him with skinny little legs.

'You stupid little COW. What did I say? Be a GOOD GIRL. You fucking idiot.' He's shaking – furious with both himself and her. Why didn't you take any precautions, Ian? Why not shut her up for good? Shoves her back into the car, feeling tenderly at his forearm where two perfectly perforated half-moon bite marks bloom against pale skin. Slams the door. Marches round to the boot for a roll of duct tape. Yanks the door open and climbs in beside her. Pulls her up out of the footwell to clamp her between his knees. Rips off a length of duct tape and smooths it down over her stupid, screaming, can't-be-trusted mouth. She wriggles under him, trying to throw him off, but what hope does she have? A skinny little seven-year-old against fifteen stone and a lifetime lugging wood? Bella growls at him, snaps at his hands. In the space of half an hour, her allegiances lie with this kid. This stupid, screaming, can't-be-trusted kid.

'Now.' He's breathing heavily, head swimming. 'Are you going to be a good girl?'

She looks up, blue eyes welling with tears, snot running freely from her nose over the heavy silver of the tape. Nods, slowly. Deep breaths. Body rigid with fear.

'Right. Come on then.'

Tries again. Pulls her over to the door and out of the car. Over his shoulder like a rolled-up carpet. There's no screaming this time is there, Ellie? In the place of a scream, a warm wetness seeps into the fabric of his shirt and the sharp tang of urine pricks the air.

Into the house. The torch, resting on the edge of the sink, throws uncertain shadows over the room. He picks his way over the floor, testing floorboards under their combined weight. Drops her down into one of the chairs. They eye each other warily. She can't scream now, but she can run. And she can kick. God, what is he doing?

He pulls the roll of duct tape off his wrist. Holds a hand around her throat to pin her in position. Draws his face close to hers so she can feels the warmth of his breath on her cheek, the flecks of spit of his careful enunciation.

'Don't move, Ellie. I can trust you, can't I? I can trust you to be a good girl? You want to be a good girl, don't you?'

She doesn't move, frozen by fear and confusion. Her jeans are cold and itchy against her leg where the urine has soaked into the heavy twill.

He backs off slowly. Don't scare her, Ian. Don't make any sudden movements. His head moves into shadow – she is alone in the torch beam. Solitary in the limelight.

He slowly pulls off a length of tape. Holds it between his teeth. Reaches for her hands. First one, then the other. She resists, a stiffening of muscle to hold them tight by her sides and out of his way.

'Ellie.' A warning.

She gives in. Sits still as both wrists are encased in a dull, sticky, silver shackle. Shaky breaths as leg is taped to chair leg, as head sags on shoulders and she stares dully at the floor. Exhausted.

He steps back. Looks at this tiny frame in the spotlight. Crumpled and grubby and broken. This tiny frame in the pink T-shirt whose princesses still dance their waltz in their floating ballgowns of blue and green. Mouth covered, hands bound. And he is horrified. Stumbles back with hand pressed to mouth, fist clutching at hair. Stumbles back to distance himself from his actions. Stumbles back into the corner of the room, where he sinks to the floor, eyes wide in disbelief. And he starts to cry. Shoulders heave with sobs and dry retches. What have I done? What have I done? What have I done?

What have we done, Ian? What have we done?

Back in town and the alarm bells are starting to ring. At almost exactly the same time, people are starting to wonder.

Rebecca Morgan, heating through a bolognese on the hob shouts through to the kids 'Ellie! Josh! Mason! Tea's on the table!'

Two boys come running through. Josh, nine, still a boy. Mason, twelve, showing the shadowy beginnings of the man he'll become. Darkening hair on an upper lip, a voice that cracks and breaks beyond his control. Limbs all of a sudden too long for his body.

Rebecca turns, puts plates down in front of them. Heads to the door through to the hallway, 'Ellie! Ellieeee! Come on! Tea's getting cold!'

A beat.

'Mason, run up and get your sister. I swear, that girl . . .'

'She's not upstairs. I don't think she's back from the

shop yet.' Head down, hand shovelling food to mouth. He sniggers at Josh who sits opposite, crossing his eyes while he slurps spaghetti strands through pursed lips.

'What?' A cold shiver creeps down her spine and makes the hairs on her arms stand to attention. 'What do you mean she's not back? She went about an hour ago.' She's never late for tea. Never late for Mum's home-made bolognese.

'Mu-um – it was, like, half an hour ago. Don't overreact.' Still shovelling, flecks of mince splashing onto the wipe-clean tablecloth, a riot of tropical flowers.

'Oh my God. Stay here. Both of you. Do. Not. Move.' She runs out of the back door, apron tied around her waist, slippers shuffle slapping on the paving slabs.

'Ellie! ELLIE! Ellie! Come on, Els, it's teatime!'

Come on, Ellie – you must be somewhere right? Wrong.

'Ellie! Richard, hi, have you see Ellie? She's not come back for her tea.'

Let's not fear the worst. Not yet.

A passing dog walker shakes his head. 'Sorry, love . . . Have you tried the shop?'

She carries on down the street to seek out her daughter in gardens, under cars, behind fences. It's only two minutes' walk to the shop – two minutes there and two minutes back and five million possibilities in between.

She arrives at the shop to find Maureen Shipley holding up a small, pink bike. Tassels on the handlebars. Barbie bicycle bell. Ellie's.

'Rebecca, hello. I was just about to send Roger up to yours. This is Ellie's, isn't it? Left the thing right in my doorway – nearly tripped up old Fred Manning and he's only just had his new hip. Must've gone home without it. Kids, eh? Don't know the value of things nowadays. I tell you, if it were my boys they wouldn't have heard the end of it. I don't work all the hours God sends for you to leave your things lying about, I used to tell them. If you want something you've got to learn to take care of it, that's what we used to tell them. Rebecca? Rebecca?'

While Maureen's rabbiting on, Rebecca's in silence. Tears pouring down pale cheeks. Teeth biting blood from bottom lip. Where is she? Where IS SHE?

'She's not at home.' A hoarse, strained whisper. 'She came down here and she's not come back.'

'I've not seen her for a while. Oh, about three-quarters of an hour, I'd say. She came in for some sweets. Roger? ROGER! What did Ellie Morgan come in for?'

I don't care, I don't care what she came in for. Where is my daughter?

'Where did she go? Maureen? Maureen! Where did she go?'

'Well, I didn't see her after she left. Thought she'd gone home, then I went out about . . . oooh . . . half an hour ago. Had to help old Fred when he nearly tripped over that bike. She wasn't there then. I just thought she must've gone home and forgotten it. Thought she'd be back for it by now. That's what I was just saying to Roger. ROGER! Don't worry about that bike – her mum's here now.'

'She didn't come home, Maureen. I've not seen her.' Fingers tightly pressed at anguished lips.

'Oh well, dear. Let's not worry. She'll turn up. Why don't you go and wait at home for her and I'll make sure to send her your way if she comes back here.'

'No! NO! She's a seven-year-old girl! I can*not* wait for her to "turn up".' She shouts out into the bruised dusk. 'Ellie? ELLIE!'

'Roger, I think you'd better call the police. Mrs Morgan's daughter seems to have gone missing.'

The police arrive with a sense of calm proficiency. When did you last see your daughter, Mrs Morgan? Rebecca? May I call you Rebecca? And Mrs Shipley, you say you last saw her at about half past six? Can you remember what she was wearing? And have you spoken to your husband, Rebecca? She's not with him?

Of course I've spoken to my bloody husband. A silent scream in the depths of her head. Among fervid imaginings and the throbbing, overwhelming, gut-churning fear.

'Yes. He's on his way home from work. He's coming straight here.'

They're gathered, Rebecca, the Shipleys, the police officers, in the tiny kitchen out the back of the shop. A beige plastic kettle roars and spits as it boils, mugs lined up for tea to press into nervous hands.

'Sir?' Another police officer appears at the door. 'Sir, could you come outside, please? I think we might've found something.'

Out in the alley, dogs and police officers scouring every inch in the dark. Working lights erected either end to throw what light they can on the situation. Halfway down they stop. A clump of grass. A pink towelling hairband, baggy from overuse, attached to a plastic disc, scratched and fading – Cinderella going to the ball.

Heads turn at a groan that turns into a scream. A drawn-out, anguished 'No' punched out from deep within. Heads turn as a father arrives at the scene of the last known sighting of his daughter and his wife collapses against him to confirm that yes, that belonged to Ellie. Yes, that was her favourite.

Back at the watermill, Ellie and I sit in the darkness. Even now, in the middle of the day, it's black as night. Not a chink of light through the armour of breeze-block windows and a curtained door.

Ian went back to town last night to help with the search and to fill the gap left by one empty house on the street. Left us here, alone with each other in the dark. He had to get out. Had to get away from the madness he's been driven to. To seek normality in the light and the fresh air. Everything looks better in the cold light of day, doesn't it?

A circuitous route home took him past the local garage on the far side of town. Thought he might hoover out the back seat while he was passing. Nothing to arouse suspicion there – bloody dog hair gets everywhere, doesn't it, Ian? And if you clean up after yourself in full view, why should anyone think you have anything to hide? He arrived home late, but not unusually so. Nothing that would spur comments from neighbours. Always been a likeable chap, has our Ian. Always keen to help out at the local fete, to be pelted with sponges on a warm June afternoon in aid of school fundraising. Although not a father himself, he's a pillar of the community. Salt of the earth. Who'd ever think he'd be salt in the wound?

But I can't get away. I have to sit there and think about what I've done. How I've taken this little girl, ripped her away from the family who love her. How I've left her alone in the dark, with the blunt ammonia stink of urine and not even a local man's dog to keep her company. How I've done this for Him. For me. How I've done this for me.

Her head lolls. It's been twenty-four hours since her last meal and she sleeps to protect herself from what she sees when she wakes.

What happens if I let her go? If Ian and I peel industrial tape from seven-year-old skin and turn her out from the boarded-up door? If we leave her to stumble over rutted mud tracks and fall into the road to flag down whatever passing car first stops? If we leave her to live? If we leave me to die?

Outside Shipley's, Ian is in the midst of the throng. Cameras point in every direction, their reporters rehashing the facts of the matter for a nation hanging on the hook of twenty-four-hour news and its flashing graphics. Not a single person bats an eyelid at dark-rimmed eyes and a slumped shoulder as he makes his way through the crowd. Not much sleep was had last night in this little town, and another yawning, staring local rubbing the grit from his eyes does nothing to raise the alarm.

He joins a search party – mainly local men who have appointed themselves saviours. All focused on a task, all thinking, hoping that they're the one. The one that will pull her out from behind a bush. Cold and scared and alive. No one wants to think of the alternative. Cold. No longer scared. No longer alive.

Down into the valley they go, a solemn column of men following the path of the river that churns through this area. A beauty spot at any other time, it now rings with one name: Ellie, Ellie, Ellie, Ellie. The water bubbles and boils with black-clad divers dredging the bottom, returning to the surface empty-handed again and again. Nothing down there so far. Nothing to see here.

As night encroaches on in this changed town, the civilian search parties make their way home. The police have thanked everyone for their efforts but as the hours pass it is specialist teams cutting swathes of light through the darkness with their movie-scene equipment who must take the weight of the investigation. The town won't sleep tonight. Ian won't sleep tonight. He lies, eyes staring into the darkness, waiting for sleep to come, the usual voices in his head replaced with just one. Just Ellie.

Five a.m. and he's up and about. Breakfast for Bella, who has adopted a permanent look of reproach, not helped by an early wake-up call from a warm bed. What time can he leave without arousing suspicion? What was it the police said yesterday? Everyone should continue with their routine? Seven – that seems like an acceptable time. An acceptable time to be heading out of town for a job.

To be a normal man, heading out for a normal day's work.

The two hours yawn and stretch as he waits. Sitting on the brown leather sofa in a sparse living room. Foot nervously tapping on a patterned carpet, thumbnail chewed to the quick. Television switched to the news – the street right outside his front door brought inside for the world's front rooms to see. What if she's found? What if, while he's sitting here, wasting time, she's found?

He moves through to the kitchen, puts together a packed lunch. He's got to eat while he's working, right? If they ask who it's for? And more than anything, he's got to fill these minutes, these hours while he waits. Has to do something to drown out the little voice echoing through his head 'Mummy, Mummy, Mummy . . .'

As he leaves the house, Dave from number 35's head pops up above the roof of his car.

'Morning, Ian! Early start, eh?'

'Yeah, um, got a job up Bakewell way. Thought I'd try and get an early start. Make the most of the afternoon, you know . . .' He swings open the car door, trying to cut conversation short before it can turn to the inevitable. 'C'mon, Bella. In you get, girl.'

'That Ellie going missing's a bit weird, innit? Just "poof", disappearing into thin air. Tell you what, Ian, some sicko's probably got her. You never know where they are, do you? Probably one been living here for years and they're never gonna tell us about it, are they? 'S only our kids at risk. This bloody country. Bring back hanging, I reckon. Eh, Ian? Ha, bring back hanging?'

'Yeah . . . Hanging . . . Bloody paedos. Hanging round schools. Our kids. Hanging.'

Stop rambling, Ian. Just shut up. Get in the car and go.

'Maybe we should talk to the police. Ask if there's

anyone we should be looking out for. They must know who has a record.'

'Good idea, Ian. We can always rely on you for an idea, can't we? You not helping with the search today, then?'

'Not this morning. Get this job out the way and hopefully get back in time to help this afternoon. Hope they find her before then, though. Poor little thing. Must be terrified. Anyway, better crack on. See you later, Dave.'

'Aye – see you later.'

And Dave stands back, watches as the car backs out of the drive and makes its way off the estate, swinging left on to the Bakewell Road. Gets in his car and heads off to the office, oblivious to the U-turn Ian's making further up the road, car accelerating in exactly the wrong direction.

And on the other side of town, in a static caravan stuffed with police officers, Sergeant Neil Edwards spots this U-turn on the cameras watching the roads out of town.

'Sir? Sir? I think you'd better have a look at this . . .'

19

IT'S A SUNDAY. ACID-GREEN SPRING LEAVES FLUTTER
against a brilliant blue sky and through the open sash
windows Tom can hear the sound of picnicking parties
heading for the Heath on the first warm day of the
year. A knock at the door. Earlier than usual. Muffled
voices. Whispering.

Tom stands in the kitchen. Eyes the locked door
warily as if the hinges are going to burst of their own
accord and open him up to the outside world. He sinks
against the cabinets as they bang a couple more times.
Alex again. And Janey. Back for another try. The
banging. The shouting of his name. The whispered
congress between the two in the hallway. Tom presses
himself up against the back of the door. Watches them
through the peep-hole, huge heads on tiny bodies.
Alex has always hated his nose and the fish-eye lens
makes it look enormous. Tom smiles to himself. A tiny,
inward smile, but a smile nevertheless. A crack. A

chink. A breakthrough. As they turn to leave, he reaches up to the latch. Turns the key in the deadbolt. The warped bodies in the hallway stop in their tracks. Turn back to the door that has stood so solidly shut for the past month. It swings open slowly.

Tom stands in the doorway. Can't speak. His stubble's grown to a beard and his hair stands on end. Skin is grey, dull. His eyes are tired. Hooded. Alex smiles at him. 'Mate . . .' Janey doesn't hold back. Runs full at him and throws her arms around him.

'You idiot!' she sniffs. 'You bloody idiot.' She bursts into tears, wiping her nose against the front of his T-shirt. Punches lightly at his chest with a balled fist. He lifts his arms. Wraps them around her in his first proper human contact since . . . well.

'I know,' he mutters into the top of her head. 'I'm sorry. I'm just . . .' The smell of her shampoo makes his head spin. The soft skin of her upper arm against his fingers makes him want to grab at her. Dig his fingers in and never let go. He takes a deep breath. Steadies himself.

'Pint?' Alex asks. Jerks his head in the direction of the street.

Deep breath. 'OK.'

Down to the local. A typical London pub straddling the corner of a busy crossroads. Wooden picnic tables flank either side, hanging baskets bloom and burgeon overhead. They perch on the end of a bench, amber pints glinting in the sun, crisp packets spread out on the table to share. Alex and Janey chat, allowing Tom his space. It's enough that he's made it outside. He can't concentrate. Can't catch the words that trail through the air in front of him like smoke. One minute they're there, the next minute they're gone. Vanished for good and he can't remember for the life of him what they were.

He shakes his head. Doesn't even try to keep up. Closes his eyes and turns his face to the sun. Smiles at the babble of voices that wash around him. It's good to be out.

He feels a nudge in his ribs. Opens his eyes to see Alex and Janey are looking at him, eyebrows raised in a mutual question. 'Well? What do you reckon?'

'Umm . . . well . . . I . . .'

'To-om! Do you want to come or not?' Janey's looking at him expectantly. Eyebrow cocked, grin wide.

Fuck. He really needs to listen. 'Come to . . . ?'

'Nekros . . . ? They're re-forming. For one gig only. Finsbury Park in July. It's going to be epic! We got tickets and they were like gold dust and Alex spent all day on the website the other day and WE got them. And we got one for you. We can't go without you! Will you come?'

The surrounding babble of voices bubbles into a flood. Blood rushing in his ears. Passing traffic deafening. Nekros. A rock band from the seventies. They had one cheesy ballad. One cheesy ballad that was theirs. His and Kate's. The last song of countless nights at uni, swaying slowly under sweeping lights.

He shakes his head. 'I . . . can't . . . it's . . . me and Kate . . . it was . . .' It's playing in his head. The chorus looping around and around. 'Don't walk away, don't turn to say . . .' He squeezes his eyes shut. Drops his head to his knees. Breathe, Tom. Breathe.

'Oh. Shit. Mate. I'm sorry. I didn't think. Of course not.' Alex glances at Janey over the top of Tom's head. Fuck. She's frozen. Staring at Tom. Unable to move.

Mortified.

Tom stands. 'I'm going to . . .' He lets the sentence hang. He needs to be alone. Alex and Janey have no words. They can only watch as shoulders slump and shoes scuff their way home to an empty flat to slam the door shut and settle the lock back into place.

Sleepless night has followed sleepless night for month upon month. Watching the figures on the alarm clock click and flick. I visit every night now, and tonight's no exception. Curl up in the leather armchair in the corner of the bedroom to watch over him as he finally falls into a restless sleep. Legs kick off the duvet and hands bunch pillows under his head. Lips mutter her name in the dark.

Tonight it's worse. As he lies in the dark with the lyrics to their song playing on repeat in his head, worming their way into his brain however tightly screwed his eyelids, however close he holds his palms over his ears. It becomes too much to bear. I can't watch this again, for another night to be followed by another and another, unchanging. This never-ending, all-consuming pain and fear and desolation.

So I creep in. I can't help myself. Climb onto the bed, onto her side. Slipping under the heavy duvet to rest my head on her pillows. I lie on my side straight in the bed, not touching him. He's lying flat on his back staring at the ceiling. Profile outlined by the green highlight of the alarm clock. Slowly, gently, I reach out a hand to rest it lightly on his chest. Feel the rough texture of chest hair under my fingertips. He doesn't flinch. Doesn't know I'm there. I shift myself over on the mattress, until the length of my body fits against his. Rest my head against his shoulder. And as we lie there, watching the green digits that light the room, 01:43, 02:17, his lids droop, breath slows. And together we sleep.

I wake to birdsong and dappled light. The room is bathed in the soft green light of new leaves. Tom is wrapped around me, stretched diagonally across the bed. His leg is thrown over my hips, his arm lies over my chest, curling around my cheek to where his fingers knot in my hair. For the first time in weeks he's not been awake to see the sunrise, and as I slip out of the bed, allowing him to curl into the warmth I leave behind, still he sleeps. I want to stay here, with him, together alone. But I have work to do. Abhorrent, hateful work. But work that will bring me here to him for good.

20

I KNOW THAT IN TAKING THIS ONE LIFE, I AM automatically signing a warrant on another. I know that in three months I'll be sitting on a metal-framed bunk, knees drawn up against my chest while Ian swings by the neck, legs kicking in mid-air to search out a chair knocked sideways, eyes bulging, his face turning purple.

Sitting on that narrow bunk when the first warder finds him and the alarm is raised and prison officers flood into the tiny cell to cut him down and lay him flat and push futilely against a stiffening ribcage.

I know that he never wanted to be here. That he never wanted to have those thoughts that have lingered for years. Never wanted to be sitting in a darkened room in the middle of nowhere with the shallow, shuddering breaths of a seven-year-old for company. He fought those thoughts. Fought them every day, year after year. Until I came along.

But now, what option is there but to get rid of her? If he lets her go and she blabs they'll lock him up for sure. And he's heard what they do to men like him in prison. To the nonces. The paedos. The kiddie-fiddlers. The lowest of the low. But he can't keep her for ever – the police aren't going to give up looking. One of these days there'll be a police dog at the door whining and whimpering like a bitch. Scrabbling and scraping at the door. Growling between gritted teeth. Biting at his heels while he's led away, head hanging, arms cuffed behind his back. The shame. The out-and-out shame of it.

If he gets rid of her somehow, though, if she becomes the case that never gets solved. If he shuts her up once and for all. Buries her in the woods. Shallow enough to manage by himself, deep enough to hide her for ever. If he does that, if he gets away with it, then he can live his life and no one will be any the wiser.

Enough of this dilly-dallying, Ian, this shilly-shallying as the days pass and the clock ticks. Time is running out for both me and Ellie. The two-week limit He gave me is fast approaching – it took a week to psych myself up to find my perfect stooge, to summon up the courage to take her. And four days in this hole leaves us with only three days to finish the job.

As the sun sets on another day of searching, Ian sneaks back from town to the watermill. Pockets of his huge parka stuffed with what he could find in the cupboards. A packet of biscuits. Lump of cheese. Two apples. Bella sits next to him on the front seat, studiously ignoring him and staring out of the window at the passing countryside.

I'm waiting with Ellie while he arrives. Waiting in the damp, in the dark and the dank. Moss-slimed walls drip, drip, drip in the half-light as the wind whistles and whispers to us through cracks in the lichen-smeared windows. At the sound of the car pulling up outside, at the sight of searching headlamps sweeping across the sodden walls, she stiffens, shrinks back against the upright of the chair.

Screws her eyes closed. If she pretends to be asleep, maybe he'll leave her alone this time. He cried yesterday and the day before. Why would he keep doing something if it makes him cry? He apologises to her again and again and again. But why would he keep doing something if it makes him so sorry?

The thing is, though, in this slimy-smudged, darkened gloom, he doesn't touch her. Not in that way. He doesn't do those things he's planned, that have so haunted his daydreams and nightmares. And he hasn't. Not yet, not since he first tied her to that chair. And he won't. Because every day, as he unlocks the door, the doubts kick and spit at the pit of his stomach. As Bella bustles past him to hurry along and lick tears from a smeared cheek, his mouth fills with saliva and he feels the retches rising. As he locks the door and leans back against it the words he has practised in his head, so jolly and forced, leave him. Trail away – a breathed, unspoken wisp of air. His limbs go heavy, paralysed by fear, by guilt, by the memory of an uncle's exploring fingers burrowing under a lumpy duvet. His nostrils fill with the sharp scent of urine and squalor, the muddied stench of caked faeces. They overwhelm him, these sights, these sounds, these smells.

He slumps against the strutted wooden door. A wail, a moan. The phantom feel of fingers from thirty years ago pressing at soft skin and stroking at silken hair makes him wonder for the umpteenth time what he has done.

So while he wants to do something – to touch her, to love her, to make her his own – mind trumps muscle and for the time being at least she is safe from his darkest thoughts.

Instead, he embraces her. Places a chair next to hers and tips wooden legs on their points to lean her body against his. Wraps lumbering great arms around fragile shoulders in a misplaced attempt to soothe, to comfort. But she won't yield, she can't. Her body is held in catatonic rigidity, limbs stiff, eyes glazed and unseeing. He tries to stroke away the fear. Tangles thick fingers in matted clumped hair. And he cries. And he whispers. That he's sorry, he's sorry, he's sorry. Forgive him, forgive him, forgive him. He lulls himself, rocking and murmuring and gazing into the past.

He revolts me.

I have to end this. For her sake. This cycle of fear in this damp-walled prison. There's only one way I can stop it happening. And that's to end it all. To take his hand and guide it over her face. Pinching closed the small nostrils and covering her mouth with a meaty palm.

After an hour of this sobbing, this rocking, this snot-smeared apologising, a switch flicks and he comes to his senses. He looks around him into the gloom. As if he doesn't know why he's here, doesn't know who she is, doesn't know what he's doing. His eyes are confused, stubby fingers rake through grubby hair and he backs away, stumbling over loose scree on the mill floor. Stumbles and fumbles his way to a corner where his body slumps against the dripping moss walls and the apologies resume. Sobbing and apologising through spit and snot. Apologising again and again and again. Ellie is motionless but for shaky breaths that rock her ribcage. The chair stands upright once again, her head a snowdrop nodding on its fragile stem. A half-eaten apple lies discarded on the floor next to her and her face is turned away from the figure in the corner.

Vacant eyes stare in sleepless exhaustion as her young mind battles to protect her from the horror with which she is surrounded. She's cut herself off. Taken herself to another world where she can see the trees and play with her brothers and curl into her mother's lap for a bedtime story. Her lips are moving in almost silent song and if I strain I can hear the faint melody of nursery rhymes from a happier time.

I make my way over to Ian through the darkness and light cast by the camping light hung from the exposed beams. He's curled into a ball and shaking. Whispering to himself over and over again, 'No. No. No. No. No. No. No. No.'

He sickens me, this curled body in this squalid cell. For that's what it is, this mill on the stream in this valley no one visits. A cell. The damp, the dark and the dank. The moss-slimed walls that drip, drip, drip in the half-light and the wind that whistles and whispers to us through those cracks in the lichen-smeared windows. It is a prison. Like mine, all those years ago. I know that other world, the one she has retreated to in her mind. Far away from this dirty little room. I know that world and she can't hide there for ever.

Come on, Ian. It's time.

I haul him to his feet, draping his arm around my shoulder to support a weight buckling on weakened knees. Lead him across the room to where she sits. Head still turned away. She can sense him moving towards her in the dim light. Can smell his unwashed skin. Hear his breath catching. Her lips start to move more quickly, the nursery rhymes blurt out a little louder, a little quicker, unnaturally quick even for their light-hearted content.

Bella runs forward to nip him on the ankle and we

kick her in tandem. A swift boot in the ribs to send her whining into a corner to watch helpless.

We reach the chair and lean forward to stroke her hair, hanging limp and greasy over a dirt-smeared face. Her body is rigid with fear. He's never come back before, never come back for more. He's always left. After the crying and the saying sorry again and again and again. He's always left her alone.

'I'm sorry, Ellie. I didn't mean to do it.'

Tears sprout once more from her eyes. Huge drops that bloom on pale cheeks and drift south. Shoulders shudder and lips move in their silent song. She pulls her body as far away from him as possible against the shackles holding wrist and ankle.

'I don't know what came over me. I don't know why I did it. But, I can't let you go now, can I? If you go, and you tell your mum and dad, then they'll come and get me and lock me away for ever. And I can't do that, Ellie. Do you know what they'd do to me in there? To people like me? You wouldn't want that, would you? Ellie? You wouldn't want them to hurt me?'

He continues his mumbling, his voice shaking, while fingers are fumbling at knots and tape. 'So it's better if I just hide you away. Let you go to sleep for ever and ever. Hide you away where no one can find you. And then me and Bella can go back to the way we were. You wouldn't want me to leave Bella all alone, would you? Ellie? Would you?'

She's gasping. Sucking in short, nervous breaths. Tiny body quivering with fear. She's heard about dead before. Heard about when people go to sleep for ever in heaven and you never see them again. Is that what he wants to do? Make her dead?

Her eyes dart to the corner where Bella cowers. Bella who tried to save her in the car and who's turned on her master from the very second he first shouted at Ellie.

'I'm sorry, Ellie.' Lips pressed against the top of her head as he whispers into pale blonde hair.

I reach for his wrist. Thread my fingers through his. Bring his hand up to Ellie's face to pinch closed those tiny nostrils and cover her mouth with that meaty palm.

She struggles against him. Arching her back and trying to bite his palm with her small teeth. And though she draws blood, though the pain slices through his hand, I hold him firmly in place, crushing him against her face. Muffled screams come from under the hand until her body starts to sag. As her eyes close, once, twice, three times, she sees me, clear in the room.

'Mummy!' A scream. In these final seconds she breaks free of her corporeal body, leaving Ian to finish the job. Runs full pelt into my arms. I can't tell her. I can't explain to a seven-year-old that I'm not her mummy. That I just look like her mummy and she'll never again see the real woman.

But I look down at her, at her soft hair and rounded cheeks, at the blonde hair that now hangs shiny and straight and smells faintly of apples. I look down at her and I know that I can't do this. That this is wrong. That I'm taking the wrong person, that I don't care about the consequences, about my future, about my life. This is the life I can't take. This is the line that I must draw. She can't die. Not here, not like this. She can't.

Where Ian crouches on the other side of the room there is a flicker of movement in a slim leg and I know I haven't got her yet. I still have time. To leave her now, to leave her to life.

A wooden strut next to me, left to one side by the door from his first entry into this space. A wooden strut with a rusted nail protruding from one end. One swing is all it takes. One upward swing to embed sharp metal into the soft, vulnerable spot at the base of his skull. He doesn't see me coming. He doesn't hear me coming. Just a groan as his back arches and his body slumps to cover hers.

To accompany his muted slump, a screech fills the air. The howl of a banshee, a fishwife, a harridan. 'You bleedin' idiot!' My foot kicks at his lumpen body and he moans. His body flops to the side to look up at me and he groans. Eyes squint and peer through the gloaming, the gloom. He can see me now, hunched shoulders outlined in the dim light.

'Mother . . .'

My hands have shrunk, gloved in wrinkled skin. Stubby nails blackened with grime. That screech, that scream, it was mine. For Ian has chosen his mother, the woman whose approval he sought for so many years, to be the one he sees, that last woman before he fades and passes. But she would not have chosen to see him again. Not for the world.

'You dirty little bastard!' we shout, her and I. A kick to his spine. He rolls from where he has covered Ellie, turns his back to her to curl into a ball, arms wrapped round his head to protect himself as blows rain from above. 'You nasty little man.' The wooden strut swings once again to swipe blows against his side, his thighs, his hands, his rear.

To his side, Bella snuffles over a small figure lying bent and broken, but alive on the floor. Licks salty tears from smeared cheeks, from eyes that blink at a soft tongue. Small barks, gruff little ruffs. She runs to the door, scrapes and whines. Runs back to Ellie. Doesn't understand why she doesn't move, doesn't follow her. But Ellie can't. Her limbs are heavy, her head filled with wool. So Bella runs from door, to girl, to door, to girl. Until finally she settles where she's needed most.

Nudges her nose under curled fingers to wait for help to come, however long that may be. Other than a snarled growl in the direction of Mrs Morris and me when that first strut was swung, she has paid no attention to Ian. Her loyalty no longer lies there.

Where Ian lies, a tirade of abuse, of insults, of derision cascades over him. High-pitched and ranting, his mother has never held him in any esteem, has never really cared. His father left before he was born, and she hated Ian for that. Blamed him for Colin walking out the door, when in reality it was that self-same tirade of abuse, of insults and derision that drove a mild-mannered man on his way. It was her brother whose fingers would creep under that thin duvet all those years ago, and her brother who she'd call downstairs when dinner was ready. If she knew what was happening she never admitted it, never tried to intervene. But he loved her all the same, did Ian. Desperate for her acknowledgement and approval. And all she could do, all she would do, is criticise.

And so he ends his life where it began. A good-for-nothing, lazy, hateful waste of space. In her words. These words that pour from my mouth.

I hate these deaths, these final moments harbouring hate. For however hateful that person is, the idea that they are so despised, so desperate for love from the one person who shuns them, those final moments are all they have left.

And so these deaths, these ones filled with hate, are the quickest. Who wants to stay around to be abused, to be hit upon and hated? So as I lay my hand on a shaking shoulder, and as these words flow relentlessly from my mouth, Ian Patrick Morris plummets to black.

*

Dusk in that prison quickly spirals into the blackest of nights, and we lie, we four, side by side as we wait to be found. For Ellie, limbs are leaden and eyes tired, her head aches and an egg-shaped lump on her brow gently throbs. Though her eyes flicker and her foot occasionally twitches, she remains motionless, sleeping the sleep of the drugged, the spent, the weakened and drained. When her eyes briefly open, she has no sense of her surroundings, no memory of where she is or how she came to be there. So heavy are those lids that the effort to look around her is too great and she quickly falls back into the deepest slumber. She doesn't remember him coming at her, can't see the shape of his body lying so close, and so she lies, she sleeps, cocooned and protected by an amnesiac embrace.

To one side lies Bella. Noses her snout into Ellie's palm. She is alert to every twitch, every sigh, every flicker of lids, causing her eyebrows to raise, a low whine to escape, a tongue to gently dab at a dirty cheek. When Ellie sleeps, Bella's chin rests on her paws and she watches. Doesn't sleep for a second.

To the other side, I stretch. Lying on my side to shelter Ellie and form a barrier to her body and Ian's, lying inert behind me. Head lolling in a viscous pool of its own blood. There is nothing there, nothing left. No soul clinging desperately to life. But I separate them, for fear that she'll wake in this hell hole, turn to the side and find her face inches from thick fingers reaching towards her to stroke once more.

A late dawn in this dim little prison. While the rest of the world are waking to a bright blue sky, to a crisp morning and the sound of birdsong, colours are muted in our cell, where windows are layered in moss and shaded by the trees outside. But as fingers of light creep through smeared windows to caress dormant faces, so they are sliced through by pulses of flashing blue. Where birdsong and the scratch of branch against glass seep to remain unheard, the screech of sirens and the rumble of engines pierce sleeping ears and stir slumbering bodies.

Banging at the door.

'Ian! Ian Morris! Are you in there?'

No reply, for the man they are looking for will never be woken again by lights, by sirens, by the rumble of engines and the shouts of men. No reply except for a bark from Bella. A whine. She runs to the door, scratches against it. Barks once, twice. Returns to Ellie, her charge, who lies still motionless on the dirt-caked floor.

A face appears at a cracked window. A gloved hand taps at the cracked pane, breaks off shards to clear the view.

'Sir! They're here, sir. Two bodies, sir, neither moving.'

A crash, a thud at a secured door. Bella's barking is insistent now. She growls, runs towards the door before another crash sends her spiralling back to Ellie, where she remains, barking at the door, protecting her friend.

Two more crashes, two more contacts between battering ram and barrier and one of the door panels falls, casting a broad shaft of light into the room. A head appears in the gap 'Sir. It looks like we've found them.'

Detective Superintendent Paul Harper steps through the hole made in the door. Hands gloved in sterile white. A female police officer by his side. She crouches beside Ellie, reaches warm fingers to find a pulse. Bella spins on the spot, barks incessantly, but makes no move to bite. They're here to help, these strange people who have arrived to bring light and hope.

'She's alive, sir. There's a pulse.'

Bodies cloaked in white move into the area. Ellie is bundled up tight, an oxygen mask gently placed over her face. Bella is carried into the back of a police Land Rover, where she runs from side to side, desperate to catch a glimpse of her friend, to check she's OK as a tiny body is stretchered into an ambulance.

They turn to Ian, the DS and his second. Reach to feel for a pulse, but finding none step back and stand upright to look down at this body, broken and bloodied.

'Looks like he had a nasty fall, sir, that's what I'd say. Must've tripped over in the dark. Knocked himself out. Bastard.'

His body is lifted on to a stretcher. Zipped into a black bag. Carted off to who knows where, and who knows who cares.

Slipping out past the men clad in white, I step out into a fresh, crisp, blue-skied day. A day of new beginnings, of spring. It's time for me to leave. I'm no longer needed here. The game is over, my time is up. While one person lies dead, it's not the person for whom I was sent, and that, ultimately, is my failure. I see Him leaning against the trunk of a young silver birch, bathed in the acid-green light of new leaves. See Him shake His head, scuff His toe against mossy ground. Turn His back on me and walk silently into the woods.

And so I slip away, in the opposite direction. To another death and my morbid life. Slip away to start again, to a chance missed and a love lost. For Tom can no longer be mine.

21

A DARKENED ROOM, LIT BY THE GREEN DIGITS ON a digital clock that flash minute by minute in the dimness, and a lamp on the landing that keeps the real darkness at bay. I know I can't have him, this slumbering body who lies next to me, but I can't keep away. It is here, in Tom's bedroom, where I find my refuge, where I find my relief. And it is here, in Tom's bedroom, where I find myself trying to block out the horrors of the week gone by, to hunker down against the screams of a fishwife that ring in my ears, and the image of thin, pale legs flailing against the bulk of a middle-aged man.

He draws me in, tucks me close. Wraps one arm around my waist, throws one leg over my thighs. He smiles a sleepy smile, sighs a contented sigh. Wriggles deeper into bed to nestle his head into the crook of my neck. And as I lie awake, fixated on the green digits that flip and blink, he sleeps.

As those digits flip from 02:28 to 02:29, I feel that lurch. The pull that tells me I am heading on to my next death, wherever that may be, whomever I may find and whomever I may become. Because what I must remember, in this sanctuary, this haven, is that I have failed. That I have no place here. And for me, death must go on.

I close my eyes, waiting for the lurch, the swirl to subside. Feel the weight of Tom's leg lift, feel his arm stretch and uncurl away from me. Hear the light tap as soft shoes make contact with lino, and open my eyes to find myself in one of the hospital corridors it has been my habit to stalk. Dark but for the working lights, I can hear the trill of the heart monitor, see bulging curtains surrounding a bed to betray the flurry of nurses working within, and I know that I have found my place.

Behind those curtains, Francis Wellesley lies prostate and helpless in the midst of nurses who bustle about, around, above and to the side. Rearranging the oxygen mask, checking the level in the catheter bag that hangs heavy from the bed frame. His blood pressure is low, the oxygen in his system dropping despite the mask clamped over nose and lips.

I slip through a gap in the curtains to take my place. Brush past the backs of nurses crouching over a motionless body to settle into the high-backed chair to the side of the bed. To the side of my husband of fifty-seven years, whom I left myself six long months before. For in this bay, next to this bed, I am Barbara Wellesley. Loving wife and mother of three. Grand-mother of seven. A woman Frank never expected to see again, despite the longing and loneliness, and his deepest desires to have her by his side once more. As I sit, I reach up to pat short permed hair into place, softly set and curled for the occasion. For this occasion. For one final goodbye.

My hand drops to the bed to cover his, to offer a reassuring squeeze. His eyes open at the unexpected gentle touch, but there is no surprise in them at the arrival of Barbara in the wee small hours. He has been expecting me. Not knowing of course what form I would take, but knowing with great certainty that death is but a matter of moments away.

'They do a marvellous job,' he mumbles in his deep, West Country burr, nodding at the whirlwind of activity around him. 'I thought that, you know. When you were here. But then I was so worried about you, and I felt so sick at the thought of you going that I couldn't tell them. And now, well, it's too late now, isn't it? For me to say thank you. Because I'm off now, I think. I hope they know. I hope somebody does tell them.'

I smile. A thin effort. Watery. The most I can muster in an effort to reassure. Pat his hand with its raised veins and broken capillaries.

'I'm sure they do, dear.' Even I can hear how dismissive my tone.

'You're quiet,' he says. 'Everything all right?'

I smile again, that same thin, sad smile. But inside I am lost. For while I have the appearance of Barbara, of a wife well loved for more than half a century, I'm not her. I can't tap the memories that ordinarily come so readily to hand. I know we have children and grand-children, but I can't capture the intimacies, the memories, the secret moments that would ease this final passage. While I try to remember, to embody her, the memories I see behind my mind's eye are all my own. Of Hywel and Rose, Rob, Ellie and Ian. Of long nights in dark rooms with Tom.

And so I answer with a non-committal, 'Hmm.' Squeeze his soft hand once more and dredge through the memories I have of visiting Barbara in this same hospital barely six months earlier. When I arrived as her daughter. Dredge through what memories I can amass to dedicate myself to the man lying beside me at this very moment.

He struggles to sit upright, raising himself on arthritic elbows from which all pain seeped at my arrival. 'I don't understand,' he says. 'You're you, but you're not . . . you. Remember when we went to Tenerife in seventy-nine? With the kids? And you had some dodgy fish and couldn't get out of bed? You wouldn't even stop talking then and you couldn't even move. What's wrong, love?'

I laugh at him, with him, a small laugh held in my nose. A forced laugh because this, this whole situation is the wrong way round. He is not here to support me, to worry for my welfare. And so I laugh to disguise my confusion, to maintain a guise that I am here for him, and that I am who I purport to be. Because in truth, I don't remember that holiday in Tenerife. I don't remember food poisoning and the inevitable fevers, being bed-bound in the August heat. I don't remember because for the first time since taking on this role, I am not who I say I am, and my own personal reality is encroaching too closely. Where I would ordinarily leave my individual self on the far side of that bulging curtain, I am here, myself, by Francis's bed in the veiled disguise of a beloved wife. I am here, myself, an unwelcome hanger-on.

'I'm fine, dear! Just fine. I just don't like to see you like this, you see.' My voice pitched high, unnaturally cheerful.

As I speak, his face contorts. A grimace. A gasp. An iron claw grips his chest, sending shooting pains through the very heart of him. He clutches at my hand.

'Barb . . .' His voice hoarse, strained. The voice of the physical man lying in that bed, not the soul I am here to soothe. My presence is doing nothing to calm, nothing to console. Nothing to alleviate the pain that tugs on every nerve of his being.

'Oh, Frank. Just wait, my love. It'll all be over soon. The pain will pass and you'll be at peace. I promise.' But the words are hollow, meaningless, and I myself am helpless. They are simply words. Not personal to him, not meaningful to them. Simple words that could be uttered by anyone.

His clutch on my hand tightens, knuckles whiten. Another spasm of pain passes through like a crashing wave. Blood pressure drops still further, oxygen can't reach where it is so desperately needed. His body lies shrouded in wires, all leading to a monitor that shrieks its high-pitched scream in an unbroken screech.

'Frank, I'm . . .' I try to find the words but they are lost to me.

My presence here is unsettling – to him and to me. And as pain takes hold, as the final breaths are eked out of a dying body, the cubicle is plunged into darkness. Not for Francis a gentle fade to black, an easy passing from this world. A switch has flicked, his soul has leapt from his body, but he is no longer in pain. It is the sole solace I can take, for I have had little part to play in easing his end.

At the foot of the bed, a young doctor stands slump-shouldered and defeated.

'We've lost him,' he says to the clutch of nurses who still surround his bed, peeling the sticky pads that monitored his vitals from delicate skin that could rip at any moment. 'Francis Wellesley. Time of death two forty-seven a.m.'

Hours pass, days pass, weeks pass, lives pass. Deaths surround me, support me, distract me, subsume me.

They are now, more so than ever before, a job. A way of life, a daily grind that must be endured. After Francis, each death fills me with worry, a fear that I will leave other souls in torment, other bodies in pain. And so I force myself to concentrate, to expel all thoughts of those that have gone before and those I know no longer have the hope of ahead. Because, ultimately, I have failed. Failed in this mission to win life. Failed in my mission to leave death far behind. In taking the wrong life, back there in that miserable little cell, I have put any chance of having my own life out of my reach. And in my failure to kill Ellie and my determination to serve those passing on from this life, I know that I must stay away from Him. Stay away from that mocking laugh, from the inevitable derision in His voice when He jeers at me, parades my shortcomings before me and forces me to relive every minute of that painful night. The shake of His head in a spring glade was enough – I have disappointed Him, His challenge has come to naught, and I don't need Him to tell me that.

But what burns at my insides, the thing that gnaws at my core, the small voice that whispers to me on the wind while I wallow in my own self-pity, my own sense of loss, is the overwhelming knowledge that I was right. The choice I made, the path I took, while sealing my own fate, was the right one. It wasn't Ellie's time. She wasn't the one to die. I know that. But as we have learned before, knowing doesn't make it any easier.

And so, Death must go on, and I throw myself fully into my old life. Focus on the lives around me as they fade to black in their homes, their hospital beds, their heavens and their hells. Offer what comfort I can when the pain threatens to overwhelm and the end is so evidently at hand. When I think of Tom I duck my head, close my eyes, block my ears. Hum a tune to drive the sound of his voice out from where it has burrowed into the depths of my being. I've lost my chance, and in doing so, I have lost him. So on I go, from life to life and death to death, avoiding Tom and avoiding Him. On I dance, a twirling dance from one woman to another and on to another. Although I can feel that something has changed in this whirl, this swirl. A new weight that I never carried before, preventing me from passing as easily from one to the next, from leaving each story cleanly at the end of their final chapters. A weight that comes with having to concentrate on each and every one, where previously I had slipped into each new skin with the ease of donning a light jacket on a warm summer's eve. But now these deaths hang on my time. I carry them from one persona to the next, the women I embody dragging in a chain behind me in their memory and their spirit. Their stories flow behind me in gossamer spider webs, anchoring me stickily to the ones who have passed before. And while those threads are fine, are light, and dance on the wind, they weigh on me these women, they slow me. They exhaust me.

22

A STRETCH OF MOTORWAY ON AN EARLY FRIDAY evening on a late May bank holiday in the Cornish sun. Visors pulled low to block a sinking western sun, drivers' brows aching from the constant squint against the rays that spread across their vision.

A foot hits the brake too quickly, a car slows too sharply. Red brake lights remain unseen from the cab of a lorry sitting high overhead, diffuse in the hazy late light. Momentum connects truck cab with car bumper, carrying them forward for one hundred yards, for two hundred, three. The articulated load behind, carried forward by its own inertia, swings into the lane alongside, sweeping a car stacked high with holiday hopes over the hard shoulder and into the earthworks. In the outside lane, a Mercedes zips past the unfolding carnage, the driver casting a glance in the rear-view mirror, 'God, I'm glad I'm not going to get caught up in *that*', before rearranging Ray-Bans and refocusing on the sunlit path ahead.

Back at the scene, burning rubber worries at nose hairs, and the heavy stench of petrol douses the sweet smell of roadside wildflowers as cars and lorries and vans settle to a standstill.

The first car, the braker, faces in the wrong direction, confronting the lorry's cab in a matadorial stand-off, its front section crumpled and crushed. The single, unbroken blare of the horn drowns out roadside birdsong, the head of Pete Maxwell pressing down on his steering column pillow, his neck bent sharply to tuck chin to chest. The driver of the lorry has hopped down from his cab. Rushes to the car in front of him, fails to open the door and fumbles in his back pocket for his phone. To press three numbers and wait for the question. 'Which service do you require?' All of them. Now. Here. Now.

Another car, the one swept forth by an articulated load before coming to a halt mid-clamber up the steep slope of the grassy roadside bank. Its occupants Brenda and Howard shake their heads as if to shake some sense into them. Clasp each other's hands and check beloved faces for cuts and bruises before tugging valiantly at door handles to open doors that won't budge. Howard winds down his window to pull himself free before trotting down the bank and back up on the far side of the car to help Brenda work her way clear. Not today for Brenda and Howard. Not here. Not today.

Behind the jack-knifed load, a scene of confusion, of impending carnage. Two vehicles have come to a sudden stop with their noses jammed under the trailer chassis, their horns sounding a two-pitched mournful wail. To their rear a small van is wedged between their back ends. Alarm sounding, its driver sits motionless in his seat, hand over his mouth, surveying the scene ahead in disbelief. Not today for this local delivery driver on his way to his last drop of the day, not today.

Behind him, more vehicles lie strewn across the carriageway facing north, south, east and west. People step out of their cars, mobile phones lifted to every ear to make calls to the emergency services, to husbands, wives, sisters and brothers. To children, waiting for bedtime stories and friends waiting for the first glug of chilled rosé into a tulip-bottomed glass. These lucky few turn their faces to the sun and wait as the distant sirens get louder, get closer, get here.

There are four. Here. For me. Four who sit crunched, broken and bloodied behind shattered glass and stricken metal. Pete Maxwell, his foot eternally pressed against the brake pedal that triggered this sequence of events, his neck snapped, a drop of blood snaking from his ear, another slipping from slack lips. Eyes open in an unseeing stare. I crawl in through the passenger door to stem the flow of blood. Wipe it from his lips and cup his cheek in my hand. At my arrival his body unfurls. His back straightens, stretches to lean back against the seat. 'Mum . . .' he breathes. 'What are you doing here? Why aren't you at work?'

I take his hand, curl it and cosset it in one of my own. Keep my other hand cupped around a cheek caked in drying blood.

'Because you needed me, my precious boy. Because you wanted me. Here. And now. So I came. Come on. Give your mamma a cuddle.'

He shifts in his seat, leans his head into my shoulder. Breathes a shuddering breath.

'But how did you know?'

'It's my job to know, my darling. It's my job to know when you need me. When you need your mum. It doesn't matter how old you are, how independently you live your life, how far away you are from me. I knew when you needed me. And I came.'

He sinks down in his seat, leans back to look at me straight. The pain and shock of the first impact abates as life seeps slowly from his being, allowing limbs to soften and relax. Strong arms wrench open the driver's door, shaking this cocoon in which we sit. Straighten a broken figure and release the pressure on the horn that has sounded relentlessly from the final resting place of the impact, at the final resting place of Pete. While those arms work, while they feel for a pulse and fasten strapping around an angled neck, he gazes at me. Tears brim in red-rimmed eyes before billowing forth to swim unchecked down blood-stained cheeks. We talk while they work. Talk about the kids, about his wife, the love of his life. About childhoods in the sun and the week ahead. About what will happen now. To them. To the ones he'll leave behind. He never once asks me about what will happen to him.

As his body is lifted from the wreckage, and an oxygen mask clamped over his face, he rallies. Neck held in place by foam blocks, face swathed in plastic and tubing, he rallies. Allowing me to move on. He will fight, will Pete. I'm not needed here – at least, not yet.

Wedged beneath the metal frame of the lorry, fifty yards from where Pete rests on his stretcher, Ollie and Jenny Freeman lean forward in their seats, facing each other in a final loving gaze. Ollie's arm thrust beneath Jenny's body in a last-minute but ultimately failed bid to save and protect. In the back seat, one-year-old Alfie cries – an exhausted sob and scream of shock, a wail of despair. Thick straps that held him in place and held him in this life hold small arms pinned to his side and try as he might, he can't strain forward enough to see his mummy's face shining with the diamond sprinkle of shattered screen.

An unknown pair of arms reaches into the back seat to unshackle him and carry him to safety. Whispered murmurings from beneath a yellow hard hat and behind a scratched visor scare rather than soothe and his solid little body twists towards the car, back arching in rage against the arms that hold him close.

When he's clear of the car I shuffle to the middle of the back seat to lean my head through the gap and speak to each front seat occupant in turn. Facing Ollie, I am his beloved Jenny, my body healthy and strong in comparison to the broken physical presence in the seat beside him. These are some of the most difficult, these co-present deaths. Not that any are easy. But these tear at my soul. He sees her lying beside him while seeing her lean over him. He smells the scent of her perfume, feels the tickle of her hair on his cheek while smelling the iron punch of drying blood and feeling the dead weight of a lifeless body pressing down on his arm. She is life and she is death. She is here and she is gone.

Facing Jenny I morph into a childhood best friend. Twenty-seven years of history bundled into this car – first kisses, first days at school, first dates, last words. Tears run down Jenny's cheeks and my own and a solemn promise is extracted to look after Alfie, to love and to cherish and to tell him every day how much he is, was and always will be loved.

But I must leave them now, alone together, while heroes work to free them from death, to keep them in life.

And so on I move to the final car, to Ben. Brought up by his gran and on his way back to a Devon cottage with roses round the door and chickens in the garden. This was his first visit home after joining the Navy and being posted to Portsmouth. His first visit, taking his final journey. Home.

He doesn't expect to see Gran here, on this hot and smoky motorway. In her crocheted cardie, with tights-clad legs in soft-soled shoes poking out from under a stiff, pleated tweed skirt. Doesn't expect to see her and can't bear to see her when I appear, tapping at the window and bustling into a compacted passenger seat. He withdraws as I settle in, tries to pull his hand away as I take it gently between mine. Tries not to breathe in the whiff of pressed powder and lavender that clouds around her. But my presence, my scent, my touch overwhelms him and he crumbles. Sagging on to a soft and solid bosom clad in wool to sob, shudder and sigh. I rock him gently, cuddle him to my chest. On the threshold of becoming a man, he is still a boy to me.

While the emergency services work – cutting, sawing, breathing life into struggling lungs, I follow them. From car to car. From Pete to Ollie. Ollie to Jenny. Jenny to Ben. Through tears and laughter, leaving them as chests are pumped and bodies surge, returning as lungs choke and a simple breath is out of reach. I follow those rescuers in a constant whirl between a mum, a lover, a friend, an anchor. Between a mum, a Jenny, a Karen, a gran.

Back in Ollie and Jenny's car, Jenny turns to look at me, perched on the back seat, and starts. Eyes wide, mouth hanging open. 'Who . . . ?' But before she can finish the question, I am gone, summoned by Ben whose heart is failing and who needs his gran. But it is not his gran who clambers into his passenger seat, and he wonders who exactly is this blonde girl pulling his head to her chest. Before he can speak I am moving on to Pete, whose heart rate has dropped and who has never before seen this old lady who smells of pressed powder and lavender, and who cups his cheek in her hand and wipes congealing blood from a split lip with a spit-wetted, soft aged thumb. His lips hang slack, his brow curled into a question mark. Where has his mother gone? Who is this old lady, and where is she going now? He watches as I disappear up the carriageway towards Ollie and Jenny, confused still further to see my morphing complete as I reach their car and watching from his prone position as his mother climbs into the back seat of a stranger's car.

Back in Ollie and Jenny's car, Ollie is still struggling to comprehend the presence of his beloved wife by his side and behind him. He turns to talk to me, to understand the situation he now finds himself in and recoils at the sight of a middle-aged woman crammed in next to Alfie's crumb-strewn car seat. He leans as far away from me as he can manage, body pressing once more against the horn, feet scrabbling in the footwell for a hold.

'Who are you?' he shouts. 'Get out of my car! Where's . . . ?' He turns to look at Jenny, so beautiful, so restful, with rainbows that dance on the shattered shards of screen in her hair. 'Jenny! Jenny! Wake up, baby. Where have you gone? You were just here!' He strokes her face. His voice drops to a whisper. Pleading. 'Jenny? Baby?'

'Darling!' I interrupt from behind. 'It's me, Ollie. I'm here. Look at me, darling – I'm here. I love you. Please, my love, please. I'm not going anywhere. Not without you.' But the voice coming from my mouth is not the voice of the woman whose words I speak. The hands in my lap are not those of the slim, manicured fingers I expect to see, instead they are age-spotted, twisted by arthritis and resting on legs clad in checked trousers. The very trousers I wore when I first arrived in Pete's car those never-ending minutes ago. Looking in the rear-view mirror, not the thick, dark hair I expect to see, but grey, curled, closely cropped.

I pull back from the divide between the seats. Reach up to feel my face, my hair. Force open the back door of the car and stagger backwards across the tarmac, watching the flurry in front of me as emergency workers continue their fight against death, against my inevitable arrival. From the driver's seat, Ollie stares out at this imposter, this stranger, who tugs at her own hair and pinches at her own cheeks.

The women I embody are dragging, being pulled by me from one death to the next – the gossamer thread binding me to the last for too long, the ties too strong. The lag lasting long enough for each person to lift their head, pull back in confusion, question the presence of this stranger in those very final, those most intimate of moments. But such is my distraction, the speed at which I work, the delusion that I am working as well as I ever have done, the arrogance that it must be they who are confused, and not I, that I haven't noticed.

I'm horrified. I can't bear that I've done this, can't believe that I've exposed these four people to an ending that asks more questions than it answers. For them, for their first meeting with me, their only meeting with me, I have brought confusion in the place of clarity, replaced a final tranquillity with tumult.

I slump down on to the hot asphalt, elbows resting on knees, head resting in hands. Eyes screwed tight against the pain I've brought about. Light fades, air cools and I lift my head to watch from a distance as four souls fade to black in the summer skies above the knot of vehicles. One by one they float, ultimately unaccompanied. They have found their own way, fading slowly, messily, without direction. The souls are bruised – pulsing through yellows, purples, blues. Before slowly, stutteringly, unguided . . . to black. They are alone and lonely, these souls.

Left by themselves, to their own devices. Confused, hurt and hurting.

The carriageway clears and traffic begins to move – slowly at first until, mere minutes after the cordon has been lifted, normality has resumed and there is nothing to denote this patch of land, nothing to suggest what has so recently passed. I lift myself to perch on the metal barrier, feet tucked up beneath me, hair blowing with every passing car. I wince at every lorry that rumbles past inches from my face, but I can't move, can't leave. Who am I and what have I become?

Dusk passes into a violet darkness and the traffic thins until minutes stretch after the passing of each searching headlamp. To the west, deep navy gives way to a slender tongue of pink that laps at the horizon.

In the night silence, the clipped scrape of footsteps on dusty tarmac gets closer until they stop dead beneath my bowed head. Facing my own feet, two black leather loafers, side by side at the end of long, slim legs in tapering charcoal grey.

'Enough, Little D. Enough.'

I say nothing.

'You've been avoiding me.'

I have.

'I've been watching you, these past few weeks. You've been avoiding me, you've been avoiding him. So what was the point, Little D? Hmm?'

No reply.

'Look at me when I'm talking to you!'

I tip my head back. Close my eyes and stretch my neck, looking up to the stars. I'm exhausted. Lower my chin to look Him in the eye.

'Why start this whole rigmarole in the first place? Eh? You've wasted my time. Taken Hywel's, what little time he had left. Ripped Rose from her family and friends. Stolen Rob from his wife and children. Given Ellie nightmares that will last a lifetime.' He's pacing, voice rising, speeding up as He works through my victims.

Then He pauses, stops in front of me. Lowers His voice to a whisper. 'One step wrong, Little D, and you run. Down tools and run. Pathetic. You obviously don't care as much as you thought.'

'Of course I care! I do! I just . . .' My voice gets smaller after the initial burst. Ashamed. 'I didn't know what to do. I saw you. In the woods that day. I saw the look on your face and the way you shook your head and . . . I knew. I'd lost everything. I'd lost your game. And if I can't have him, and I have no hope of getting him, then I can't keep watching him go through that pain. So . . . I . . .'

'You hid, Little D. You buried your head in the sand and you hid. And in doing so you went off half-cocked and started letting down the deaths you were tending to. You failed them – these four aren't the first. I've been watching you, Little D. You failed yourself. You failed . . . Tom, is it? And you failed me.'

'I know! I don't need telling! Why are you even here?' Once more, a petulant child responding to His confrontation.

'You're very quick to get chippy, you know. When this little . . . "situation" is all your fault. When you have let us all down. You are very quick to snap at me.'

'Sorry.' A mutter. A shamed stutter.

'What you don't seem to have taken into account, though,' He settles down on to the barrier beside me, legs stretched, ankles crossed, 'is that I'm actually quite enjoying this little game of yours. D'you know, I like watching you squirm and struggle. Fight with that conscience of yours . . . And I had such great plans for your final task! Such great plans . . . But, if you're not bothered, then . . .'

'I am! Bothered. Please.' Tom's face, fresh in my mind's eye. Tom's voice breaking through the white-noise hum. I need him. I want him.

'Go on, then. Go back to him. Get yourself back on track. And when I'm ready, I'll find you. And we'll see, shall we? We'll see what future we have.'

A coach thunders past, blowing grit into my eyes, my hair into my face. When the dust settles, leaving the carriageway bathed in a milky moonlit wash, He is gone.

The possibility of a second chance. Do I deserve it? Should I take it?

Of one thing I am sure – I have to see him. I have to see Tom.

23

THE LOUNGE LOOKS LIKE A BOMB'S HIT IT. IN THE corner a standard lamp rests its head awkwardly against the wall, shade cocked on its broken neck from being hurled to the ground. Hurled to the ground and then kicked when it was down. At my feet, a dark, wet stain where an overturned mug has spilt cold, milky tea to soak slowly into the pile. A bookshelf has been tipped, volumes lying open on the floor, their pages spread to flutter in the breeze. Faint strains of an opera swim through the early morning air and through the window, the first buds of spring blossom wait, poised, to bloom on naked limbs. Tom is nowhere to be seen.

Through to the kitchen. Letters lie on the lino, swept from their heap by the phone. Plates, smashed to pieces, form a pathway that crunches under every step. A cupboard door hangs limply on one hinge to reveal a motley assortment of cups cowering on the shelf. Anything that can be thrown has been. A lone red warning light flashes on a washing machine stuffed with damp clothes left to slowly mould.

And on into the small dark passageway that links the rooms of this tiny flat. The music gets louder as tenor weaves with soprano to billow softly from the bathroom door, mingling with the gentle pitter-patter and clouds of steam of a too-hot shower.

He stands before me, under the shower at the far end of the deep, white tub. Stands with his back to me. Head bowed on strong shoulders as scalding water rains down on the nape of his neck, turning it the fleshy pink of a fresh slap. On the radio, Rodolfo clasps Mimi's cold hand and in the bathroom Tom's shoulders begin to shake. Kate had loved this opera.

He'd taken her to see *La Bohème* at the Opera House years ago. In their early twenties, living the life of the grown-ups they thought they should be. Perched high up in the slips on those hard wooden benches, looking down at the audience below in their opera finery. When the lights dipped and the horns burst forth in the opening bars, she'd leaned forward as far as she could over that balustrade. As if those extra inches could somehow help her absorb the music better. And as she watched the stage, so he watched her. Couldn't look away from wide eyes fixed on the love story unfolding below. He watched as the tuberculosis took hold far below prompting tears to chase themselves down hot cheeks like raindrops on glass.

He can barely remember seeing the opera himself, so much did he focus on the girl sitting beside him.

And here, in this bathroom, as the crescendo builds, the memories of that night, of that girl, are overwhelming. He slumps against the cold white tiles before his body slips and slides down the smooth wall to curl into a tight ball. Cocking my leg over the high side of the tub I climb in. I know that he has no idea I'm there, but I also know that he can sense me. In his office, in his bed. In his head. He can sense me. And I know that as long as he is life and I am Death I can offer no tangible solace, no physical body to cling to, but I can't just stand back and watch. I won't just stand back and watch.

As I settle down, press my lips against wet hair, there's a shift in his shoulders. A slight turn to allow him to rest his head against mine. To drop his chin to tuck his forehead into the crook of my neck. He hooks his fingers around my forearms to draw my embrace tighter round him, to swaddle him like a blanket. Hot drops rain down on naked skin and his shoulders shake with finally released sobs. Sobs that rip and tear at his throat. Sobs held back for weeks.

We rock back and forth, we two. We cry together. For Kate, for Hywel, for Rose, for Rob. For what I have done and what I have become. For what I want, for what he can't have. Gradually those anguished cries that have ripped from his lungs begin to subside, settle to a groan, a gentle moan. To whispered words over the raindrops of the shower. The same word repeated over and over. 'Why? Why? Why?'

I don't know, Tom. I just don't know.

Together we rock gently, limbs entwined as I hush him, I shush him. Calm him as he clutches at me in his grief. Tom, my Tom.

24

WHEN I WALK INTO THAT LITTLE RECORDING studio, in that run-down little industrial estate off the Westway, there's a spring in my step. The sun shines brightly against breeze blocks, the sharp angles of those squat buildings throwing the door I'm looking for into deep shadow. He's waiting for me. Sitting in the corner, head bent over the neck of a guitar, fingers working the frets as He makes minute adjustments to tuning keys. The same sequence of chords, played over and again. A tweak. A twitch. A thrum. The same chords, over and again.

I knock. A tiny tap on the doorframe to let Him know I'm there. He ignores me.

I clear my throat. A soft cough. Open my mouth in greeting. His hand flies up to silence me, pick pinched between finger and thumb. 'I've waited long enough for you, Little D . . .' His voice weary, carrying a warning.

The spring in my step softens, slowly deflates in His presence. So I stand. And I wait. Stand awkwardly and wait in silence in the doorway, eyes following the slither of black leads that snake their way across the floor from mic to amp to keys to amp to guitar.

Finally, He speaks. 'So you've pulled yourself together, have you?' He settles the guitar into its stand. 'Had a good, long think to yourself about all of this?' Leans back on the bench to rest against the wall. Long, slim fingers pinch the bridge of His nose in louche, studied exasperation.

'Let's go over a couple of things shall we? Hey? I didn't force you into this, remember? This pernicious little game of yours. You came to me. *You* came to *me*.' He crosses His long legs at the knee. Bounces His foot gently. 'And how do you repay me? The going gets tough and you disappear on me. You kill the "wrong person" and you go to ground. I told you, Little D, I was watching you. While you were avoiding me. Watching you supposedly getting on with your job, but ultimately, let's be honest, failing. Failing those people while you flail around trying to carry on. People aren't getting the deaths they deserve – won't get the deaths they deserve – all because you're moping around. Beating yourself up because you "failed". Because you've had a taste of something you want and you don't think you can have it any more.'

'You were clear! You told me I had to kill those people. Those particular people. And I didn't. I did fail. And do you know what? I'd do it again in a heart-beat. I'd take that option every time. Ellie didn't deserve to die. It wasn't her time!'

He snorts. 'Didn't deserve to die . . . Who exactly does deserve to die, Little D? Did Ian deserve that? When he'd been lured by you? Ellie dangled in front of him like bait? He wouldn't have gone near her if it wasn't for you!'

'But he would've gone near someone! He had those thoughts – you put them there! It was a matter of time before he did something like that and I stopped him before he could.' I'm resolute. I was right. And I disappeared to accept the consequences alone, in my own time. 'What were you even thinking? Ellie's a child! What kind of person even thinks of doing that?'

He holds both hands to His forehead and smooths back a lock of hair that has fallen over one eye. Mouth twists into mangled grin as He nods slowly. 'I get it now. That's it, isn't it? This is my fault. You going missing. Hywel dying. Rose. Rob. Ellie. Ian. All of this is *my* fault, isn't it?'

He waits for an answer. I don't have one.

'The thing is though, Little D. It's *not* my fault, is it? You ask me what I was thinking? What *I* was think-ing? D'you know, I do wonder what I was thinking, even going along with this stupid little idea of yours in the first place. "I want my soul", "I don't think I can do this any more", "A seven-year-old?"' All of this said with a mocking whine, a merciless whinge. 'Boo hoo, Little D. Poor Little D. Boo fucking hoo.'

He gets to His feet, and strides across the room towards me. Brings His face close to mine. Coffee-laced breath warm on my cheek. He speaks through gritted teeth. 'None of this is my fault, you little idiot. *none* of it. And what kind of person thinks of doing this? You tell me. Because let's not forget, you came to me, Little D. You came to me. You might do well to remember that.'

With each spat syllable I flinch, eyes lowered to avoid His stare. He grabs hold of my hair, pulling my face up until there is no choice but to raise my lids and look Him straight in the eye. The initial grasp softens as His fingers massage the base of my scalp, and His voice softens to the gentlest of purrs. 'I have done nothing, nothing, but support you, offer you my years of experience to guide you through this whole ridiculous process. And you don't even have the decency to thank me? You refuse to come near me for weeks?' His thumb strokes my cheek, the palm of His hand cupping my face. And His voice hardens once more. 'This isn't a game, Little D, and I never asked to play it. And now, now that I'm actually beginning to rather enjoy it, you're trying to take it away from me. No dice, Little D. You started this, and I have the mother of all plans for you to finish it. Now, do you want this "life" of yours or not?'

We hold the pose. Hold the stare. Blue eyes so cold they burn.

'I do. And I will. Finish it.' A long breath, emptying my lungs, my head, my heart of everything that's gone before, filling my mind's eye with Tom, slumped and sobbing in a steaming stream. 'I'm ready. If the offer is still open, I'm ready.'

He releases His hold. Breaks the stare. Leaves me to slump, exhausted, to the floor.

'I've lined this one up for you, Little D. I know who, I know where, I know when. Most importantly for you, I know how. And, d'you know, I'm rather pleased with myself. I think I've come up with rather a fun plan.' He pours me a glass of Scotch. Clinks His glass against my own before we tip our heads back in unison. Even I, with my limited senses, can feel the burning liquid scorch the back of my throat. It's vile. I bare my teeth with a hiss while He swirls His own mouthful beneath puffed cheeks to savour the peaty flavour.

We're sitting side by side on the floor of the studio, legs stretched in front of us, backs against the wall. A song plays over the speakers. A classic from the seventies, the obligatory ballad offering from a popular rock band who are gearing up for a final reunion concert. A classic ballad with a big chorus that will have the crowd roaring the lyrics in unison while the tiny figure of the lead singer conducts them from the stage. 'Don't walk away, Don't turn to say, I love you . . .'

On the other side of a huge window, a man sits behind a vast desk studded with buttons and knobs, with sliders and switches. Remastering the track for a new audience, for a younger crowd whose ears jar at the flawed, scratched perfection of the original recording.

'He hates this song, you know,' He says, cocking His ear towards the speaker.

'Who?'

'Stephen. Stephen Saunders. Number five. Of course, he's the one you should aim for. He's the one you need to "get", so to speak. To win this funny little game of yours. But there will be others. Almost certainly I'd say.' He chuckles to himself. Toys with an ice cube with the tip of His tongue while He waits for me to speak.

'Others? What are you talking about? We agreed five. One more. No more.'

'We agreed you'd do things to my satisfaction, Little D. And let's just say that recently I've been finding you sadly lacking. My game. My rules. And Stephen is the target, he's definitely the target. There's no avoiding that.' He takes another swig. 'But for you to achieve what you've set out for, there has to be more than one, Little D. At least one more. And you of all people can't avoid that. You didn't think I'd make it that easy, did you?'

My head falls back against the wall and I close my eyes. Of course. It makes perfect sense.

'Me.'

I feel the jog of my arms as He clinks my glass with His own once again. 'Quite right, Little D. Quite right.'

'All along. It's always had to be me, hasn't it? The others – Hywel, Rose, Rob, Ian even – they were just, what? For your own amusement?'

'Now now. Not my amusement per se, little one. What do you take me for?' He has the audacity to look hurt. 'No. I told you at the beginning. Every action must have a reaction, and if you wanted to go back on our agreement then there would have to be consequences. You would have to earn that right. That's what the others were for. They were payment, Little D, payment for the return of your own soul. But the actual process of regaining it, the actual manner in which you are able to live again? Yes. For you to live, your incarnation as Death must die.' He smirks. Laughs that irritating little inward laugh of His. 'I must admit, Little D, I thought you might have cottoned on a little sooner than this. I mean. Five deaths? What are they to anyone? How could they possibly be worth the return of your soul?'

What are they to anyone? They're everything. Everything.

To Darren's mother. Getting the bus out to that prison week in week out. She'd known her son was in with a bad lot. Known deep down that he hadn't kicked the heroin. But murder? He was never a murderer. And yet she lives her life in the shadow of one night with Death in tow.

To Hannah. And Dom. Turning to share a joke with the one person who can no longer laugh with them. Catching the flash of blonde in a scruffy ponytail ahead of them in the queue, on the train, in the shop window reflection. Hearing the howling miaow of the cat as he pads from room to room but never finds who he's looking for.

To Beth. Fighting the urge to vomit when she hears his voice. And she hears his voice wherever she goes. Fighting the urge to push the kids away when they crawl into bed after the nightmares take hold and they call for Daddy and Daddy isn't there. She loves them with a fierceness she didn't think possible, but their touch burns with an indelible reminder of his absence.

To Rebecca. Sitting late into the night on a single bed shrouded in candy floss cotton, cuddling a tiny frame who is now terrified of the dark, of shadows, of the sight of headlights sweeping across the wall of her bedroom. On Rebecca's wrist, a talisman. A pink towelling hairband, baggy from overuse, attached to a plastic disc, scratched and fading – Cinderella going to the ball. She stares, night after night, at the pile of toys in the corner of Ellie's room, lips dry, lost in a terrifying world of what might have been.

They were everything, those deaths, my actions. Everything.

'So if it's about me, why does there have to be

anyone else? Why does this . . . Stephen . . . why does he have to be involved? Can't we just stop it? Stop it now. You've had your fun. Why do I even have to die? What's the point? This whole thing was designed to enable me to live.'

'Don't you get it? Must I spell it out?' Apparently so.

'When I came to you in that market square, you made me a deal. You exchanged your soul for eternal life. And you died, in the fire, burnt to the core while the crowds howled and the smoke blotted out the sun. You are still apparent to me, to those people you help day after day, but to those around you – your family, the outer world – you were gone. For ever gone. And because you made that deal, because I benefitted from your willingness to relinquish your inner being, I smoothed the way. Your death was pain-free, you slipped from one side to the other with the minimum of fuss. You didn't feel the bones crack and the flesh cook on your bones. You didn't feel your skin peeling and fat melting in that searing heat. You slipped, softly and gently. Passed seamlessly from a living incarnation into the life of death. And so, for the reverse to be true, Little D, for you to live as normal, for you to return to life, so you must relinquish your current incarnation. For you to live, you must die as Death.'

'But what happens then? After I've died?'

'The reverse of what happened last time. Your body will become apparent to those around you. All those things that you so desire, you'll be able to feel. Food will have taste, the sun will have warmth. You'll be able to take that lungful of air you so crave. And feel the touch of Tom's fingers trace your skin. You won't see me any more – you'll have passed once more into the world of the living. But the thing is, I don't have the same disposition from all those years ago. I have no interest in making this easy for you, Little D, in smoothing the path and clearing the way. You've escaped it once, so this death, this rebirth of yours, will carry along with it everything you would expect to feel. The helplessness and hopelessness. The searing pain, the choking, the gasping for breath. All the things that people usually feel. You will come through it, you will see life on the other side, but you're going to have to fight for that life.'

'And Stephen? What's he got to do with this? Why not just me? Just count me as number five.'

'Well, you don't count, Little D. Not as one of the five. It's not all about you, you know. I said the game would be conducted by my rules and so it shall. Stephen is your cypher – the one you must kill for the game to be won, for your life to be lived. And, as I say, he hates this song. Above all else, he really, really hates this song.'

'So what do you need me to do? What is this final grand plan of yours?'

'All in good time, Little D, all in good time.' He

raises His glass once more. Chinks crystal against crystal while amber liquid swirls against ice.

'To Death.'

25

IN THE MARCH OF 1983, MALCOLM SAUNDERS, father of one and model husband, pillar of the society and friend to all, was found hanging by his neck from the cold, steel beams of the barn round the back of Bill Cook's farm. He hung up there for two days before they found him. I was there as he fell, holding his hand for the tell-tale crack of vertebrae and wiping the spit that bubbled and drooled from drooping lips. It takes so much longer than you would think, hanging, and while he waited we talked. About Stephen, that little five-year-old lad with solemn eyes and few words.

It was out of character, this disappearance, and that twenty-four hours was the longest Susan Saunders had ever known. She daren't leave the house. Daren't risk missing him. Missing the call from the local bobby to say, 'He's fine, Mrs Saunders. There was a bit of an accident, but he's fine.' How was she supposed to know, after all, as she cleaned the same spot on the kitchen floor over and over and over and waited for him to come home? How was she supposed to know that at that very moment, there was another her? A twenty-five-year-old version of her balanced on hay bales in a draughty barn with a hand cupped against the face of her beloved husband as he swung gently in the breeze.

Though when they came and knocked at the door, she'll say she knew. Knew what those two police officers were going to say before they said it. People always do, don't they? Say they had 'a feeling'. Say they'd known all along. But there's no way of proving that, is there? Because to voice that knowledge before the final confirmation is surely the ultimate betrayal of faith.

In the weeks following that terminal drop, the lives of Stephen and Susan Saunders were turned upside down, flipped on their backs, shaken until they were empty and tossed to the side. All the money was gone. A series of bad investments and a well-hidden love for the nags had led him down the path to the noose that left Malcolm Saunders' wife and son high and dry. The brand-new Ford Capri sitting in the drive was collected by a man called Ken with a bristling 'tache and a nervous, barking laugh who ruffled Stephen's hair and cleared his throat awkwardly when Susan handed him the keys. Neighbours dipped their heads as they passed – not wanting to be caught gawping at the house, catching the eye of that poor woman, that wee bairn.

The house had to be sold. They moved out on a

Saturday. A mother and son and a jumbled pile of cardboard boxes waiting at the kerb for the removals van. They didn't have much to take with them. Couldn't keep the furniture. That had been sold with the house. Eking every penny they could from under that roof. It had sold for far less than it was worth, but still, there was cash in Susan's pocket – enough for a deposit and three months' rent on a grotty little flat on the first floor of a red-brick terrace in Holbeck. And so they upped and left. Neither of them looked back as the van pulled down the tree-lined avenue and turned into the nose-to-tail traffic of ring-road rush hour.

Stephen can barely remember his dad. He recognises him in the pictures his mum had on the bedside table, but he can't remember the details. Can't remember ever speaking to him. Ever being tucked up under the covers or listening to a story while shadows danced on a wall lit dimly by a bedside lamp. For Stephen, it's as if his life started on the day his father's life ended.

And what a life was starting. Watching his mother as she sank, swaddled in a blurred blanket of depression. At times she'd fight, floundering against the pathos that threatened to drown her. Gasping for air and grasping at Stephen to wrap him in a tight squeeze and press her lips to his hair, muttering tight-lipped promises that he could barely hear before pressing kisses onto his cheeks so hard he thought he'd be able to see them the next morning.

More often though, she'd succumb. There were whole weeks when Stephen couldn't even be sure she knew he was there. When she sat on the sofa, ash building on a forgotten cigarette while she stared into the ether. Eyes glazed as she watched memories of a different life. And there she'd sit for hours, not moving. In the same place on the sofa at 3.30 in the afternoon as she had been when Stephen had left for school at nine. The only change in the scene a growing pile of crushed cigarette butts in the ashtray at her feet.

The only movement, the only chink in this frozen state, was to reset the old record player that perched on the nesting tables at the side of the sofa. One of the only things from the old house that she had refused to leave behind. It played the same song over and over – Susan's arm would reach out to replace the needle at the beginning of the track time and time again. The vinyl wore smooth and the needle skipped and jumped from chorus to verse, but still she played. A token ballad from one of the rock groups of the late seventies. Whining electric guitar and yelping vocals that entreated, 'Don't walk away, don't turn to say, I love you . . . But I'll leave you . . .'

Stephen hated that song. Hated it with every fibre of his being. The opening chords fuelled an anger that built up behind his eyes, pressing his brain against the inside of his skull until he thought his head would burst. It was the last thing he heard when he left the house in the morning, the first thing he heard when he got home. The only thing he heard through the long light evenings while he sat by her side on the sofa and held her hand in his until her head drooped and dropped against the arm of the sofa and long, deep breaths betrayed sleep. Only then would he stand, lay her hand in her lap and stub out the half-smoked cigarette. Tug the blanket off the back of the sofa to lay over her sleeping form.

Lift the needle from vinyl to still the never-ending spin for six precious hours of silence. Six precious hours before he'd be woken again by scratchy static and those hated opening chords.

It never occurred to him not to go to the little red-brick school at the end of the road, if only for the promise of a hot lunch and a morning bottle of creamy milk. More often than not, and depending on who had visited from their former life this week brandishing casserole dishes that were popped in the fridge with a note proclaiming 'Gas Mark 7! Forty-five minutes!', this would be his only meal of the day.

He never dreamed of bunking off. Avoiding the shoves and the shouts. The yells of 'Stinky Stephen! Stinky Saunders!' that echoed round the playground from one end to the other when the kids caught the musty whiff of his unwashed uniform. On rainy days, they'd tip the contents of his satchel into puddles, shattering oily rainbows with the clatter of pencils spilling from their case.

At first he tried to talk, tried to make friends with the twins, at least. Daniel and Matthew Cole. With their shock of ginger hair and spattering of freckles, they too were all too often to be found scrabbling for their belongings in the puddles that ringed the small tarmacked yard. But even they kept their distance, the thought of another reason to be targeted by the schoolyard bullies too much to bear.

So gradually, one day at a time, the words disappeared. Day after day of thinking of things to say but not daring to open his mouth for fear of exacting the wrath of the Junior Three boys. Day after day of keeping his mouth shut until eventually, the words just disappeared. Upped and left.

Susan can't see it. Doesn't see it. To her, that summer is a tiny sliver of her life. Three months when she couldn't get off the sofa before a switch flicked deep inside and she emerged, gasping, back in to the real world. When she remembered that first and foremost she was a mother. Got off the sofa and popped to Tesco's. Stephen came home to find her standing at the stove in front of a huge pan of bubbling mince. No rhyme or reason. Nothing to indicate that today should've been any different from every other. Welcomed home for the first time with a hug and a kiss and a 'How was school today, pudding?' She looked at him warily, waited awkwardly, hip cocked against the cabinets, unsure of the damage she'd done. But he just sat at the kitchen table in silence. Took his books out of his bag and got on with his maths homework. Same as he had done every day for the past few months. Watching her when her back was turned, then ducking his head when she turned to smile at him. She couldn't bring herself to talk about the previous few months, so the two of them carried on as if they had never happened. Well, she carried on as if they had never happened. For Stephen, that summer was to mark him for the rest of his life.

At fourteen, Stephen is a quiet lad. He stands alone in the schoolyard, tucked into the gap between the science block and the bike sheds. He's tall. Thin. But his stance is stooped, as if the body inside has grown faster than the skin, drawing thin shoulders into a hunch. The words never came back. Not after that summer.

Silence now manifested as a stutter that chokes and catches at the back of his throat. Under hooded brows he watches the other kids – the boys kicking a ball around the asphalt, the girls gathered in gaggles to watch. Twisting long ponytails around fingers stubby with bitten nails. The same boys who taunted him, who threw pencils into puddles, now ignore him. Not deliberately. They don't turn their heads as he approaches. Don't jeer at his stuttered, stammering answers in lessons. They simply don't see him any more. To them, he simply doesn't exist.

Occasionally, one of the girls will break free from the group. Trot over, ponytail swinging, to lean against the wall and ask what he's up to, if he wants a fag. Bite their lips and tilt their heads as they flirt and flatter. 'I love your coat, Steve. Where did you get it?', 'Did you see *Top of the Pops* last night, Steve? Michael Hutchence looked so fit. I said to Jodie I thought he looked like you, but she said you were more like Brett Anderson. Did you see it?' Over their shoulder he can see the rest of the gaggle watching, waiting, whispering. He can't answer, can't get the words out. So he stands, mute. Glowering. Breathing heavily through his nose as the anger and frustration build and have nowhere to boil over. He feels his head get hot, and all he can do it grunt. Scuff at the ground with the toe of his shoe and wait for them to give up. To leave him alone. And they always do. Finish their cigarette and blow smoke in his face before trotting back to the group to be sucked back into the fold. They take it in turns, the girls. It's a game to them.

They couldn't give a shit where he got his jacket from. And they certainly don't think he looks like Michael Hutchence. They just insist on this relentless game, egging each other on to see who can stay with him longest. Who can get the most response. And when they don't, by the time ash has burnt down to filter, they toss their manes and run back to the rest.

There's one who's different. Who secretly does think Steven looks a bit like Brett Anderson, with his long limbs and curved spine. She takes part, of course she does. She is, after all, a fourteen-year-old fighting for survival in the tundra of a school playground. But she's different to the others. Softer somehow. When she comes over it's with a shy smile and a flushed cheek, looking up at him through her lashes. She asks about his mum. If he saw *Red Dwarf* at the weekend. She doesn't expect him to speak. Seems to be happy with a nod, with a hum of agreement. Offers him a drag on her fag. He accepts, always does. Tasting the fruity blur of lipgloss with the tip of his tongue. It doesn't matter that he can't speak. When she looks him straight in the eye and smiles his stomach flips and he finds himself smiling back. Grinning like idiots at each other, until with a flick of hair, and a cloud of smoke, she's back in the pack. Fran. Frannie.

Frannie left him though, at sixteen. Went off to the Sixth Form college with some of the other girls in a cloud of Fuzzy Peach and a stomp of platform shoes. She left with promises that she'd stay in touch, that she'd come and see him on a Saturday afternoon, that she'd lend him the Suede tape she'd bought a week earlier for him to copy. But promises are fleeting at sixteen, and intentions, though well meant, slide in their quicksand foundations. It didn't take long before she was deep into her new life – flirting with boys, going to gigs in town and proffering drags on fags with their fruity tips to the long-haired, doe-eyed lads of A-level art.

He doesn't forget her though, the smile on her face and the look in her eye. The kindness. The boy she saw at fourteen when all around had turned their backs. He may have lost her temporarily, but he'll never, ever forget her.

'Argh. God. Ow! Watch where you're . . .' A blur under his chin of shiny brown hair, rustling shopping carriers and a tote bag slipping off a slim shoulder.

'God, I'm sorry . . . Here, let me . . .' He tries to rescue tumbling groceries before they hit the floor, juggling bags of oranges in long arms, supporting sagging sacks with his knees.

He steps back, hooks long fingers through plastic straps. Blows a straggling lock of hair away from his eyes. Proffers the rescued bags. To . . .

'Fran? Frannie?'

The girl looks up from where she's crouched on the floor, shoving used lipglosses, receipts, and a dog-eared *A–Z* into a gaping shoulder bag. She's been chuntering to herself since the moment he knocked her. The sound of her name brings silence and she peers up at him, squints through a thick, shiny fringe.

'Stephen? Saunders? Wow, you look . . .'

Different? Older? The lean frame has filled out, hair no longer greasy and dull. Teenage blackheads and angry outbreaks have cleared in a twenty-five-year-old face. He's become a handsome boy, our Stephen. Classic. Slim and angular. And finally, after three years of university, of a new job and a new life, with new friends who value his thoughts, no longer pursued by the burden of a teenage shyness, the words have come back.

They both start to speak. Both stop, waiting for the other to continue. 'How've you . . .'

'God, you look . . .'

'Sorry, you . . .'

'No, no, after you . . .'

They laugh, self-conscious. Silence falls. Stephen breaks it. And in starting to speak, in finding out how she is, how she's been, what she's up to, who she is, years fall away and they stand, chatting over each other, finishing each other's sentences, grinning at each other like idiots. Without asking, without thinking, they start walking, side by side. A coffee? Sure. My local's just round the corner? Fish and chips? Why not?

And that evening led to the next, to a visit to the cinema, to a walk through Greenwich Park. To their first official date and a laughing kiss perched on the edge of a fountain in Trafalgar Square while she tried to splash him in the dying sun.

With every date, with every meeting, he falls harder for her. Glimpses of the fourteen-year-old girl seen in someone who has grown into a strong woman who loves him unconditionally. As the years pass, they meet each other's friends, his mum and step-dad, her parents. They move into a flat together where they dance around to Suede and watch old episodes of *Red Dwarf* and sit as happily in silence as when they're gabbing away. And when he looks at her, every time he smiles down at her to drop a peck of a kiss on her forehead, he thinks, 'I'd do anything for this girl.'

Which is why when the city is abuzz with the news of a reunion, of the one-off return of that rock group from the seventies with that ballad that everyone knows and everyone loves, he agrees when Fran suggests that they should get a bunch of them together and make a day of it. And why, when tickets go on sale and people spend hours online glued to their computer screens in a desperate bid to secure them, he gives Fran his credit card details for her to ring up and book. And when he thinks back to that summer and that ballad playing again and again in a smoke-filled stuffy flat, he pushes those thoughts down and packs them away where they can't be seen and where that pain can't be felt. Because although it hurts, and the memory of that summer makes his stomach curl, Fran is desperate to go. And he'll do anything for that girl.

26

ALEX AND DAN ARE IN TOM'S SITTING ROOM, throwing a rugby ball between them in that way men have. Incapable of not playing with a ball if there's one lying around. The place is spotless, a fresh pot of coffee chortles on the stove.

'What do you reckon then . . . ?' Alex tosses the ball to Dan.

'To what?' Tom comes through from the kitchen, mugs in hand.

'Nekros . . . Remember? Finsbury Park? It's tomorrow. We've got a ticket. You've got a ticket. You know, if you want it . . .' He catches the ball. Tosses it back to Dan with a spin.

Tom stiffens. He's come on leaps and bounds, but some things . . . Some things just don't sit right with him. 'Mate, I dunno . . . Thanks and everything, but . . . It just feels weird, you know? Going to that without her? It was our song . . .' He trails off, lost in a thousand memories.

Alex opens his mouth. To convince him. Dan shoots him a look. A tiny shake of the head. Don't push him. He'll come round. Slowly slowly and all that.

'OK. Well, the ticket's there if you want it, I mean. No biggie.'

'I know. And thanks. But it's too . . . big, I think. I mean, the pub's one thing. Massive gig with meaningful songs? And booze? I'm not ready for it yet. Jeez – I don't think you're ready for it yet . . .'

Alex laughs. Holds his hands up in acceptance. 'All right. Well, as I said . . .'

'I know. It's there. And thanks.'

As afternoon light fades into a pinkish evening sky, stomachs grumble and the rugby ball is tossed to one side for the final time. 'Curry?' Dan asks.

'Thought you'd never ask.'

On the way to the curry house they're distracted, as is often their wont, by warm lights, smoked windows and the promise of a pint. Hunger pangs momentarily pacified with cheese and onion crisps and amber nectar, and three boys shoulder their way through their fellow drinkers to a tiny table in the corner of the bar.

Tom takes a sip of his pint. Nods towards the bar. 'Alex, do you know that girl? At the bar?'

And there, feet resting on the brass rail, elbow propped on polished wood, I stand.

He's looking at me. Straight at me. Like he knows

who I am. Knows where I've been and who I will be. For the briefest moment the lights dim, the crowds fall into darkness, and he and I stand alone, lit in high relief. Eyes locked. Breath held.

Alex looks over. Sees the girl next to me. Standing alone at the bar waiting patiently for a pint of Guinness to swirl and settle.

'That's Fran, mate. What are you on about? Steve's girlfriend. You've met her, like, a million times . . .'

'Not her,' he replies. 'Her . . . I keep seeing her around.' Nods his head towards the bar once more. But when he looks back, that girl, of locked eyes and held breath, is gone. To him, Fran stands alone, waiting patiently for the pint of Guinness to settle and swirl.

And I've gone. Vanished to carry on my life, my deaths. He has been seeing me most days now, this face he can't place. This face that replaces Kate's on every street corner, with every reflected headlight on rain-soaked tarmac. In the corner shop as he picks up a pint of milk and stops to have a chat with Aasim. Crossing at amber flashing lights on the road ahead. He's the only one who sees the real me. Hair tied in a knot, body clad in the simple shift that I've worn for hundreds of years, but almost passes for modern. He smiles when he sees me. Always a smile. Raises his hand in an occasional greeting, a puzzled smile playing on pursed lips when once again I get away from him, when once again he can't get close enough for a hello.

But I can't let him too close. Certainly can't let him close enough to speak. And so I vanish. Behind a parked car, a budding tree, a shelf piled high in a packed corner shop. Keeping my distance until the time is right.

And on I go, vanishing from Tom's view to morph into the mothers, sisters, daughters I embody. Leaving on the wind to tend to the many, to occupy the very final seconds of all the ones who are ready to go. It isn't our time yet, Tom. Not just yet.

The pint turns into two, three, four and the curry house swings open its doors to three friends as the pub closes its own. It's the longest he's been out of the house in months. He realises as they're plied with poppadums, as they muse over madras, that for the entire evening he hasn't turned mid-conversation to include Kate, hasn't heard her voice from across the room. She's with him, but she's not there, not the ever-present presence of the preceding months. A weight is lifting. Day by day, it's taking its time. But it's lifting.

He walks home, heads straight to the shower. There's only one toothbrush in the mug by the sink now. Only one bottle of shampoo by the taps. Towels hang, straight and dry on the rail, no longer left to moulder in a damp heap on a sodden bathmat.

Walks through to the bedroom, a towel slung loosely around his hips. I sit in the corner and watch as he dries off. Content in his solitude, he walks round the bedroom naked, hanging his trousers in the wardrobe and chucking his T-shirt into the laundry basket. The trail of destruction that has followed him for the past few months has petered out to a restored order. Eventually, everything is in its place, and he settles into bed.

Breathing becomes deep and even. His limbs lie heavy, head tucked into the crook of his elbow, legs sprawled to cover the width of the bed. I pull back the duvet. Slip naked between the sheets. Run my hands down his chest. In his sleep he twitches. Reaches up to scratch at the feather-light touch he can feel on exposed skin. He finds my hand, entwines my fingers with his. I move closer. Press my lips against his. And he responds. Kisses me back. Reaches his hand up to cup the back of my neck and draw me in deeper. To flick his tongue against mine. I shift in the bed to straddle him. Sit astride his waist and lean forward to drop a smattering of kisses across his chest. Hands hook under hips while lips dip to nip lips and soft skin slips beneath calloused fingertips.

When he wakes the next morning, he wakes with a smile. Hardened by the memory of a dream, of bodies moving in sync, of the unknown girl in the pub stretched the length of his naked body, and driving him to orgasm. Of limbs linked in ecstasy and skin that prickled and shivered at her touch. Of light hairs that stood on end as lips lingered and fingers fluttered. It's so clear in his mind, so real. But it was just a dream, nothing to waste too much time on.

Of course it was, Tom. Just a dream.

27

HE MEETS ME IN THE DRESSING ROOM. SLIPS IN between the curtains to hang a selection of clothes onto the hooks on the wall. Steps back as I move forward to look at them, to feel the weight of the fabric. My first set of my very own modern-day clothes.

'Are you just going to stand there while I get changed?'

'Nothing I haven't seen before, Little D, nothing I haven't seen before.'

He settles on to the stool tucked into the corner of the tiny cubicle, legs stretched out in front of him. 'Can't have you reappearing to the world looking like you've just been dragged out of the sixteenth century, can we? Imagine the headlines!' He smirks. 'And I think you deserve a treat. A new outfit to celebrate your re-entry to the world. You've not made it easy for yourself, have you? Far too emotional . . .' He tuts under his breath. 'But you've nearly done it. I have to hand it to you. One more teeny-tiny death and you're free.'

One more teeny-tiny death . . . And the rest. Deep breath. One more day of this and I can get on with my life, with living. I can't let myself think of the people out there, going about their day-to-day lives, looking forward to the gig they booked tickets for months before. Some of them just like me, crammed into a cubicle to find the perfect outfit for the perfect night. Some already in the pub – lunch and a couple of pints before they head over to the park. Some of them have been looking forward to this for years. For a lifetime. The unexpected reformation of a classic rock band from the seventies, music they've grown up with, that they first heard on vinyl records with their dads. Music that bonds them with the generation before, an overlap to tie them together despite the multitude of differences between them. One last chance to see legends at work. Not that they know it yet, but today for them is one last day.

I reach up for the skinny jeans that hang from the wall beside me. Wiggle and tug them up my legs underneath the brown hessian dress that I've worn day in, day out for the past four hundred years. Bounce on the spot to drop into them. How do people wear these things? I feel trapped – lower body encased in rigid denim, waist cinched into a tight belt. When I appear to the dead, to the dying, I've never realised until this moment that I never feel the clothes they're wearing.

Never really noticed the difference between those and my own plain dress. But Lord above, these things are uncomfortable.

I look over my shoulder to where He sits in the corner, waiting for my full transformation. My own need for privacy and personal dignity is completely disregarded – I am His project and He'll be as involved as he wants. Back turned, I lift the heavy dress up over my head to expose my naked back and shoulders, masked only by the curtain of hair hanging down my back. I loop the arms of a bra over my shoulders and my breasts strain against the thin fabric as they're thrust forward for me to reach round to my back and try once, twice, three times to hook the two ends together. I don't hear Him move, but a finger is drawn down my back while hands push mine out of the way to finish the job. A kiss dropped on my shoulder seals the act. My skin crawls at His touch. Get off me. Just get off me.

Arms scoop into a silk blouse that droops casually off one shoulder. Feet slip into ballet pumps to wiggle toes to the very end. My transformation is complete. I turn to look at myself in the changing-room mirror. A girl stares back, kohled eyes peeking out under a heavy fringe, recently streaked blonde hair styled into shaggy layers. My face. My body. I barely recognise her, but staring back from that changing-room mirror is a modern-day me. Lizzie, Lilibet, Bess.

*

At this height, in this tiny flat at the teetering top of this towering block, birds swim languidly past in the humid summer air. Once again He watches me dress. In the nondescript bedroom of a nondescript block. The council cleared the flat last week, shunting squatters from a safe haven.

The air in here hangs heavy and thick. Thick with the musty smell of the unwashed, of lingering stale smoke. A broken glass pipe lies abandoned by the wooden leg of a cracked leather sofa and the door sags sadly on splintered hinges.

I stand before Him. Exposed in a white cotton bra and white cotton pants. Stripped to the essentials, skin tacky with sweat. He places cold hands on my shoulders.

Cold hands that offer misplaced relief on this stifling day. Those same hands turn me around, to face myself in the mirror. Though I can feel Him behind me, can feel the ice-light touch of His fingertips and squirm at cold breath on exposed shoulders, in the reflection in front of me I stand alone.

He takes my hand in His. Twists His fingers through mine and brings my hand to rest softly at my waist. Cold breath teases tiny hairs upright to prickle and shiver.

'It's time, Little D.'

My reflection stares back at me, its gaze unavoidable.

It's time.

He lifts my arm and in the mirror glass I watch as it raises slowly, gently, floating in the fug as if of its own accord. Shoulders shrug into soft, cream calico. Heavy. Weighted. Through thin fabric I can feel every lump. Every bump. Pockets and seams bulge lightly and droop under the weight of the nails, the screws, the lethal ball-bearings packed into secret compartments waiting for their moment. Brown paper packages plugged into pockets. Brown paper packages waiting patiently for their moment. For the flick of a switch that will send them on their way to unleash their hell. Twisting into soft flesh, grating against bone. Ploughing messily through spongy tissue that cedes too easily in their path.

My skin pinches between the leather and metal as fingers fiddle with buckles and straps. Soft cotton straps threading through shining buckles. He tugs. Cinching me in until my breath comes in short gasps. He smooths the fabric where it catches. Rearranges the packages for a smoother line. Slips a silken blouse onto silken shoulders and stands back as my fingers fumble with buttons.

I don't look away from the reflection standing in front of me. Won't look away. Stare myself down in the mirror. Throw down the gauntlet. Who blinks loses. Reach into the pocket to trace the edge of the trigger and straighten my back against the weight hanging heavy at my shoulders. What if I did it now? Flicked the switch here, in this tiny room. Stopped this whole sorry mess before it even has a chance to start. It might blow out the windows. Might hit a passer-by in the street, cause a passing car to swerve and crash. But in the main, those ball-bearings firing out would lodge into plaster instead of flesh. Would smash through windows instead of bone. The nails would hammer into wooden struts, not slice silently through tissue.

But as I stroke that smooth plastic disc, I know I can't. His words have run circles in my head all morning. 'This is my game, Little D. If you want to play it, you play by my rules. And today, I say where, and I say when. And if you don't like it, well, you know what you can do . . .'

So I stand still. And I stare. Watch myself in the mirror, the lumpen lines under soft folds of silk. I watch my reflection run its fingers down from my shoulders, over the lumps and the bumps to rest on my waistband. Smoothing. Soothing. I watch this reflection that stands apart from me. And I wait.

'Hands up,' He commands.

I raise both arms above my head. Drop into cotton-soft darkness as a huge sweatshirt is slipped over my head. Pulled down over my ears, my arms fed through ballooning sleeves. He dresses me like a child. It swamps me this sweatshirt. Too heavy, too hot for this weather. But it hides what lies beneath.

Those lumps, those bumps. Those brown paper packages packed full of sin.

He rests both hands on my shoulders. Gives them a squeeze. Turns me back around to face Him.

'There,' He says. 'Done.' Strokes His thumb along my lower lip. 'I want you to stand proud today, Little D. Go out there with your head held high for the world to see. None of this hiding away until you're needed. When you set foot outside this flat, I want you visible to the world.' He squeezes my shoulders once more. Tucks a strand of hair behind my ear. 'Now. Ready?'

My mouth is dry. A droplet of sweat winds its way down my back, picking a cautious course beneath a fatal shroud.

I nod. 'Ready.'

He turns me back around to face the mirror. And once more, in that reflection I stand alone.

Ready.

28

FIVE P.M. AND I'M ON MY WAY. HE LEFT THE FLAT an hour ago, squeezing out between boards hammered across a busted doorframe. Leaving me to make this final journey on my own.

Soft-soled shoes pad along sun-softened pavements. Tarmac, melting in the heat, yields with every step and the North London streets wallow in the warm late afternoon light. My hair, drawn into a ponytail, hangs limply, trailing tendrils that cling wetly to the damp skin on the back of my neck.

At the station, lift doors open and hot air blooms from within. Sucking passengers in and down to the hell of a summer's afternoon underground. The carriage is packed with excited gig-goers crammed together to get an early start and a good spot on the grass for lazy beers while the sun's still up. They sing despite their confines, snippets that fly from one group to the next until the length of the carriage hums to the same tune. I tuck myself into a corner. Tight, rigid against the wall of the train. Holding my body, my bulk clear of anyone who risks brushing too close. Anyone who risks feeling the hard edges and unnatural lumps beneath an unseasonable, unreasonable outfit.

I hold my breath. Close my eyes against the surrounding melee. The nerves have set in and my lips move in silent prayer. Whispered words to comfort, to protect. Mouthing them to the rhythm of iron against steel: 'It'll be over tonight, It'll be over tonight.' I block out what I can of the surroundings. The sounds of singing dulled to a muted mumble. The movement of the figures around me softened to a Vaseline-smeared sway. My head feels unsteady. Too heavy for my neck.

The stuffed vest is tight. Too tight. Breathing is hard in this saturated air, and the earlier trickle of sweat has become a torrent. 'I have to get out, I have to get out.'

Doors slide open. Gig-goers swell through parted doors in a laval ooze. Swim to the surface to gasp for fresh breath, although the overground world offers little relief. The air is still thick, still heavy in this heat, though the sun has fallen far from its zenith.

On the street outside, I bend. Crouch to the floor. Bottom lip is sucked and scraped between teeth until I can taste the iron tang of blood. I take what gulps I can of what air there is. Breathing becomes more regular and the melody returns clearly on all sides.

Snippets of songs pitched high, pitched low. I stand straight, using all of my strength to pull my body upright. To rearrange the straps on my shoulders and face the walk ahead.

I'm ready.

Along the Seven Sisters Road we're driven forward in a herd of excited bodies swarming towards the gates, tickets clutched in sweaty hands. Shouts of excitement pitch and swirl in the air around us and the singing continues – a chorus of a greatest hit sung by one group of friends bounces through the crowd until snippets are heard from all directions. There's a festival atmosphere – the smell of grilled burgers and hot-dogs hangs in the late afternoon air to tempt and tease. Long-limbed girls ride on the shoulders of broad-backed men as kids grip on to the hands of parents and leap from foot to foot in excitement and we flow relentlessly towards the ticket gates.

At the entrance the bubbling, churning flow swirls and slows to a pool of people lapping at the gates. Luminously clad security check tickets, check bags. Pat down jackets and usher the clamouring congregation into the field within.

Luminously clad security check tickets, check bags. Pat down jackets. All jackets. I hadn't thought.

A fresh bouquet of sweat blooms on my upper lip. I look from one queue to the next to the next. I assumed I would pass through no question, the ticket He gave me curled damply in my fist. But they have dogs, these guards, and the dogs will sense me. They always do. Even if I wasn't standing before them cloaked in explosives and oozing the sweat-sharp tang of fear. They sense me. Barking into thin air with a snarl. Drool dripping from slavering jaws. While their owners droop in this heat, the dogs are eager. Fresh. Sniffing at bags, nipping at heels.

As I slip through the turnstile, head down and ticket held out, the head of the Alsatian ahead is already turned in my direction. Low growls emanate from choked throat as he tugs on his lead, tugging the arm of the burly guard he has in tow. He barks. Snarls. Pulls hard to leap at me. His paws, huge and heavy, brush at my chest. His face, hot breath panting, inches from mine. But the burly guard tugs him back without even a glance in my direction. As he's dragged in the opposite direction, off to a group of lads doing their best to smuggle cans of lager in the hoods of their jerseys, the dog turns back to me. Confused. A soft bark. A gruff ruff. Teeth bared in warning.

But he can growl all he likes. I'm through. Shaken but undeterred.

Although the band isn't on until nine, the grass in front of the vast stage is filling up with the crowds flooding in from outside. I need to find Stephen somewhere in this soup, this mob. I take a wander, check out my best position. Somewhere to herd him to when I track him down. Too far back, not enough people. Too far forward and we'll have to force our way through a tightly packed throng to get into position and risk someone feeling misshapen lumps beneath a well-worn sweatshirt. I settle in front of the sound booth, watching and waiting as the tide of fans ebbs and flows around me. There's time. Time to catch my breath, collect my thoughts. I have to find him before it gets dark and faces merge into one, blurred and distorted by setting sun and swooping lights. Here seems as good a place as any from which to set forth – a stoma in the continuous skin of bodies stretched across the grass. I'll lead him here. But how to track him down in this throng?

More fool me. For as we know, the Devil Himself is on my side. A voice, speaking on a phone to my left. I turn to see a tall figure – slim build, broad shoulders, longish hair messy. Finger pressed to one ear, phone to the other while he shouts into the mouthpiece. Stephen.

'Mate? Can you hear me? Yep – we went through already . . . In front of the sound booth . . . No, we're waiting for you before we go to the bar, cop a spot and all that . . . What? I missed that. What did you say? . . . Wicked! That's wicked news . . . OK, yep. Yep. Front of the sound booth . . . Yep. Laters, mate . . .'

He hangs up. Leans down to the girl next to him to peck her on the lips and wrap her hair in his fist. 'That was Alex . . . Tom's coming! Rang him this morning apparently.'

'Amazing! God, I've been so worried about him. Janey's been filling me in, but sounded like he was in a pretty bad way.'

Fran. Shiny brown hair waiting for a glossy pint of Guinness in a North London pub. Feet resting on brass rail as elbows are propped on polished wood.

Alex. A daily vigil outside a North London flat. Tom.

Fran. Alex. Tom.

Sweat-slicked skin freezes to ice. Tom. My Tom. Coming here. To meet Stephen. My Stephen.

I should have known. Should have seen this coming. This must have been His plan.

'Mate! You came!' Stephen spots Tom approaching through the crowd. Grabs him round the shoulders to pull him into a hug.

Tom shrugs. Shy. Apologetic. 'Yeah, well. It's about time I reckon. And she'd bloody kill me if she knew I was moping about.' His voice is thick, the words forced past a lump in his throat. But he's there. He's made it. And he's proud. He clears his throat. Chokes back the wobble that threatens. 'Right then. Pint? They'll be on in a bit.'

Fran and Stephen stay put, staking a claim on this small patch of grass and establishing a base for the boys to head for when the drinks are in. They don't notice me, another body in an ever-growing crowd. Too entwined in each other to notice a stranger sitting only a stone's throw away and watching their every move. I stay with them, close but not too close. A trio lined up against the fence, faces turned to catch the last warmth of the summer sun. I can't risk losing him now, when he's landed so easily in my lap, but the urge to follow Tom, to push him away, distract him, lose him in this billowing crowd is almost overwhelming. But, I know this is it. My last chance. My only chance to finish what I've started.

And so here I stay. Lined up with Stephen, our backs to the wall.

When Tom and Alex return, the sun is setting over the stage roof, smudging the heavens with pinks and purples, sliced through by the flaming orange streaks of high flying clouds. As the day draws to an end and the sun dips below an unseen horizon, the pinks and purples deepen to a violet bruise and anticipation within the bowl reaches fever pitch. Lights either side of the stage pulse and flare, sweeping over a bouncing crowd in blinding arcs. A burst of fire from the roof of the stage and the opening chords of a classic song vibrate beneath our feet. The crowd roars.

It's nearly time. It's so very nearly time.

Tom is grinning. For the first time in months, he has a smile on his face and his thoughts are not swallowed whole by the gaping hole in his life. Alex and Dan flank him on either side as the three of them leap to the music, arms around each other's shoulders, voices roaring familiar lyrics at the tiny figures on stage. The crowd ahead is a sea of waving arms bathed in the blue, purple and red lights swooping from the stage. For the first time in months he feels like himself again, like he can live his life again. He's swept up entirely in the tidal force of the crowd and for the first time in months he's living. Properly living.

Stephen and I push forward through the crowd, easing our way past bodies swaying in rapt homage to the riffs and refrains on stage, searching out Tom, Alex, Dan and Fran from where we left them half an hour ago. No one pays any attention to a tall messy-haired boy and his shadow weaving their way through the crowd. And for his part, Stephen still hasn't noticed me. Why should he? Just another face in an overwhelmingly huge crowd. And as the pints flow, so the faceless crowd blurs into one swaying mass.

With every jolt and shove I feel my cargo digging into me. Lumps and bumps that press on flesh and nip soft skin. But the dancing bodies around me are oblivious. Softened by the sun, blurred by the booze, none of them notice the bulk burrowing past them and deeper into the crowd. As one song finishes the crowd pauses, panting, giving us a chance to stop, look around.

We've found them, swept from their original spot by the flow of bodies, but we've found them. And they leap on him – Tom, Alex and Dan. Like he's been gone for years. Leap on him, throw arms around his shoulders and throw their heads back to howl the chorus of the band's biggest hit.

As I manoeuvre myself behind him, I feel a hand on my shoulder. 'Little D!' a voice yells in my ear. I can barely hear over the screaming of the electric guitar, but I would recognise that cold grip anywhere. I turn round to see Him looming above me, jogging from one foot to the other. 'You didn't think I'd let you go without saying goodbye, do you?'

'What?' It's impossible to hear. I can't believe He's here. If there had been any lingering doubt in my mind, I can't back out now, not when He's standing right there.

'I came to say goodbye! Goodbye!' He motions with His hand, fingers curling to meet palm in a tiny wave. 'And well done!' This accompanied by a thumbs-up. 'I wasn't ever sure you'd do it!'

'You knew, didn't you?' I yell back. 'About Tom? And Stephen?'

I'm shouting directly into His ear, but the words are getting lost in the lyrics that are being shouted over our heads. Jumbled into the stream of noise. If He can hear me, He makes no sign of having understood. His only concession is a smirk in the direction of where

Tom stands, one arm thrown around Stephen, one fist pumping the night air, mouth wide in roared song.

'I'll leave you to it! Good luck, Little D! One more! Just the one!' He pulls me into an awkward hug. I can't pull myself away quickly enough. I glare at Him, but time's running out and I can't waste precious minutes with Him when I have to get to Stephen and get him away from Tom before our time is up. An argument with Him is always futile, and never was that more true than at this very moment.

He steps back to merge into the crowd. Loops an arm around the waist of a tall, slim girl with long, blonde hair. Eyes closed, swaying hips in time with the melody, she waves one arm languidly above her head. As she reaches up, her top rides up to reveal a toned, tanned belly, marred only by the slim red slash of a birthmark running from hip to navel. How can she bear that proximity? I can only think that in the oppressive heat of the packed crowd the frigidity of His presence is undoubtedly a welcome, if unexplained relief. A breath of cool air in the sweat of the mosh pit.

The opening bars of that familiar song pulse out across a sea of waving arms.

It's time.

I can see Tom from where I'm standing, tucked in behind Stephen, trying to get close. Can see him falter. Where the rest of the crowd sways, leaps and whoops, he stands still. Mouth slack. Eyes fixed on the stage. A silent prayer muttered in the dark. Be safe, Tom. Keep clear of what's about to unfold.

Please, please don't let the past few months have been in vain. I shift to Stephen's other side, step forward to try and push him further from Tom, to create a gap between the two, to give him a fighting chance of steering away from the immediate blast. But Tom's approaching, coming towards Stephen, towards me.

I turn my head, tuck my head behind Stephen's back. Pray that Tom can't see my face, doesn't recognise that girl he sees crossing the street ahead of him, in the shop, in the park. Not now, Tom. It's not our time.

Stephen's lost in the song. Taken back to that lounge in Leeds, to ash hanging from an unsmoked cigarette and a scratchy LP being played again and again. His thoughts are interrupted by Tom, tugging on his arm. 'Mate. Steve.' He has to shout over the crowd, over the riffs.

Stephen looks over. Tom's eyes are hollow, black. The joy of the previous hour has plunged into a darkness that only Kate's memory can cause. He leans in to make himself heard, leans so he's speaking into Stephen's ear, inches from the top of my head. 'Steve. I'll see you in a bit, yeah? I can't . . . I thought I could, but . . .'

'I'll come with you. Come on, let's get a pint. Get away from it.' No.

Stephen. No. Let him go.

Tom smiles. A tired, small smile. 'Thanks, mate. But I need to be by myself.' We watch him walk away. Head bowed, slumped shoulders push their way through the crowd until he's swallowed, lost. Fran reaches up to kiss Stephen. 'I'm going to check on him,' she says. 'You wait here. Don't move. We'll need to find you!'

The breath I'm holding releases with a rush. He has gone. We're clear. And so we're left: Stephen, Alex, Dan and me. With minutes to go of a classic song and only one thing left for me to do.

I step forward to Stephen. Loop my arm around his waist. The crowd around us pitches and swells with every beat, forcing the full length of my body up against his back. With each surge I lose my footing, and it's all I can do to cling on to him and stay upright. Squash up close, pressing the lumps and bumps of this stuffed vest into him. Taking his hand in mine, threading his fingers through my own. He looks down with a smile. Thinks Fran has decided not to bother, that she'd never find Tom in this crowd. But it's not Fran, who threads his fingers through her own. Not Fran winding her body against him in the heat of the summer night. Eyes widen when he sees me. Tries to pull away, to wrench his hand from mine, to apologise. You must think I'm someone else. But I don't. I know exactly who he is and why I'm there. And the trigger is cupped in the palm of my hand and that tug, that wrench is all it takes. To flip the smooth plastic button that is the only barrier between us and . . .

Click.

My body is ripped, torn. Flesh stripped from bone. The pain is immense – searing, aching, stabbing, tearing. All feelings, all sensations, all at once, all encompassing.

I float.

No longer feeling. The pain receding. Too much for my body to bear, for my mind to compute. So I switch off. To drift. To float. I can hear the screams issuing from my throat, but I cannot feel them leave. They are distant, detached. Mine, but no longer of me. Separated in space and time from the mouth that forms them.

And yet simultaneously, I am on the ground. As I have lived my life as Death, so in my death I am everywhere and nowhere. While I float, I am grounded to live the moment in its full Technicolor horror.

The noise is like nothing I've ever heard before, a crack that rips through the air above us. A blinding white light slices through the crowd, lighting it brighter than day as the tsunami from the blast floods out from Stephen's epicentre. For the briefest millisecond the cries of 40,000 are sucked into a vacuum of silence and disbelief – words punched from gasping lungs with the force of the explosion.

And then they come – the screams, the groans, the

crying, the shouts. The band have stopped, the shriek of feedback piercing the night sky as electric guitars hang forgotten. They stand on stage, the four untouchables looking down on the crowd from on high, uncomprehending. Roadies bustle onto stage to hustle them to safety, but they can't tear their eyes away from the carnage unfolding at their feet. Paramedics flood into the ground in their luminous jackets as fans stream out, running to put as much distance as they can between themselves and the death and the destruction and the desperate screams. I stand in the middle, standing over Stephen's body lying ripped in two at my feet. Stand motionless as the streams of people flow around me, babbling and blurring into each other in the purple half-light.

From where I float, people scurry below, bathed in the ubiquitous blue flashing lights that so haunt my life as I know it. But the scene dims.

Flashing lights slow and darken. A twisting, shifting kaleidoscope of bodies and light swirl beneath me. Flashing lights slow and darken and far below me the unfolding bloodshed, the havoc I've unleashed, fades to black.

Back on the ground huge arena lights switch on with a clunk and a buzz and a flash, flooding the place with a light as bright as day. Bodies lie strewn around me. From one to another I pass, morphing as I go, my life's work continuing while my corporeal body fades and stutters. One last day to bid these final ones on their way while I straddle the hinterland between my own life and death.

Faces choke at me from where they lie, their wounds healing and pain abating as life seeps away and they pass from the living to the dead. Bones knit and skin is sewn as we lie under the flashing blue lights for those final moments. I crouch beside a man lying at my feet. The full force of the blast had ripped flesh from half of his face, exposing his teeth in a rictus smile. As I bend to him, lips soften to cover the gritted grin. His arm, hanging by a single thread from his shoulder, twists back into position as skin smooths over exposed bone. Yet his clothes remain tattered, clinging in threads to fresh skin only recently burnt through to flesh. He looks up from where he lies into the eyes of his mother as I shush and hush and rock his ravaged body and he sobs into my arms. Time slows around me as I turn from one to another, to another, to another. And they fade to black, to black, to black, to black.

With Mark I lie in silence, holding his hand in mine. The first silence he can recall from a four-year-old daughter who chatters to the cat, the fish, the rows of beans in the back garden. With James, a game of backgammon in this theatre of the macabre, played with a grandmother passed long before. Over to Helen for a hand of gin rummy and a small sweet sherry that causes her to shudder and suck her aching teeth. All around me they lie in wait, patient and still as my seconds expand and my hours contract to a pinprick.

All around me they lie in wait as my appearance changes and I pass from one to the next. From a teenaged girl cradling her widowed father, to a young bride back in the wedding dress worn only a week before. From sisters clutched in a clenched embrace, to an aged mother gently picking curled iron shavings from my son's scorched skin. A young boy, this his first gig, curls into a foetal ball to be embraced by his mother – ending his life where so relatively recently it had begun. I go to them, one by one. No need to rush, no need to hurry. They'll wait, lying there in their final moments. As life expires, as painful final breaths are gasped from choked lungs, they'll wait. And when I do get to them, I'll take all the time they need. Sing their songs and paint memories in their minds' eyes. Kiss away the sting of screws twisted into their bones. Massage bruised chests thumped and thwacked by the shockwaves chasing that initial blast.

As I work, He watches. Standing tall and slim and rooted in a bed of twisted limbs, He watches. Looking down His hooked nose as I rush from one to the next, breathing deeply as their souls expire, unwittingly nourishing Him in their deaths. But it's not only me He watches. Something else is catching His eye.

Something else that prompts the occasional nod of approval, that smirk of satisfaction. I can't make anything out through the melee of bodies and the thick smoke hanging heavy over our heads, but there's something. Something or someone to tickle his fancy.

On I scurry through the flurry of lives lived and lives lost. Get my head down and help smooth the way for this most horrid of endings. Gradually, minute by minute, hour by hour, the ground is clearing, leaving green grass dyed red with bloodshed. The physical bodies littering the grass are lifted on to stretchers and escorted from their resting place to more permanent lodgings, and their remaining souls fade to black under a navy-blue sky. The screams of fear have quietened to a gentle hum now. A soft whisper, the occasional terri-fied whimper.

And as the space clears, as bodies are removed and their spirits dissolve, I take a moment in the whirl of confusion to breathe. A deep breath in. A long, slow exhale to the night sky above. With each breath a twinge in my chest, a sharp pain that stabs at my ribs. As the death around me is carried away, so life seeps into my being. And with that life comes feeling. The pain in my chest. The hard ground beneath my feet and the stench of the acrid smoke that still hangs in the air. The nervous feeling in the pit of my stomach at the thought of seeing Tom, at the thought that he may not have got far enough away, that he might be lying hurt out of sight unseen, as yet, by me. I turn full circle to take in this final scene. To see what I've done, what I've caused with this relentless desire of mine. The lives of so many torn apart, ripped asunder to facilitate the happiness of so few. Of me. And of Tom. If, indeed, happiness is what I will bring. He's right, my friend the Devil. Selfish doesn't even start to describe it.

I scan the area for Stephen. My last task, before I can truly live, is to finish what I've started, and oversee the death of the final person I have killed.

Two bodies lie left in this amphitheatre. Two bodies prone on the ground.

The first. Chestnut hair matted with blood. Slashed through the torso, a gaping gash opens organs to the night air. Skin sliced and shredded. An arm, ripped from its socket lies tossed to one side. Abandoned. Forgotten. It's not needed now. His mouth hangs ajar, teeth torn from their roots, tongue lolling and swollen. My presence does nothing to heal, nothing to close those lacerations, nothing to soothe that pain. He's gone and I am no longer able to take him. A dark-haired girl, glossy locks softly sweeping a rigid cheek, crouches over him, leaning to kiss a blood-stained forehead. Fran.

To the side, paramedics restrain a screaming girl who claws at them, runs at huge men who stand steady in the face of her onslaught. Her dark brown hair hangs lank and stringy, her face red, streaked with tears that flow unchecked. She screams his name again and again, her cries echoing in the cooling air. Fran.

Two Frans, of which I am not one. Two Frans: one calm, the other frenzied. And if I am not one, then who, pray tell, is the other?

A voice, behind me. 'You abandoned me.' He speaks clearly, without emotion. 'And after years of having you there, of taking these souls and ushering them in my direction, I couldn't imagine life without that. And so, a replacement. You'd like her, I'm sure.'

She's me. That girl dancing with the Devil on a hot July night. Blonde hair and bronzed skin. My successor. Doing what I do, tending to those who pass from this life into the unknown. Smoothing that directionless path. And my last death has become her first.

It's over. I'm free. Replaced to live my life. And I need to find Tom, my Tom. Find my Tom and start living that life. I turn back towards the bar, take one step, two. And see that second body lying on the grass ahead of me. The body of a girl. A silken blouse slides off one shoulder, legs clad in skinny jeans are bent unnaturally beneath her and a dark red sweatshirt has been bundled under her head in a makeshift pillow. I can't see it, but I know it has a hood. Know it was too hot, too heavy for this weather. Three steps, four. Each step is now an effort. Breath held as intermittent stabs of pain jab at my abdomen. Lips pressed together and mind set against the dull ache. Ahead of me, a man crouches above the girl lying broken on the ground. Dark curly hair scrunched in a fist, navy blue eyes clouded in grief. For she is me, that girl on the ground. And he is Tom.

Behind them, a tall, slim figure in a well-cut suit dangles a ripped and torn calico package from one finger, roughly torn from slim shoulders in a silken shirt. Unseen by those on the ground, He turns on His heel and walks briskly away to dispose of the very instrument which has brought so much panic and hate.

One more step towards these two. One step, two. One more push. The scene around me flickers, the pain stabs deeper. My knee buckles and I fall to the ground.

Cut to black.

29

A VOICE, THROUGH THE DARKNESS.

'Hey. Hey. Can you hear me?'

The voice fades. Trails away to be swallowed into the black.

A hand taps at my face. A tap that softens to cup my cheek, to rub a thumb gently at my temple.

A whisper in the black.

'Hey. Come on. Open your eyes. For me. Open your eyes.'

The hand drops away, knocked to one side in the shadows.

A weight pins me to the ground. A searing shot of white hot pain as my leg twitches involuntarily causes sparks to fly behind closed lids and a mind to shut down. Black.

*

Blue lights flash through the dark. The voice is more urgent now. 'Please! Wake up! Come on!'

Lids flicker open. A face looks down at me with a smile. 'There you are.'

Tom. Leaning over me on this blood-soaked plain. Staring down at me, blue eyes wide and concerned. One hand is wrapped around my own. The fingers of the other gently tuck hair behind my ear. Fingertips trail across my cheeks, across my lip.

'Hey, you.' His tone is gentle. 'I thought you weren't going to wake up. I'm Tom.'

I know.

'You're OK now. The paramedics will look after you. What's your name?'

Lizzy. Not Little D. No longer Death. I'm Lizzy. Lilibet. Bess.

'Lizzy.' My voice is thick, rasped. Choked with blood. My mouth dry, gritty. Talking hurts. Breathing hurts. A brutal return to sensation after hundreds of years of nothing but numbness.

'Well, you're OK, Lizzy. I thought I'd lost you there for a second. And I can't lose you now – we've only just met!' A throwaway comment to lighten the mood. But it hits home, oh how it hits home. He doesn't know how close to the truth he is. I can't lose him now. 'Are you with anyone? You were just lying here alone. And I couldn't leave you. Do you have any friends with you?'

I shake my head. Wince. Any movement is a bad idea. Pain slices through.

'You live around here? I'm sure I recognise you. I've been seeing this face for weeks now in the shop and on my street and, well, everywhere really. And I'm sure it's you. I mean, it's hard to tell, but . . .' He's gabbling, nervous. Attempting to keep me distracted from the pain. The paramedics try to move him but he won't leave my side. So they work round him, inserting needles, bandaging the wound that slices across my midriff. My head feels heavy. Cushioned from the ground in a way the rest of my body is not. Every lump, every bump of that hard ground digs into my back, my legs.

'Hampstead.' A whisper. I have no home now, no place to belong, but that is where he's seen me and for now that's enough.

'Same as me. I knew I'd seen you!' His eyes are locked on mine, his voice softens. 'I knew I'd seen you.' A whisper.

A cold fluid flows into my veins through the paramedics' cannula. A cold fluid that softens the mind, blurs the edges. The pain ebbs, seeping from my core as the fluid works its way into my system. My head feels woozy, my eyelids heavy as I snuggle into the warmth of this morphinic blanket. Keeping my eyes open is more effort than I can manage, and I swoop, drift, settle. Tom's voice a distant call – far from my ears, but so close to my heart. And I float gently into the softest grey.

I wake in an ambulance. Tom's face still close to my own. A drip hangs above me, swaying in unison with Tom and the movement of the ambulance.

'Hey, you're back.' A whisper. He leans forward. Slowly, softly, his lips meet mine. Eyes close into the kiss. Soft, firm.

He pulls back. 'Oh God, I'm sorry.' Reaches up to rake his fingers through dishevelled dark curls. 'What am I doing? I'm so sorry. It's too soon. You're stuck in an ambulance and I'm . . . I'm sorry. I just feel like I know you. And . . .'

I smile. Eyes locked. Reach my finger up to hush, to shush. 'Please. Don't. Don't apologise . . .' Will him to dip his head again, to brush his lips once more against my own. To kiss him back, to feel the heat of his breath against my face, his fingers twisted into my hair.

'I couldn't leave you.' He smiles down at me. 'Not there, not alone. And I won't. Leave you, I mean. Not until you're in and they've got you safely tucked up. You're stuck with me, I'm afraid.'

That's fine by me.

A wave of morphine and once more I sleep. No longer the black of pain, of death behind these lids, but the dove grey of peace, of tranquillity, of calm. He's here. With me. And he wants to stay.

*

A shadowy figure seen through sleep-smeared eyes looms over Tom's shoulder. Swaying with Tom, with the movement of the ambulance. Tailored suit, crisp white shirt unsullied by the events of the evening. For the first time in over four hundred years, a blemish marks that porcelain cheek. Our bond is broken. He gazes down at me, at my inert body on a narrow bed. Arms bound in place by unseen shackles. The machine that monitors me speeds up its rhythm. Urgent, relentless, warning beeps. But no one can see the cause. No one but me. A medic appears beside me, moves Tom down the bed. Checks my levels. Oxygen low, dropping. A mask pressed over my face. And He stands, swaying above me. And He stares.

Cool air floods into my lungs. Gulping breaths. Tom's fingers twisted through my own.

'You did it then.' He speaks. 'Finished the job and got the boy. I must say, you've made it look positively easy. Give or take the odd . . . hiccup, shall we say?' My body is paralysed as I stare up at Him. I can feel the pain in my abdomen starting to nag, feel the morphine in my system starting to seep away in His presence. Why is He here? Our time is through, my job is done. Will He never leave me alone?

'Why are you here?' Still my voice rasps, grates through crushed cords.

'I wanted to say my goodbyes, Little D. Or should I call you Lizzy? We've had a long ride the two of us. And all good things, as they say, must come to an end.'

'But we said our goodbyes. We're done. You can leave me alone now. Please.'

This wasn't part of the deal, Him hanging around after I'd fulfilled His demands. I glance at Tom, willing him to notice, to shove this man out of the way, to protect me from this presence that is no longer wanted, no longer needed. But he remains at the foot of my bed, reaching up to hold my hand in his, oblivious.

'But Lizzy! I said goodbye to Little D back there. To my partner for all these years. She's the one I'll miss. But now I'm leaving you, Lizzy. The girl I met in that Scottish market square on that freezing cold day. You don't look all that different, truth be told, with that blood smearing your face, shackles holding your arms. And that hunted look in your eye. You've never been able to disguise that, have you? I suppose you smell a bit better than you did back then . . .' He leans to peer out of the tiny window etched in the back doors of the ambulance.

I glance once more at Tom, internally screaming for him to notice. But still he is oblivious. To him I lie sleeping. Eyes closed, pain muted, the monitor beeping a more regular tone. Hurt but safe. Safe but sleeping.

'Anyway, I digress. The thing is, Lizzy, this will be our last goodbye. All good things must come to an end. And then, after our last goodbyes, you really will be free of me forever. Once I give you up, little one, you really are on your own. And I can't help what happens to you. Alice!' He calls through to the front cab.

The blonde girl appears at His shoulder, ducking through past the drip.

'I don't believe you've met, have you?' He asks Alice. Then turns to address me. 'I think Alice was a little busy when you saw her last. I thought it was only right you should meet your successor. Then you'll know her when your time comes, Lizzy.'

We eye each other, Alice and me. My gaze is wary. I'm open, vulnerable. Unsure. She is confident, arrogant almost, retaining the louche demeanour I saw earlier, looping a long slim arm through His and smirking down at me. They stand united, He and His female twin. She reaches up to His cheek. Dabs at a drop of blood with her fingertips before sucking it clean between smiling lips.

'So, that's me.' He says, smiling down at me. 'Done.' He leans down, brushes a cold kiss against my forehead. A damp trace from His lips lingers against my skin, but with bound arms I can't rub it away. My lip curls, my fists clench. Skin crawls under cotton sheets. My head presses back into the pillow – mere millimetres of distance between my face and His, but those millimetres are miles when they're all I have.

'Goodbye, Little D . . . Lizzy. Congratulations. You won. Enjoy him while you can.' He nods in the direction of Tom, who has my fingers pressed to his lips. 'Have a good life, Lizzy, it's been a pleasure.'

And with that, He's gone. Leaving Alice to sway

with Tom, to sway with the movement of the ambulance. Fade to grey.

A jolt. The ambulance comes to a stop. Doors open and bright light floods in. Tom lets go of my hand, steps aside to allow the paramedics to lift the bed on to its wheels, to unhook drips and gather tubes and get me out of there.

And still Alice is by my side. Looking down at me with that twisted smile on thin lips. The medics swim around me in slow motion, Tom stands alone at the open door to the ambulance.

She leans down, taking one of my hands in hers, cupping her free hand around my cheek. Brings her lips to my forehead. I'm frozen, locked inside my own head. Words won't come, I'm paralysed in body and mind.

'I'm sorry,' she breathes. 'But you made your choice, Lizzy, and you chose to make a deal with the Devil. But He always wins, my darling, He always wins.'

Me. Her first task to oversee the death of my last. Her second to seal the deal and finalise the sale of her soul to my nemesis. Me.

'I have no choice, Lizzy. I'm so sorry. I have no choice.'

I find the strength from somewhere, deep within. A stamina and strength I didn't know I had. My body goes rigid, legs kick against straps, arms strain against shackles. I try to scream. Struggles that go unseen, a throaty gurgle that goes unheard. Tom, the medics, the nurses that wait patiently by open doors oblivious to this final fight. I have to get up, I have to get out. But she's in control. I've been there, I know this. She holds all of the cards.

But I won't let her. I can't. You can. And you have to. Hywel, Rose, Ellie, Stephen. Lives lost in my quest for my own. And now that is taken from me before it's even begun.

Her face has softened, filled out in the cheek. Older. More familiar. Laughing lines crinkle at the edges of her eyes, and she smiles down at me, peaceful, beatific, calm. A face that morphs as I look at it, as blonde hair darkens and blue eyes melt into a chocolate brown. A face that settles into one I haven't seen for four hundred years, a face last seen slumped at the stake in a cold market square. The face of my mother, looking down at me on that narrow bed. Her hand is held over my mouth, her fingers press gently at my nose.

My mother leans forward. Presses her lips to my cheek, to the top of my head. 'My darling girl,' she breathes through a kiss. 'I've missed you so very much. Through all of these years.'

The machines beep. Long pulses, shorter beeps. A Morse code to warn them, to save me. Bodies flow around me, reattaching the oxygen, pumping my chest, desperately trying to stem the blood that flows freely from my chest. My body fights against her hand, my head twists from one side to the other to free myself from her grasp.

But it's too late.

With her free hand she smooths my hair, reaches to take my hand. With one hand she cares, with the other she kills. A searing pain shoots through to my very core. The injuries I've sustained leave me gaping and exposed. No one could survive them, I've been kept alive merely by His desire to see me suffer. To give me hope and snatch it in the very final seconds.

Strange noises come from my chest. Blood gurgling into my lungs. Breath wheezing as if from the bellows of a cracked accordion. I feel like I'm drowning. Lungs tight, they won't fill. They can't.

One final kiss. 'I'm sorry.' A tear, drops onto my face. Mingles with my own to track down my cheek.

One final squeeze, holding her hand in place against my struggling body, the world around me morphs and warps. Everything blurs, as if a heat haze fills this tiny space. From a distance, I can hear a man calling my name again and again. Lizzy. Lizzy. Lizzy. I feel my shoulders being lifted into an embrace, feel my head fall back on my neck. She is gone, slipping away from me and on to the next. Whirling and morphing from one woman to the next to the next. Herself and yet never herself. She will learn. She will see.

The very edges of my field of vision are darkening – a looming shadow encroaching by the second. Until all I can see is Tom in the very centre. His face hovering over mine. Lips lowered to mine to breathe air into lungs filled with blood. The aperture is closing, a darkness that seeps into my vision blocking my view of everything except his face. Until slowly, gradually, even that is absorbed into an eclipse. And with his name breathed from cracked lips, slowly, quietly, softly, gently . . . my final death.

Fade to black.

ACKNOWLEDGEMENTS
AND THANKS

Lucy is unable to thank those many people who helped her and encouraged her to write and complete her novel, but it would be remiss of us (Lucy's family) if we failed to acknowledge the great support she received from her friends, colleagues, doctors and carers at the hospice.

There are so many people to thank and her friends know how grateful we are, but we would like to specifically thank:

Lucy's university friends: Karen, Dave, Rachel, Christine, Van, Adam, Mariel and Slim.

Lucy S & Little Beth for being as daft as Lucy was!

Kyna, Sally and Jill.

Her colleagues at Rattling Stick, particularly Ringan and Katie.

School friends: Nikki, Juliette and Kate.

The 175 crew: Deep, Steph, Walks and Fodes.

Dr Emma Spurrell, the chemo nurses, Helen and all the doctors and nurses at the Whittington Hospital, who were unfailing in the care they gave to Lucy.

Dr Adrian Tookman, Glynn Thomas and their colleagues at the Marie Curie Hospice in Hampstead for treating Lucy with such care and kindness in her last days.

Lucy's literary agent, Rachel Mills, without whose help this book would never have got to publication.

Lucy's godchildren: Anna, Jude, Otto and Noé of whom she was so proud.

And the rest of Lucy's friends, too many to name, who supported her (and us) through a time we wouldn't wish on anyone.

We thank you from the bottom of our hearts for looking after our Luce.

Alan (Pa), Jackie (Ma) & Analie (Fanners)

Unbound is the world's first crowdfunding publisher, established in 2011.

We believe that wonderful things can happen when you clear a path for people who share a passion. That's why we've built a platform that brings together readers and authors to crowdfund books they believe in – and give fresh ideas that don't fit the traditional mould the chance they deserve.

This book is in your hands because readers made it possible. Everyone who pledged their support is listed below. Join them by visiting unbound.com and supporting a book today.

A.Flo
Celia Adams
Martin Adams
Sharbari Ahmed
Rochelle Alahmed
Koos Alders
Fede Alfonzo
Rachel Ali
Susan Allen
Iain Anderson
Judith Anderson

Jane Angell
Ann Ankers
Tom Appleby
Julian Apps
Sandra Armor
Edith Athey
Tim Atkinson
Michelle Ayling
Averil Bailey
Patrick Bailey
David Baillie

Matt Baker
Lara Baldwin
Helen Ball
Jason Ballinger
Clare Barker
Andrew Bartel
Ann Bate
George Bate
Hanna Bayatti
Bob Beaupre
Joanne Bednall
Alex Beidas
Martin Bell
Stuart Bentham
Kate Bhamra
Suchada Bhirombhakdi
Cecilia Blanche
Gavin Bluck
Fizz Bolton
Alan and Jackie Booth
Alfie Booth
Analie Booth
Ruth Boreham
Matt Bounsall
Elizabeth Bradley
Ruth and Lorcan Brennan
Linda Broadbent
Louise Brown
Erica Buist
Jason Bulley
Dave Burgess
James Burgess

Ali Burns
Philip Byrne
Bryony Cale
Kimberley Cameron
Nathan Camponi
Rachel Carling
Debbie Carmichael
Joshua Carpenter
Philip Carpenter
Kelly Cartwright
David Casdagli
Nicki Casey
Denise Cassar
Philip Cassidy
Ed Cave
Nick Chappell
Mary Cheney
John Christian & Linda
    Monk
Luke, Debbie, Max and Ellie
    Clark
Paul Clarke
Heidi Clover
Shirley Cock
Clive Cockram
Juan Coello Hollebecq
Gina R. Collia
Laura Colvin
Hilary Colyer
Gilly Combe
Helen Connor
Heather Cook

Toby Cook
Jenni Coombe
Penny Cotton
Nicola Coulson
Tobi Coventry
Robert Cox
Susheila Cox
Matt Craigie Atherton
Matt Cresswell
Russell Curtis
Riccardo D'Amico
Alan Dagger
Nicola Dale
Becca Day-Preston
Rawdon de Fresnes
Caz Deery
Oly Dempster
Jane Dilworth
Johnny Donne
Martyn Donoghue
David Doran
Karen Downs
Clara Downton
Tim Dowse
Alexandra Duffy
Neil Duncan
Kirsty Dye
Caroline Eales
Robert Eardley
David Eastaff
Wallis Eates
Patricia and Malc Edwards

Michael Elliott
Sally-Ann Elliott
Samantha Ellis
Richard Eno
Louise Evans
Gavin Eyers
Christiaan Faberij de Jonge
Sophie Farrah
James Fassnidge
Jennie Ferrar
Erin Foden
Graham and Trish Foden
Matthew Forrester
Lindsay Fox
Debra Franks
Davey Fraser
Luke Fraser
Alan Friel
Karen Fyfe
Caroline Gale
Claire Gallagher
Mr Gammon
Isusko Garcia
Barbara Gartside
Lorraine Geoghegan
Martin Geraghty
Morgan Gillespy
Christine Gilmour
Jessica Gioia
Steve Giudici
John & Carol Gleave
Adam Goldwater

Bobbi Goldwater
Gill Goodswen
Johnny Goonan
Rachel Goswell
Edna Gray
Nicola Graydon
Jackie Green
Sarah Gregory
Joanna Grey
Cathy Griffiths
Lisa Grigoriou
Chris Gunn
Sharon Gunnell
Joanna Gupta
Parveen Gupta
Sophy Gupta
Vandana Gupta
Gretel Hallett
Tessa Hamilton
Jo Hardman
Laura Harrison
Sally Harrison
Anne Hastings
Monica Hastings
James Hatcher
Anwen Kya Hayward
Barbara & Iain Hebenton
Brenda Henderson
Gemma Henson
Rachel HG
John Higgins
Karen Hinojosa

Peter Hodgson
Liz Honer
Sam Hope Claus
Clare Houston
Gus Howells
Otto Howells
David Hughes
Jenny Hughes
Julie Hughes
Claire Hugman
Nadine Hulston
Austen Humphries
Gemma Humphries
Sally Humphries
Raphaël Iberg
Susie Innes
Hermione Ireland
Jamie Jackson
Mike James
Christine Jenkins
Lisa Jenkins
Katie Jewell
Kate John
Karen, Dave & Jude
   Johnson
Kitty Johnson
Margie Johnston
Stuart Johnston
Jim Jolliffe
Cat Jones
Sara Jones
Savana Jones-Middleton

Sandra Jordan
Josie Juneau
Mandeep Kandola
Lizzie Kaye
Katie Keith
Chris Kelly
Ella Kennedy
Morgan Kennedy
Nicola Kenney
Liz Kessler
Dan Kieran
Ben King
Laura King
Rachel King
Louise Kingman
Maureen Kingman
Reg Kingman
Sylvia Kingman
Eloise Kitchen
Margaret Kitchen
Daniel Kleinman
Nicola Ladbrooke
Doug Laird
Tony Lambert
Tee Lapan
Cara Lari
Alistair Lavin
W Tom Lawrie
Barnaby Laws
Paula Le Flohic
Christopher Lear
Jane Learner

Ringan Ledwidge
Mike Lindgren
Jim Lindsay
Kirsty Lister
Victoria Lloyd-Hughes
Andrew Local
Barbara and Hugh
    Logan
Marian Lomas
Jimmy Lou
Kate Lowe
Declan Lowney
Claire Luke
Rachel Lum
Jennifer Lynch
Elizabeth Lyons
Paul Mackay
Tiwirayi Magwenzi
Alice Maltby-Kemp
Paula Marcantonio
Evelyn Marr
Richard Marshall
Jessica Martin
Oliver Martin
Jan Mather
Melinda McCheyne
Pat McCrudden
Alison McDonnell
Helen McElwee
Gareth McEwen
Marie McGinley
Alex McLay

Andy McLeod
Kathleen McNeill
Sarah Mead
Ann Menzies
Glynis Milburn
Rachel Mills
Roger Mills
John Mitchinson
Simon Monhemius
Beth Montague
Penny Montague
Kate Moore
Natalie Moorse
Paddy Moran
Charlie Moreton
Leonie Moreton
Hilary Morris
Jenny Morris
Alison Morton
Linda Mulholland
Judy Munday
Dom Murgia
Alexandra Murrell
John Napier
Linda Nathan
Carlo Navato
Jill Neill
Howie Nicol
Alexander Nirenberg
Gabi Norland
Paul and Elisabeth Norman
Chaz Northam

Eva Ntoumou
Michelle O'Brien
Spob O'Brien
Scott O'Donnell
Winnie O'Neil
Fiona O'Riordan
Heather Ocego
Colin Offland
Tessa Oldham
Andy Orrick
Rich Orrick
Giusi Orsini Shaw
Kyna Palin
Lynton Parmar-Hemsley
Will Paskins
Richard Paterson
Lesley Peak
Eddy Pearce
Thomas Phillips
George Pitcher
Katherine Pitman
Justin Pollard
Marion Poole
Helene Poursain
Elvin Prentice
Rhian Heulwen Price
Llinos Mair Pritchard (Ll's)
Julia Prola
Hector Proud
Sarah Rafati
David Rainford
Helena Reis

Pat Renwick
Karen Reynolds
Nikki Richards
Rosemary Richards
Simon Richards
Carol Roberts
Dennis Roberts
Katie Roberts
Philip Robinson
Rachael Robinson
Alison Roe
Lou Rossiter
Antony Rowe
Lian Rowlands
Claire Ruocchio
Polly Ruskin
Cala & Garry Russell
Melanie Ryder
Monica Saksena Joye
Kate Salmon
Teraza Salmon
Hannah Samantha
Shelagh Sanderson
Amanda Sands
Di Scott
Patrick Scott
Juliette Seddon
Jane Seymour Brooke-
    Taylor
Jenny Shaffstall
Laurence Shapiro
Heather Sharp

Mandy Sharpe
Carol Shaw
Lucy Sherwood
John Shirley
Ged Simmons
Matt Sinclair
Robin James Sinclair
Algy Sloane
Bill Smedley
Nick Smee
Andrew Smirthwaite
Dan Smith
Nikki Smith
Suneeta Soni
Richard Sorensen
Quentin Spender
Emma Spurrell
Teresa Squires
Anouska Stahlmann
Elizabeth Stahlmann
Emer Stamp
Kirsty Stanley
Harriet Staples &
    Ross Duffy
Andy and Sue Stapley
Juliette Stern
Christine Stevens
Hannah Stewart
Brendan Strong
Carrie Sutton
The Swanns
Karl Taggart

Ross Taggart
Claire Taylor
Jessica Taylor
Kate Taylor
Laura Taylor
Linda Taylor
Rachael Taylor
Mariel Thomas
Phil Tidy
Robert Toft
Ben Tonge
Joanna Tonge
Jeremy Tribe
Denise Trueman
Daniel Tubby
Janet Turnbull
Jenni Turnbull
Lindsay Turnham
Cara Usher
Akane Vallery Uchida
Robin Van Calcar
Seema Varghese
Gary Varney
Lou Vasey
James Vella-Bardon
Jo W
Karen Waldron
Andrew Walker
Matthew Walsh

Sue Walsh
Karen Walton
Lawrence Wan
Jon Ward
Tessa Webb
Helen Weir
Kathryn Wells
Ella Wendon
Verity White
Jack Whiteley
Zoe Whittaker
Lois Whittle
Andrea Wilkinson
Rae Williams
Ranjana Williamson
Derek Wilson
Preston Wilson
Chris Winter
Georgina Winter
George Winterburn
Jill Winters
Sue Winters
Valerie Wolf
Loren, Paul & Ava Wood
Jill Woodland
Anna Worley
Gemma Wrigley
Jessica Wylie
Annaxue Yang